Praise for
The Eternal Messiah: Jesus of K'Turia

"Theology in a new code."
> —Dr. Harvey Cox, Harvard Divinity School and author
> of *The Future of Faith*

"A marvelous book. Jesus' words and actions ring true, with a contemporary feel. You'll be torn between wanting to stop and reflect on each chapter and continuing to read to see whether Jesus will once again have to make the Ultimate Sacrifice."
> —B. C. Aronson, author of *Grace* and *Love*

"*The Eternal Messiah* is an intriguing blend of theology and science fiction, highly recommended."
> —*The Midwest Book Review*

"An elegant and gentle treatment of the transformative power of faith."
> — Keryl Raist, *The Indie Book Review*

"I was quickly drawn into a fascinating story and I absolutely loved the paradoxical question that ended the novel. I look forward to seeing how the rest of the series develops…"
> —*Sojourner's Journey blog*

"A refreshingly creative re-telling of the mission of Jesus."
> —Father Jerry Wooton, Parochial Vicar, Virginia

"From my perspective as a Christian historian, this tale is just as compelling as any Apocryphal literature or heralded classic writing, and one that could be treated as social history…"
> —Dr Wesley L B Rose, ThD

More praise for
The Eternal Messiah: Jesus of K'Turia

"A contemporary novel that can speak to any individual about their needs, their desires, their search for what their life means—hopefully, a life of helping others, a life of sacrifice when required…a life with freedom to choose…"

—*GABixler Reviews*

"A rich, well-written story with compelling characters, taking you on a journey of belief."

—Dallas Hudgens, author of *Wake Up, We're Here*

"This book reminded me a bit of *The Shack* in how it inspired me to reevaluate what I believe, how I have come to those beliefs, and which ones I need to let go of in order to submit to love, forgiveness, and sacrifice that is indeed eternal."

—Trisha Niermeyer Potter, *Prints of Grace*

"Regardless of your own beliefs, this story is certainly worth the read."

—Grace Krispy, *MotherLode blog*

"Pursche and Gabriele challenge us to think about people's thoughts about religion, their fears and insecurities, and why religion has such a profound effect on the relationships between people."

—Rabbi Bruce Aft, Adjunct Professor, Marymount University, Arlington, VA.

"A page turner for anyone who enjoys a story that will stay with you long after you finish the last page. Highly recommended!"

—WV Stitcher blog

IMMANENCE

The Eternal Messiah Future
Book 2

W. R. Pursche
Michael Gabriele

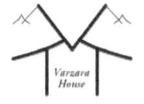

Varzara House
Marshall, VA

Published by Varzara House

Copyright © 2015 by William Pursche and Michael Gabriele.

Cover artwork by Michael Gabriele.

Varzara House books are available for educational use and to book clubs at a discount for multiple copies. Please contact info@varzara.com for information.

Library of Congress Control number: 2014958692

ISBN: 978-0-9753-7930-1

20 19 18 17 16 15 14 13a/6h

IMMANENCE

What has gone before

Treb Win has left his home and joined the Science Corps to escape the memories of the loss of Sooni, his life mate. Bereft of purpose, he tries to lose himself in his work, his goal of achieving personal enlightenment now an impossible dream without the support of his mate and his people.

Win's research ship is commandeered by the military to undertake a covert mission to find a missing freighter carrying illicit weapons. Along on the mission are two troublesome humans: a shady government official who isn't telling Win the whole story, and Kalinda Prentiss, scientist who has developed a controversial theory about the connection between religion and cultural advancement.

Prentiss is a renowned expert in her field of cultural anthropology. In her work with indigenous cultures she begins to see amazing similarities in their path to advancement—similarities based on their acceptance of a religious messiah. Yet when she documents her work and presents it to the scientific community, she is ridiculed for her theory and is demoted from her prestigious position and sent to work on Win's obscure ship.

When their mission leads to K'Turia, they witness something extraordinary: the appearance of a religious preacher named Jesus. He brings a compelling message of faith and sacrifice, encouraging the people to break free from their meaningless lives. His gospel threatens both the local religious leaders and an oppressive occupying power.

Prentiss believes she has the ultimate proof of her theory and Win is curiously drawn to this preacher, kindling a spark in his long lost sense of purpose as he listens to Jesus' gospel. Drawn into an unfolding drama that is eerily familiar to what happened on Earth, they are forced to make a desperate choice: save the galaxy or save Jesus.

Jesus, however, has other plans . . .

Cast of Characters
(major characters in **bold**)

Trebor Win	The seeker; a Treb
I'Char	The helper; an Illian
Sooni	Win's life mate
Perin-Ta	Council President
Rios Waren	Council member
Volenar	League General and Council member
Symes	Old man on K'Turia
Johearim	Secret Pertise follower of Jesus
Tsaph	Follower of Jesus on K'Turia
Coru Chiths	K'Turia miner and follower of Jesus
Tthean	Disciple of Jesus on K'Turia
Arca	Woman visitor to the Core
Lornay	Arca's grandmother
Drason	Carthlanian who offers to help Win
Aralyn	Young woman on Carthlana who befriends Win
Varshan	Rebel whose daughter dies in fire
Breal	Varshan's son
Miera	Old woman shopkeeper who helps Win
Kesh	Rebel leader in safe house
Listra	Rebel woman
Tekton	Mason who is rebuilding a house
Tu Vos	Man who owns house where Win stays

Characters mentioned but not appearing in this story

Prentiss	Scientist with Win on his first visit to K'Turia
Garrick	League official with Win on his first visit to K'Turia
Methurgem	Leader of the Pertise religious order on K'Turia
Liall	K'Turia miner and follower of Jesus

Preface

THE DESERT STRETCHED OUT BEFORE HIM, melding into the sky. To almost anyone it would appear endless, but he understood the true meaning of endless, and even this expanse was far from it. Nothing really ever ended. That was the deep secret of the infinite.

His time on K'Turia was coming to an end. He had finished what he came here to do. Whether it was enough was not for him to decide.

He had left behind what he could, what they would need, if they chose to accept it. He had left them a path to follow, just as his footsteps now would leave a path. His guidance could take many forms: a story, a touch, even a line of prints in the sand. But even he would never be able to foretell what the results of his guidance would be.

This was the longest time he had spent in this desert wilderness, a full turn of the moon, longer here than on many planets. On each, he would end his time with a walk in the harshest environment without food or water, for a length of time he did not command. He had nothing with him except the clothes on his back and the universe around him, and within him.

Even with his strength and purpose, he was affected by the heat and the hunger, wearing down his physical body, sapping him until his physical needs challenged his spiritual desire.

But it could not be any other way. He had to face the greatest of all challenges when he was most vulnerable, when he had only his spiritual strength to save him.

Far in the distance a black splotch appeared, ruining the beauty of the alluring sand and sky, a dagger in the harmony of the horizon.

As he had before, and would again, he stumbled forward to meet it, growing physically weaker with each step as the black blemish took on form. It flared up, a mirage promising of water to quench his thirst, of relief to end his suffering. All he had to do was accept it, to succumb to its darkness.

The darkness of temptation. The darkness of deception.

The darkness of evil.

CHAPTER 1

I'CHAR STOOD IN THE OPEN DOORWAY to Trebor Win's apartment, the orange Trioconian sun setting behind him, turning him into an ominous silhouette. He pounded on the open door as if it were closed.

"An open door bids welcome, does it not?" asked I'Char.

Not today, it doesn't, Win thought. He sat facing an inactive vid monitor, staring at the reflection of his wide face, distorted just enough by the screen to make him look like someone else. It was not unusual for I'Char to simply show up at his door, but tonight Win preferred to be alone. He sighed and rubbed at his almost bald head, motioning for the lithe Illian to enter and join him.

I'Char held up a small container. "I thought you might be hungry," he said. "And maybe you need some company?" He set the box down on a nearby table and pulled up a chair across from Win. "I have not heard from you."

Win eyed the container of food and bottled beverages. He took a deep breath, knowing he should eat, but he had no appetite. He'd been holed up in his apartment for a month since his return from K'Turia, unable to shake the disturbing memories of that troubled world. And of those he left behind: Kalinda Prentiss, the cultural anthropologist who had forsaken her breakthrough theory about the linkage between religion and science after discovering a religious preacher on K'Turia—a preacher named Jesus. And Jamis Garrick, the mysterious

League agent who ultimately gave his life to save Win, I'Char and Prentiss.

Win's thoughts of Jesus were the most troubling. Even now Jesus was having an unsettling effect on Win. He had worked so hard to repress the pain over the loss of his mate, Sooni, who had been killed in a freak lab explosion that Win still blamed himself for. He had fled to the League Science Corps, taking a deep space assignment in an attempt to escape that agonizing memory. On the night she died, Win died too. Yet no matter how far he ran, he had not been able to escape his suffering.

But Jesus had forced him to confront his depression, making him face his destructive denial of Sooni's loss. Now he was caught in a netherworld—no longer protected from his sorrow by a retreat into numbness, yet nowhere near the enlightened acceptance that would allow him to move on. He was torn between being thankful and angry.

"I have not heard from you," I'Char said again.

"I am not particularly hungry," said Win, dragging his attention back to the present. I'Char was difficult to ignore. He was so—in the moment. "But since you went to all this trouble I will eat."

"I think you will enjoy this. I brought you an authentic Salvenar dinner—which I believe is one of your favorites—and a bottle of Verkush." I'Char dangled the bottle in front of Win.

The aroma of the sautéed vegetables and legumes had escaped into the room. Win was hungrier than he was willing to admit. He took the bottle from I'Char.

"For myself," I'Char continued, "I have two delicious Dacun-Semage cakes and a bottle of Oonvam. None of this is beneficial to my health, of course, but for now I simply will not care."

Win allowed himself a brief smile. He truly was grateful for I'Char's friendship. The Illian had been a source of stability and strength in Win's self imposed exile. Win admired the directness and intensity with which I'Char met life. An intensity wrapped in calmness, so easy to be misunderstood. So easy to be underestimated.

"I made that sure the Verkush was made with the sharpest fruit," I'Char said. "The winemaker insisted this was his finest bottle."

Win drank a mouthful. His face curled up and he held his breath as he swallowed. It took a moment before he could speak.

"The winemaker—did not lie—to you," Win said, gasping. "It is—exceptionally sour."

I'Char took a swig of the even sharper Oonvam. "I am pleased that you are enjoying it. But I did not come here merely to eat and drink."

Win nodded. "You wish to discuss the hearing." They had been summoned to appear before the League's Joint Civilian/Military Council to answer questions about what happened on K'Turia. Neither Win nor I'Char were affiliated with the military, but the Council wielded tremendous power and was behind the covert mission that had sent them to K'Turia—a mission that had essentially failed.

"No," said I'Char, taking Win by surprise. "What I must say has nothing to do with the hearing."

"What is it then?"

"I wonder why you have not been out of your home since our return from K'Turia. I wonder why you have not contacted me. I wonder why your messaging system has been deactivated."

"A lot has happened," said Win. "I simply needed some down time."

"No doubt. But I fear you are embarking on a dangerous path."

Win held back a reaction. "I appreciate your concern, but I prefer not to discuss my—path. I am tired and I need time to recover. I am simply taking a sabbatical."

"You are entitled. But what are you recovering toward? To what you were before K'Turia, or to what you almost achieved while there?"

The words hit Win hard. I'Char had touched upon the very thing that he'd been brooding over.

"I do not care for you in the role of therapist, I'Char," Win said, more harshly than he had intended.

"And I do not care for you in the role of ongoing victim," I'Char replied in his calm way. "This is not the Win I know. The Win I know would not choose a life of sulking."

Win moved his hand over an armrest sensor and a nearby window slid open. The evening breeze moved the curtains, carrying the cacophonous hum of insects in the early dusk. The buzzing mirrored the flurry of thoughts in his mind.

Win said, "I am considering leaving the Science Corps. I have grown weary of searching for things that have lost meaning to me."

"I believe some of our discoveries have been worthy of the search," I'Char said.

"I am bored and tired. I am no longer interested in analyzing gas clouds or charting spatial anomalies." Win paused, searching for the right words. "When we are away, traveling through the depths of empty space, it reminds me that I, too, am empty. Without Sooni I will never be complete. I will never be full again."

"You mean you cannot hide anymore. Who are you trying to deceive?"

From anyone else this rebuke would have upset Win, but I'Char had seen right through him, as always.

"Does it really matter?" asked Win. "I am tired. I want to rest."

"You've been resting. Are you better for it?"

Win's eyes flittered around the room. "I wander around here day and night and expect her to step from around a corner, even though she never even lived here. I hear her voice. When I re-member things she said, I feel—I *react* just as I used to when she was with me. I've always felt that when someone dies, they leave a part of themselves behind in others, in those they knew and loved. We Trebs believe that there is an everlasting essence of the spirit. I thought if I meditated enough, if I spent enough time alone thinking of her, not her physical body but who she was, I might be able to—hold onto more of her in some way. Not like some kind of ghost, but rather a capturing of not only what she was, but what we had." Win was frustrated; this was the most he had spoken in days, and he couldn't articulate his thoughts. "Sooni had achieved the ultimate goal of our people, the highest level of enlightenment possible in this world. If anyone could be touched by me, or touch me, it would be her. Us."

Win turned back to I'Char. "I was wrong."

I'Char stood up abruptly. "You must come with me."

"Now? Where are we going?"

"You will know when we get there."

"I'm not particularly in the mood for an evening stroll."

"Your mood requires a severe readjustment." I'Char stepped closer to Win. "Please. Come with me."

Win slowly rose and followed I'Char outside. Win's housing unit was in a small complex at the very edge of the town, as far from everyone and everything as possible while still being within the environs of civilization. The complex backed up to an ancient grove of woods. The evening air was comfortably cool. I'Char led them along a pathway lined with wild gar-wood trees, their fluorescent leaves illuminating the way. A flock of colorful tanes flew overhead, screeching as they soared into the distance. Several young p'tas darted across the path and into the woods, quickly followed by their mother who playfully chased after them.

The trail entered a thickly wooded area. They walked on in silence for some time, the path lit only by the glowing leaves of the gar-wood. When I'Char turned left at a fork in the path, Win knew where they were headed. The Gardens of Na-Shay, one of the most revered places on Triocon. People from all over the planet would make their way to this natural wonder to meditate, reflect and search for understanding. In spite of his reluctance to continue, Win knew, above all, he desperately needed to understand.

They passed through a garden of herbs, the aromas combining

into an indescribable palette. Then came a glen of moss, a spectrum of greens and blues. Into the woods again, the way lined with stately bamboo. The trail opened up to a glistening spring in the center of the Gardens, water rising from the ground into a whispering natural pool.

"This is what you need right now," I'Char said.

"All I wanted was a quiet evening at home."

"You've had enough quiet evenings at home," I'Char said gently. "It is time for you to come back to the world. You cannot continue sitting in your apartment feeling sorry for yourself."

Win was about to argue, but the sound of the water soothed him. The peacefulness and tranquility of the Gardens made even a minor disagreement hard to voice. He watched the cascading flow of water. It was more alive than he was.

"Perhaps you are right," he said. He turned back to I'Char. "I appreciate your efforts and your patience, old friend."

"You will feel better once we return to the *Anatar* and make our way into open space."

"We will see," said Win.

After a time, I'Char said, "When I said that some of our discoveries had been worthy of the search, I wasn't referring to gas clouds or spatial anomalies."

"You mean Jesus," said Win. "We weren't really searching for him. We just found him."

"Searching, finding, who's to say you can have one without the other?"

Win watched the water splash by his feet, single drops splitting off from the spray, escaping momentarily from the grouping, only to recombine within a puddle, pulled inexorably back into the mix. Into the flow.

When Win looked up, I'Char was gone.

CHAPTER 2

WIN MET I'CHAR OUTSIDE the League Council building at the
appointed time. A wide stairway led up to the main entrance
where four strategically placed guards monitored the busy passage of ambassadors and legislators from planets across the
system. A massive transport vessel roared overhead, the ship
itself obscured by thick rain clouds.

"You look well rested," I'Char said.

Win smiled. "Apparently my time in the Gardens served me
well. Maybe next time you won't have to go all the way to Triocon to bring me to a place I live right next to."

"Let's not need a next time," said I'Char.

The two headed up the stairs. Halfway up they had to run a
gauntlet of protestors holding signs demanding more government
services and chanting *Honor the promise!* Maintenance personnel
were busy scrubbing graffiti covered walls, the harsh smell of
sanitizers overwhelming. Once inside, Win and I'Char stepped
onto a moving platform that took them to the Office of Inquiry,
where they were scanned by two security guards.

"Captain Win," said one of the guards. "You will be first."

"We are not being interviewed together?"

"The President left instructions that you were to enter first,
alone. Mr. I'Char can wait here."

Win shrugged and followed the guard into the President's
chamber, uncharacteristically ornate for a military room, its
walls lined with bright panels depicting star clusters, the ceiling

patterned with bejeweled parquet. Win was surprised to see only three of the council members sitting at the long semi circular table. League Council President Perin-Ta, in the middle, wore an uncomfortable looking metallic brace to support his fragile Lensian skeletal structure, which sharply poked through his spindly translucent flesh. Sitting at Perin-Ta's left was Ambassador Rios Waren. Win had encountered Waren once before at a science convention; Waren's pomposity had made for an unpleasant experience. Adorned with extravagant jewelry, Waren's corpulent face was nearly covered by oversized dark glasses. The Ambassador was of royal blood, his demeanor one of someone annoyed with the entire galaxy. Though he could not see Waren's eyes, Win was feeling his stare. To Perin-Ta's right was General Zendra Volenar. Win had never met her but recognized her from the news; she was a heavily decorated military hero. She sat tall and proper, her pale skin and flowing white hair sharply contrasting with her jet black uniform.

A single chair faced the Council table, and Perin-Ta motioned for Win to be seated.

"Good morning, Captain Win," the President said. "We appreciate your willingness to appear at this hearing. Due to the sensitive nature of what we are about to discuss, the Joint Council decided it would be more appropriate if a smaller group conducted this debriefing. We are a special Investigative Committee which will review what happened on your mission to K'Turia. General Volenar sits on the Military Council, and Ambassador Waren is its civilian liaison. We would like to begin with your own description of the events which took place on the planet K'Turia, as further elaboration of your original reports."

"Those reports left much questioning amongst the full Council," said Ambassador Waren. "They suspect omissions of certain information, as does Waren." The Ambassador tapped his chest.

Win leaned forward to speak but Perin-Ta cut him off. The President shifted in his harness to face Waren.

"Ambassador Waren, we are not here to accuse Captain Win

of anything. This hearing is simply to give him a chance to offer his personal account and explain his actions. You will have ample opportunity to question him at the appropriate time. Is that clear?"

Waren waved his hand dismissively. "Very well, let's get on with it."

Perin-Ta turned back to Win, the servo motors in his harness a whisper in the large room. "Captain Win, we do appreciate the cooperative attitude you have shown regarding this matter," he said smoothly. "However, your report was a bit short on specifics."

"What do you mean?" Win wasn't fooled by Perin-Ta's friendliness. The Military Council didn't care about Win's attitude as long as he did what they wanted. Win was still seething from being ordered by the military to go to K'Turia in the first place. "It's all there. We were ordered to K'Turia. We looked for the freighter and found it, empty. I'Char destroyed it. End of story."

Perin-Ta sighed. "Let's start at the beginning. What was your exact understanding of the nature of your original mission, prior to going to K'Turia?"

"We were assigned to join the armada in orbit around Colltaire, to support the fleet against the Lemians. I made clear my disapproval of these orders. My ship, the *Anatar*, is a research vessel and not equipped for any sort of military confrontation. We were forced to join the armada."

"You were then sent to K'Turia?"

"We received a priority message ordering us to leave Colltaire to search for a missing cargo freighter. It was believed to have disappeared in the vicinity of K'Turia. En route we were to first stop off at Sector Four Station to pick up a special representative from the League, Jaims Garrick."

Win shifted his gaze to Volenar, looking for any sign that she might have known about Garrick's involvement, but the General betrayed no reaction.

Waren raised a wrinkled eyebrow. "This Garrick was in charge?"

"While Garrick never officially took command, he made it

clear what we were being ordered to do. And once we were on the planet he—he took matters into his own hands."

"Could you elaborate, Captain?" asked General Volenar. "In what way did he take matters into his own hands?" Her sharp eyes seemed to glow, reflecting light from the gilded lamps.

Win wondered why Volenar was asking about Garrick. Surely she knew his mission. Choosing his words carefully, he said, "I believed the best way for us to proceed was to move cautiously through the community, to stay together and remain as inconspicuous as possible. We were warned by one of the first locals we met that the Lemians were looking for offworlders—and might I add, the very presence of Lemians on the planet was something we were little prepared for. Garrick didn't tell us the Lemians would be there until the very last minute. The local was friendly and seemed genuinely concerned for our safety. He offered to hide us in his home for the night, so that we might enter the city in the morning when we were more likely to blend into the crowds. Garrick originally agreed to this plan, but during the night he disappeared."

"You looked for him, of course?" Perin-Ta asked.

"Yes. We went to great lengths to locate him. Eventually, I'Char found him badly injured. He had been tortured by the Lemians."

The three Council members exchanged glances. "If you found him, why was Garrick not rescued?" demanded Waren.

Win took a deep breath. He would not allow Waren to intimidate him. "Garrick told I'Char that the Lemians were stepping up their search for offworlders. He said he would lead the Lemians away from us, giving us the opportunity to escape."

Volenar bowed her head. "The act of a brave warrior."

"Yes," Win said. "He saved our lives. But still, from the beginning I was not in favor of his presence. He was not forthcoming about his role, or even if his mission was the same as ours. His actions put us all in great danger."

Perin-Ta tapped at a panel in front of him, skimming through a copy of Win's report. "You said you found the freighter with the help of some locals. Exactly how did they come to know about the freighter?"

"Many of the locals did not seem to mind that we were offworlders. Some helped to hide us from the Lemians. But the K'Turians were naturally curious as to why we were there. We told them we were looking for something that belonged to us. They did not know anything about the freighter specifically. Later we learned that they had discovered an offworld object which turned out to be the freighter."

"Your report says Mr. I'Char went off alone to check out the freighter. What were *you* doing?"

"I was—looking for Prentiss."

Perin-Ta leaned forward. "What happened to Kalinda Prentiss?"

Win did not answer immediately. Prentiss's decision to remain on K'Turia still haunted him. Waren's suspicions were correct— Win had in fact left a lot of detail out of his report, especially concerning Prentiss's association with the preacher named Jesus. Would the Council understand her decision to stay on K'Turia? "How well do you know Prentiss?" Win asked.

"I don't know her personally, but I know she had some difficulties with the League's Science Council," said Perin-Ta.

"She has—a strong personality," said Win. "She —"

"Waren knows about this human, Prentiss," Ambassador Waren interrupted, banging his stubby fingers on the table. "Waren had numerous encounters with this one, this pseudo-scientist immersed in religious fantasies."

Win, annoyed by Waren's constant reference to himself in the third person, was trying not to react. Keeping his voice as even as he could, he said, "Her theory regarding the development of cultures as a result of religious factors was certainly controversial, but that does not make her a pseudo-scientist." Win paused. "In fact, much of her hypothesis was, to some degree, verified on K'Turia. Some kind of religious intervention was leading to the advancement of a stagnant culture which had been holding on to unyielding beliefs."

"Precisely what kind of religious intervention are you speaking of?" asked Perin-Ta.

Again Win contemplated how much he should reveal about Jesus. He sensed that this group would not be open—or even truly interested in—a possible connection between religion and science. "There was a preacher on K'Turia," he said carefully. "He was not part of the established religious order. His teachings were quite radical, and were having a profound effect on a people who had become complacent and lethargic—the very combination of events that Prentiss had built her theory upon."

"Prentiss remained behind," Volenar said. "Why?"

"She wished to continue her research. She was only on the mission to provide insight into the local culture and help us blend in with the indigenous people. She saw the events on K'Turia as a once in a lifetime opportunity to prove her theory."

"But it was dangerous to be there, you said so yourself," said Volenar. "Didn't you try to stop her?"

Win fought down his growing anger. "What would you have had me do? Force her back to the shuttle? The planet was under Lemian attack. We had a hard enough time escaping, and I'Char and I *wanted* to leave. And remember, she was not technically under my command—she reports directly to the Science Council. I did not feel it was my place to interfere."

"It is difficult to believe she would take such a risk, and you would allow it," said Volenar.

"I told you, I do not have a military crew," said Win. "I can't just order people around like you do and expect them to blindly obey. But why don't you ask her yourself? Certainly you got her off K'Turia by now."

Perin-Ta glanced at Volenar before replying. "As far as we know, Specialist Prentiss is still on K'Turia."

Win was momentarily stunned. "What? I made clear in my report that she would be in great—and increasing—danger the longer she stayed on K'Turia. You need to get her off that planet."

"You are in no position to dictate that to us," said Waren. "Especially since you are the one who left her behind."

"But—I thought she would only stay for a short time, and she would hide with—the locals who had befriended us. Certainly it would not be safe for her to be there this long. She was somewhat naïve about the Lemians—she thought she could just walk up to them and identify herself as a scientist and they'd leave her alone. We warned her this would be impossible. You know what happened to Garrick, they tortured him." Win shook his head. "She didn't sign up for that."

"As you said, it was her decision," said Perin-Ta. "Your concern is noted."

"So you aren't going to send someone to get her?"

"This is a military matter," said General Volenar. "The situation on K'Turia has escalated, and the Lemians are there in larger numbers."

"The League is helping people all over the galaxy to fight off Lemians," argued Win. "This is what you do—it is what we do. You need to get Prentiss, and you need to help the K'Turians."

"As General Volenar has said, this is a military matter," said Perin-Ta. "We cannot interfere with K'Turian politics unless they ask us to."

"Interfere? Since when is protecting innocent people interfering? The K'Turians are not an advanced people. They probably don't even know the League exists. How are they going to know to ask us for help?"

"So you would have us start a war with the Lemians to help the K'Turians, who might not even want our help? This is strange logic," said Waren.

"I'm not saying that," said Win, trying desperately to keep calm. "Isn't it the League's duty to help people who can't defend themselves? You have to go and at least find out if they need help. And you have to get Prentiss. Now."

"These matters are very complex," said Volenar. "You don't understand."

"Maybe not," said Win. "But I do know that Prentiss is in danger. If you don't go get her, I will take a leave from my duties and get her myself."

Perin-Ta breathed deeply. "I am afraid that will not be possible."

"What do you mean?"

"As I explained, the situation on K'Turia has become extremely volatile. The Lemians are there in force. The League has ordered that no one is to go to K'Turia."

"This is ridiculous," said Win. "My knowledge of the planet makes me the right person to go. I'll know what to do and how to hide from the Lemians."

Perin-Ta edged his harness forward until it hovered directly in front of Win. "Captain Win, you are expressly forbidden to go to K'Turia. If you do so you will face *severe* consequences. Is that clear?"

Win looked at each of them. It was obvious they had already made up their minds. Nothing else could be done here. He turned to Perin-Ta, but his thoughts were focused on Prentiss. And Jesus.

"Yes, Mr. President," Win answered. "Very clear."

* * *

Later that day Win and I'Char sat in the transport terminal, waiting for their separate shuttles to arrive.

"You are not thinking clearly," I'Char said. "If you are caught going to K'Turia you may be court-martialed. We were on a military mission—they will claim jurisdiction. That's why only council members friendly to the military conducted this farce of an inquiry."

"I'll take that risk," said Win. "And knowing that the situation on K'Turia has deteriorated is all the more reason I must go. If Prentiss and Jesus are in trouble, I must help them."

"That is not your fault," said I'Char. "Jesus was taken into custody. We have no idea what has become of him. Prentiss is reckless. She follows her desires without considering the costs. She may be dead. Why would you risk your career—perhaps your life?"

"Volenar was right about one thing. I left her there. We could have forced her to come back—you said so yourself at the time. I never got through to her what the risks were from the Lemians. I can't live with that. So I'm going to K'Turia, one way or another. Neither you nor the League will stop me."

"And precisely how do you plan on getting there?"

"I will find passage aboard a merchant ship."

"No merchant ship will go near that planet now that it is off limits."

"Then I'll steal a ship. I will do what I have to do."

I'Char eyed him suspiciously. "Have you ever stolen a ship?"

"Of course not," said Win. "Have you?"

"As a matter of fact, yes," said I'Char. He cocked his head. "You might need my help then."

Win eyed him suspiciously, yet another surprise from I'Char. "No, you were right. This will end my career. I wasn't happy with it anyway, you know that. But there is no need for you to involve yourself."

"I have been through the same questioning as you. I am already involved." I'Char looked off in the distance. "And I too have been affected by K'Turia."

"I cannot ask this of you."

"I did not hear you ask. I have offered." The Illian rose as his transport was announced. "One last thing. Much may have happened since we left K'Turia. Do not be surprised if what you seek is no longer there." And with that I'Char was gone, swallowed up in the crowd steaming toward the departure lanes, leaving Win wondering once again how I'Char seemed to know his innermost thoughts, just as Jesus had on K'Turia.

CHAPTER 3

WIN STRUGGLED TO FIND A POSITION where he could get comfortable in the small seats of the cargo ship. Built for long, monotonous hauls between far flung space ports, the seats were thickly padded but had been designed for passengers far smaller than Win. It was even worse for I'Char, but he didn't seem as bothered.

As things turned out, they didn't have to steal a ship after all—I'Char had instead used his military connections to gain access to a depot where the League retrofitted captured Lemian spacecraft for covert missions. Innocuous and non-threatening, a cargo ship would be less likely to arouse suspicions. The Lemian pass codes would be out of date, but this was common for cargo ships. This one had most likely been used by an indie hauler, carrying low value material between Lemian outposts. It wouldn't make it through a detailed examination, but should get them past standard scans.

The ship needed a test flight, and the depot manager didn't ask many questions; it was hard enough to find someone willing to do these bothersome shakedowns.

All perfectly legitimate, provided they got the ship back in time.

Win and I'Char were technically still on duty, and should have been contacting their crew for the next tour of the *Anatar*. But the scheduling of scientific missions was haphazard and not well coordinated by the Science Council. Even so, it would not be long before someone realized that the *Anatar* was not underway—and that Win and I'Char were missing. That would likely get reported to Perin-Ta, who might suspect that Win and I'Char had disobeyed orders and had set off for K'Turia.

Though Win was counting on the usual inefficiency in both civilian and military channels, he knew they didn't have much time.

Now, approaching K'Turia after an uneventful trip, there was another danger. If the Lemians still had a command ship around the planet, or if they had installed advanced scanning equipment, not only would the cargo ship be spotted, but their pass codes would surely be questioned.

I'Char plotted a course somewhat oblique to the planet to test whether they would be intercepted. Their scanning capability was limited, but it would have indicated a large Lemian force. After the first pass, they took a chance and swung around the other side of the planet.

"Nothing," said Win. "If there is a Lemian command ship, it is too far for us to scan."

"It is gone," said I'Char. "If it needed to be near the planet, it would be right here, not off somewhere—they have no need to hide."

"The Lemians still could scan us from the planet," said Win. "And they might be on the lookout, since they know we—or someone—from the League was on K'Turia. Surely they would have figured that Garrick was a League spy."

"They've probably found the freighter by now," said I'Char. "There isn't much of it left, and they'll know someone from the League destroyed it. They won't expect the League will be coming back here. We'll have to worry about them more when we're on the planet."

"The Lemians must have known that Garrick was not acting alone," argued Win. "They might think we've been on the planet all along, waiting for someone to come get us."

"You are imagining how *you* would act, not the Lemians. They wouldn't go and rescue a team in that situation."

"But the League would, wouldn't they? And the Lemians would know that."

I'Char didn't look up from the scanner. "It's a good thing that you have me as your military adjunct," he said. "It keeps you from making naïve assumptions."

Win was accustomed to I'Char's directness and did not take the rebuke personally. "So much for the League being different from the Lemians."

Now I'Char did look up. "As for what we stand for, we are different. But when it comes to the tactics of war, no one is really different. Softhearted governments almost always lose."

"Pretty ruthless," said Win. "I couldn't do it."

"Wait until you face such a decision—with the consequences of what might happen if you are wrong and lose—before you decide what you can and can't do," said I'Char.

Win wondered if he could make a choice like that, to not rescue someone he knew needed help. A choice that could lead to someone dying. He thought of Prentiss, still on K'Turia. He *had* left her behind, but at her own request. That distinction would not mean much if she had been captured by the Lemians.

Win decided. "Let's go in, then."

I'Char had already set the approach vector which would bring them down to the planet's surface. They didn't want to risk using the same landing site they had used on the earlier mission, and it was too close to the city and the Lemian base anyway. So they were forced to pick an alternative spot farther away.

The main city, Merculon, was bordered by a series of ridges to the north and east, and beyond that, a vast desert. Their first landing had been on the far side of a ridge away from the city. I'Char kept them on that same side, but now at the very edge of the ridge. He brought the ship down gently onto the sand and powered down.

"Good spot," said Win. "On a quick scan it might be hard to

distinguish the ship from the edge of the ridge. Might buy us some time."

"Or they already know we are here," said I'Char.

"Well, if that's the case, we better get going," said Win. But he paused, remembering his previous visit here, when his Treb *gheris*, his ability to sense extreme emotions, had nearly overwhelmed him. He took a deep breath and opened the door.

Nothing hit him but the stagnant heat of the desert.

He waited, reaching out with his senses. But he could feel nothing like what he had before, that powerful reflection of what he later learned was the passion of the people, stirred by their reaction to Jesus.

Win slumped, not prepared for this. Behind him, I'Char said, "Trouble?"

"I don't know," said Win. "It's—different, from last time. I can't sense what I did before."

"Something wrong, you think?"

"More like something missing," said Win. Had something happened to Jesus?

He dropped down onto the sand. As before, they wore the clothing that had been prepared by Prentiss to help them blend in with the indigenous people: dark colored hooded robes and sandals. On their backs, under the robes, a small sling of water and food, carried as the locals did. But no technology of any kind. Even the smallest scanner could be detected by the Lemian defenses and would be immediately suspicious, since the K'Turians had no advanced technology.

In preparation for their earlier mission they had been bio-immersed in the local language, and except for a few complex words, would have little problem communicating. Some of the local people had recognized them as offworlders, especially Win, but no one seemed to have been bothered by this. Though without their own technology, K'Turians were familiar with space flight and had received offworld visitors in the past. Yet given the presence of the Lemians, Win was determined to maintain a low profile. I'Char had the ability to mimic other races by resetting his facial muscles in a way that changed his features, and he could even shift his coloring; it could fool even a close inspection. Win could not, and if the Lemians were on the lookout for offworlders he would certainly be recognized if they saw his face.

Pulling up their hoods to brace them from the heat and the sand, they set off in the direction of the road to the south which would lead them into the city.

* * *

It took the better part of the afternoon to reach the road. Along the way they had met no one, nor had they seen any Lemian shuttle patrols overhead. If the Lemians were out looking for anyone, they weren't doing it here in the desert.

The road too was empty. From their last visit they had learned that most of the population kept to the cities, and few people traveled between them. At one time many pilgrims had come to Merculon to see Jesus, but the local religious leaders, the Pertise, had cracked down on this. Fearful of Jesus' influence, they had taken him into custody. Win and I'Char, forced to flee K'Turia, did not know his fate.

They spoke little, having talked about their plan on the long flight. They would approach the city the same way as before, over the low hills to the west, down into the valley, and then past the outer farmlands. This is where they had met Symes, the rather eccentric old man who thought they were pilgrims coming to see Jesus. A secret follower of Jesus himself, Symes had warned them about the Lemians and the Pertise, offering to hide them and then get them into the city.

They had first come to K'Turia knowing the Lemian presence would make their mission difficult and dangerous. They had not expected how much more complicated it would be due to the undercurrent of rebellion stirring against the traditional religious leaders.

A rebellion stirred by Jesus.

Prentiss, the cultural anthropologist, had held a long standing, controversial theory that many pre-technological societies could only be set on a path to advancement by the appearance of a "messiah." For this theory she had been demoted from her prestigious position in the Science Corps, exiled to serving on Win's remote ship. She had vowed to herself she would never mention her theory again. But the discovery of a religious preacher named Jesus, on a planet across the galaxy from Earth, had changed her mind. She was certain her theory was correct, and she now had the evidence to prove it.

Prentiss began following Jesus to document her findings in order to provide proof to her superiors and regain her reputation. But as she listened to Jesus she came to realize that his teachings were more important than her theory, more important than her work. She became a true follower. She had stayed behind on K'Turia to document Jesus' words, more for the local people than for any selfish goal of achieving anything to do with her reputation or fame.

Win, too, had been greatly moved. Jesus seemed to understand exactly what he was going through, what it was he had lost. Like most Trebs, Win had been on a quest to achieve *ana,* the highest spiritual plane of his people. The death of Sooni had shattered his resolve and left him drifting, and he had joined the League to hide in the minutiae of scientific research. But Jesus had seen right through Win's cloak of denial and had shaken him to the core, forcing him to confront his fears and his loss.

But unlike Prentiss, who had embarked upon a new path after hearing Jesus, Win could not make such a leap. Now he was tormented in a different way, half awake, all the possibilities of starting anew on his search for *ana* before him, but with the pain of Sooni's loss reignited.

Though he was intent on finding and rescuing Prentiss, he knew he had also returned to K'Turia with a personal agenda—to get help for himself. He too needed rescuing. He needed Jesus to help free him from his purgatory.

* * *

Once atop the final hill, Win and I'Char had a clear view of the approach to Merculon and the city itself. As before, everything appeared deserted. The isolated huts that lined the road were the homes of the lower classes of the K'Turian caste system. Most of them would be working as laborers in the city or in the fields off to the southeast, only returning to these houses at dusk. In the morning a huge exodus of people would make their way into Merculon and the fields. If all went well, that would be their chance to enter the city, losing themselves in the crowd.

"Looks the same," said Win. Just outside the perimeter of Merculon sat a set of prefab structures, ugly and incongruous against the well crafted handmade city walls. The Lemian garrison.

"No," said I'Char. "There are more buildings in the Lemian camp. They must have increased the size of their force."

Win couldn't tell the difference, but this was one of the things that I'Char was good at. "Well, hopefully we won't be going anywhere near them."

"If they have more troops, they'll have more patrols," said I'Char. "The Lemians don't like idle soldiers."

They would face harsh consequences if captured by the Lemians, who would certainly consider them spies. Though not officially at war, the League and the Lemians were bitter enemies. Covert military missions were common, and prisoners taken by the Lemians were tortured and usually killed. Win hoped that the League was not so ruthless but for all he knew the League did exactly the same thing. He didn't trust the military arm of the League, and his original mission to K'Turia, forced on him by the military, had only added to his suspicions.

"If we can find Symes, he might be able to tell us about the Lemians," said Win, leading them down the hill. "That is, if he has his wits about him. He was pretty incoherent when he was nervous about anything."

"If he is nervous, that will tell us a lot," said I'Char. "He's still our best hope for getting information. Otherwise we are going to have to ask people in the city, and we don't know what has changed—or how we will be received."

"You still think the people may blame us for Jesus being taken into custody," said Win. He thought back to the day when Jesus had confronted Methurgem, the high priest of the Pertise, in front of an enormous crowd at the temple. The Pertise had captured Prentiss, trying to use her to get to Jesus, and Jesus had given himself up to the Pertise in exchange for Prentiss's freedom.

"Us, or offworlders in general, it doesn't matter. The population was ready to erupt after Jesus challenged the Pertise. The priests would do anything to silence him. If they still have Jesus—or he has been killed—we don't know who will be blamed."

I'Char had said what Win could not bring himself to consider, that Jesus might be dead. It would explain why he had felt nothing with his *gheris* sense, why the powerful reflection of Jesus' presence was totally gone.

Win pushed the thought away. Jesus had said, *Belief is not a fate or a destiny, but a choice.* Right now, he chose to believe that Jesus was alive.

* * *

The road crisscrossed its way down the slope and then they were in the valley, the road running straight as an arrow to the city, precast synthetic material laid by the Lemians. Symes's hut was one of the first they would come to, his low rank putting him way out on the city outskirts.

The door of the first hut hung ajar, sand blowing inside. A livestock pen alongside stood empty. A hundred paces away on the same side of the road was Symes's hut, crude but neat, the stepping stones from the roadway swept clean.

The door opened as they approached. Symes appeared in the doorway, looking the same as before, and yet different in some way. His beard was just as scraggly, his face just as gaunt. But he stood taller, his shoulders no longer hunched, and now his eyes sparkled.

"I have been waiting for you," he said, with a hint of excitement, yet exhibiting nothing like the distraught demeanor they remembered.

Maybe he was senile after all, thought Win. "You were waiting? Didn't you know we had left?"

Symes smiled. "Of course. But Jesus told me you would return."

CHAPTER 4

I'CHAR STEPPED PAST SYMES and disappeared into the back room of the small house. In a moment he returned, immediately peering into the adjoining storeroom.

"We are alone," said Symes. "Please, sit. You must be tired. May I offer you something to drink?" Without waiting for an answer Symes went to a small sideboard and poured drinks from an earthenware pot.

Win was astonished by the change in Symes. When he had last seen the old man, Symes was at times barely cogent, subject to fits of rambling and incoherent mumbles. Now he seemed calm, lucid.

Symes set the drinks down on his small table. "Please, sit," he repeated.

Win took the offered seat and accepted the drink. Symes turned to I'Char, holding up another cup, but the Illian shook his head and went to stand by the front window, looking out.

"You are safe here, at least for now," said Symes. He sat down across from Win.

"What has happened?" asked Win. "Please don't take offence, but how did you —" He didn't quite know how to ask.

"Regain my wits?" said Symes. He laughed. "I'm not sure I ever lost them, they were just—hidden, I think. After you left I was able to spend some time with Jesus, and so much became clearer to me. He helped me to find a new purpose. And to do that I had to rediscover who I was."

"So Jesus is free?" asked Win. "And do you know of Prentiss? And how did Jesus know we would return?"

Symes laughed again. "So many questions! But of course you must be curious. I can make you feel better about one thing. Jesus was released by the Lemians."

"The Lemians?" Win was confused. "He surrendered to the Pertise. How did the Lemians get him?"

"I will tell you what I know," said Symes. He looked over at I'Char. "The Lemian patrols are very punctual—and predictable. They won't be back on this road until a little before sunset, and even then they no longer bother to search the houses."

Without turning his head, I'Char said, "Complacency is a dangerous thing."

"He hasn't changed a bit," said Symes.

"It's part of who he is," said Win.

Symes stared at Win. "You however, have changed, haven't you? You're more—alive. You have come to see Jesus, haven't you?"

Win was taken aback. Was his change really that noticeable? "We do want to hear about Jesus. But we came for Prentiss."

"Hmm . . ." said Symes. "Very well." He took a sip of his drink. "You really should try this. Tthean was kind enough to give it to me, a fresh fruit wine. You remember Tthean?"

"Yes. One of Jesus' followers."

The old man leaned back in his chair. "Let me tell you as much as I can about what happened after you left. Later we will find a way to get you to Prentiss—and Jesus. They have left the city and are in hiding."

I'Char looked over. "'We'?"

"There are many secret followers of Jesus still in Merculon," said Symes. "They will help you. But let me start at the beginning. Just as Jesus was taken into custody by the Pertise, more Lemians arrived."

"We were here for that," said Win. "We saw the Lemian ships landing just as we were escaping. Are they still here?"

"The ships are gone, but there are many more Lemian troops," said Symes. "The people were very angry at the Pertise for taking Jesus. It all happened so fast. Some thought the Lemians had something to do with it."

"Why did they think that?" asked Win. He knew the truth—that Jesus had given himself up to the Pertise in exchange for Prentiss, who had been captured by the priests.

"Mostly because the Lemians showed up at just that time. Others think it was the Pertise's idea, because Jesus was becoming too powerful. Still others think that Jesus wanted to be taken. It doesn't really matter, he is free now."

"How did that happen?"

"After the Lemians landed there was a lot of confusion, a lot of questioning. Many people stopped listening to the Pertise. The Pertise didn't like that at all, and the Lemians—the Lemians don't abide disobedience. So the Lemians locked up some of the more vocal supporters of Jesus. But once he was let go, things calmed down a little."

"Why did the Pertise let Jesus go?" asked Win. "I thought they were afraid of him. After that scene at the temple, when Jesus argued with the high priest Methurgem, I would have thought that the Pertise would have done anything to stop Jesus from preaching as he did."

"You are right," said Symes. "But it wasn't the Pertise who let Jesus go, it was the Lemians. The Pertise had turned Jesus over to them. I think the Pertise were afraid of what the people would do if they punished Jesus themselves. When the Lemians let Jesus go, the Pertise were furious."

Symes took another sip of his wine. "This really is quite good! Where was I . . . yes. The Lemians let Jesus go, no one knows why, and the Pertise were furious. So they again tried to capture Jesus. Jesus said this would happen, and so he fled to the desert with most of the disciples. Your friend Prentiss went with him. They are in a secret place—more than one, actually. They move often to stay safe. I was lucky enough to spend some time with

Jesus in one such place. I don't even know how he knew who I was, but I was sent for by Tthean and taken to a cave in the desert. There I listened to Jesus for many days, and that experience has changed my life. I can now—see. I know what I must do in life. Jesus has shown me the true Way—not the thing called the Way that the Pertise had taught us, with its shallow rules and rituals, but the real path to Paradise. This is how I now live."

Win was trying to absorb it all. "And Jesus? You said he told you we would return?"

"You sound surprised," said Symes. "Certainly you know that Jesus is aware of what each of us wants. Even I could tell you were searching for something, and that you did not find it. Jesus would certainly know that you would want to come back."

"We were searching for a ship—from our world," said Win. "We did find that."

"Really?" said Symes, his eyes widening in surprise. "Do you think that's why you first came to K'Turia?" He smiled. "No matter." He refilled Win's cup. "So that is the story. I had to leave Jesus. Though no one really misses an old man, some patrol would realize my home was suddenly empty." He looked around at the small room. "It is odd. I had no family, few friends. But now I do have a family. All who love Jesus are my family. They are the ones who would miss me. And there are more of us than the Pertise know."

"What do the Lemians think of all this?" asked I'Char.

"I don't know," said Symes. "Since the uprisings have subsided, they don't bother us as much. Jesus made it very clear that he does not want us to fight the Lemians—or the Pertise either. Not all the followers are happy about this. Some want to start their own temple, proclaiming the new Way of Jesus. Others don't like that Jesus says the Way is for offworlders as well. They don't really understand Jesus. The Way he teaches is for everyone."

"And Prentiss?" asked Win. "You have seen her?"

"Yes. She is writing down the words of Jesus, preserving his teachings for all of us."

"Did the Pertise tell the Lemians about her? About another offworlder besides Garrick being here?" asked I'Char.

"This I do not know," said Symes. "Why does it matter?"

"We are at war with the Lemians," explained Win.

"I don't understand," said Symes. "You and Prentiss are at war with them?"

"Not the two of us," said Win, "but our people . . . our government. It's called the League. The League and the Lemians have been enemies for a long time."

"But if you two are not at war with them, why should they care about you?"

"I'm afraid it is not so simple," said Win. "The Lemians are not very trusting. They will think we are spies—that we are on K'Turia to harm them."

"And if they know Prentiss is here, they will be looking for her," said I'Char. "If they catch her, it could lead them to us." I'Char turned to look briefly at Symes before resuming his vigil out the window. "You said before the Lemians no longer search the houses. When did they do this, and why did they stop?"

"Right after you left, when the new soldiers arrived, they searched everywhere. We didn't know what they were looking for. We asked but they would not tell us. After a few days they stopped." Symes considered. "Were they looking for you?"

"Not us specifically," said Win. "But someone from offworld. The object we were searching for, the freighter. Somehow the Lemians knew about it. They would have been trying to find anyone who came to retrieve it." He turned to I'Char. "Why do you think they stopped looking for us? They must know someone destroyed the freighter."

"Yes. The question is whether they knew that the freighter was destroyed before or after they captured Garrick. That would tell them whether he could have done it."

"Maybe they concluded he was alone," said Win.

"Better to be safe and assume they are still on the lookout," said I'Char.

"What I can't figure out is why they didn't just tell the K'Turians that they were looking for offworlders," said Win.

"You're not thinking like a Lemian," said I'Char. "They wouldn't believe anything the people told them. They don't trust anyone."

"Unless they found someone who would turn us in," said Win.

"I don't think anyone would do that," said Symes. "They might tell the priests, but no one really likes the Lemians."

"I wonder," said Win. "There was this one man who told us about the freighter. We were there when he told Jesus he had been helping the Lemians."

"You mean Tsaph," said Symes. "You don't have to worry about him. He has become a follower and is now in hiding with Jesus."

"Still," said Win, "you understand we have to be careful. How are we going to be taken to Prentiss?"

"Don't worry," said Symes. "I told you we knew you would come. Not the exact day, but that you would be here. Some were keeping their eyes out for you in the city. But I had a feeling you would come here first. I have waited for you."

Win was touched. "Thank you. So what do we do now?"

"We eat, of course!" said Symes. "Then tonight I will go get someone who will tell you how to find your friend—and Jesus."

* * *

Win was anxious to get going but realized they could do little without Symes's help, so he surrendered to the old man's request. I'Char was not one to surrender, but agreed to at least wait for the Lemian patrol to pass. Just as Symes had said, a two seat Lemian ground craft sped by in the very late part of the day, heading away from the city. Win watched as I'Char split his attention between the Lemians and Symes, as if he still suspected Symes might give them away. But the man just kept on with his dinner preparations. Shortly thereafter the Lemians came back along the road, moving even faster this time.

"They certainly don't seem to be looking for anything," said Win, who had joined I'Char near the window, both of them standing back so as not to be seen.

"Sloppy," muttered I'Char.

"Better for us," said Win.

"Maybe," said I'Char. He lowered his voice. "It all seems too easy."

"I know," whispered Win. "But if they were still looking for us, why be so surreptitious? They certainly aren't afraid of the K'Turians." He indicated Symes. "I don't even think he has the capacity to be deceitful. And we know he is dedicated to Jesus. I believe him."

"I do, too," said I'Char. "But that doesn't mean we aren't in danger."

"Come here and sit," said Symes. "I have only meager offerings, but what I have is yours."

Win sat down. "We have some of our own food. We do not wish to take what little you have."

"Jesus says we will be provided for in times of need," said Symes. "I do not worry about that. Please eat." He put some food in a bowl and brought it to I'Char. "I see that I cannot convince you to leave the window."

"I thank you for your hospitality," said I'Char, "but excuse my caution. It is —"

"Who you are!" said Symes. "I know. Someday you will come to trust more." He returned to the table. Bowing his head, he said, "We are thankful for our bounty, and are blessed for our lives."

"A prayer from Jesus?" asked Win.

"A K'Turian prayer," said Symes. "Some of the old ways are still good to keep."

As they ate they asked Symes more about the Lemians and the situation in the city, but learned little more beyond what he had told them.

After the meal Symes said, "Soon it will be sunset. Right now the farmers are leaving the fields, the builders are packing their tools. Many people will be coming and going. You must hide here while I go into the city and bring back someone who will tell you what to do next."

"Wouldn't it be better if we just come with you?" asked Win. He did trust the old man, but was heedful of I'Char's warning.

"No," said Symes. "They are used to seeing me alone." He searched Win's face. "You must trust me in this."

"I do," said Win.

Symes looked over at I'Char. "And you?"

"How many people will you tell?"

"Just two," said Symes. "One of them will tell another, someone even I do not know. That one will show you how to reach Jesus. The other person I tell will go into the desert to the caves to let them know you will be coming."

"Cells," said Win. "You are operating like spies. No one knows the whole story."

"Except Jesus, of course," said Symes. "He knows everything."

* * *

They watched Symes from the window as he walked down the road toward the city. He was trying to act nonchalant but Win could sense his excitement.

"Quite a remarkable change in him, don't you think?" said Win.

"Remarkable is an understatement," said I'Char.

"Perhaps miraculous is more accurate," said Win. He watched until Symes was out of sight. "I know you are still cautious. But would the Lemians go through all this deception to find us?"

"They would do whatever it takes," said I'Char. "I still think we need to be on guard, although I admit getting Symes on their side and weaving such an elaborate hoax doesn't feel like a Lemian approach. Unless Symes was helped with drugs—Lemian drugs."

"I'm sticking with miraculous," said Win. "Or simple belief."

"We'll know soon enough," said I'Char. "And just to be sure, as soon as it gets darker I'm going up the road toward the city to find somewhere to watch them as they come in. I suggest you go back to that deserted hut we passed. Will you be able to sense anything amiss using your *gheris*?"

"It must be emotional," explained Win. "And strong, if at a distance. Extreme fear would do it." He had never sensed much about I'Char with his *gheris*. "Have you ever felt extreme fear?"

"Once," said I'Char.

Win thought he was going to learn something new about I'Char, but the Illian didn't elaborate.

"If the Lemians show up or Symes comes back with more than one person," I'Char said, "I'll do what I can to stop them. That should trigger enough—emotional response—for you to read. It will give you a chance to get back to the ship."

Win knew it was useless to argue with him. I'Char's suspicions were perfectly reasonable. But in his heart he knew that they were in no danger, at least from Symes.

* * *

Just after dusk they left the hut, I'Char watching Win retrace their steps on the road toward the hill. As Win walked off, I'Char said, "If you sense anything at all out of place, get away. I can deal with this better than you."

Win gave a slight wave and kept going. I'Char wasn't sure what Win would do. He suspected Win would not leave him if there was trouble, but he couldn't do anything about that now.

The Illian headed in the opposite direction. He moved quickly along the road, checking each house. Nothing seemed amiss. Most of the houses were empty, but showed obvious signs of being lived in: curtains in the windows, swept stoops, livestock in pens. In only one house did he see any signs of activity, two old women feeding their animals. They either didn't notice him or paid him no mind.

Up ahead the houses began to cluster, where it would be harder for him to hide unseen from someone inside. He chose a hut with two livestock pens, one on the side and one behind. Circling the house to make sure it was empty, he settled in between the pens, giving the animals time to get comfortable with his presence. After some cursory sniffs, they left him alone.

I'Char knew exactly how long it would take to walk to the city; he had done it before and it was the kind of thing he remembered. He added in an estimate for how long it might take Symes to meet his contact and make it back to the hut.

While he waited a few people did return to their homes, but he knew that many took meals in the city and would come home very late. The house he hid behind stayed dark.

At almost exactly the time he had predicted, he heard the sound of quiet conversation above the sniffling of the livestock. He crept around the pen, his keen eyes now accustomed to the dark.

There on the road he could make out the figure of Symes, talking in a loud whisper. And next to him, someone much taller, hidden beneath a robe, but wearing an unmistakable hat. A high ranking priest.

Symes had brought one of the Pertise.

CHAPTER 5

I'CHAR HESITATED ONLY LONG ENOUGH to be sure that no one was following Symes and the priest. He crept away from the animal pen, then circled around the back of the house after they passed by.

"Symes," he said quietly, his tone commanding.

The old man and the priest spun around, startled. "Oh, it's you," said Symes, visibly relaxing. "Why are you out here on the road?" To the priest he said, "This is one of the men I was taking you to see."

"This must be the one you told me about," said the priest. "The cautious one."

"Who are you?" asked I'Char.

The priest carefully removed his hat and pulled back his hood. "I am Johearim." He took a few steps toward I'Char and held out his hand. "I have come to help you."

"You are a Pertise," said I'Char, shifting his position to block the road to Symes's hut.

"Yes," said Johearim, "but a follower of Jesus." He dropped his hand. "I mean you no harm."

"I didn't know Jesus had followers in the Pertise," said I'Char.

"Not publicly—yet. But he has many followers in the Pertise and even the general priesthood. Perhaps even more than I know of."

"We should get off the road," said Symes, looking up and down the street. "If someone were to see us . . . it is not common to see a Pertise here."

"I could not come disguised," explained Johearim. "If I had been recognized out of my robes, leaving the city, it would have aroused suspicion. And there is much suspicion in the city these days." He held open his robe. "I am unarmed."

"That's not what concerns me," said I'Char. He wasn't worried about being able to deal with the priest if necessary, armed or not.

"What is it then?" asked Johearim.

"I question the too visible path," said I'Char. "We arrive, and you are here, waiting for us."

"As do I. Yet I have found that there are few unintended coincidences when Jesus is concerned. But I can explain more. Please. Symes is right, we should get off the road, or at least move on."

I'Char had to decide whether to lead them to Win. He was not one to believe in coincidences. Perhaps others already knew that he and Win were here and where they were hiding. The more who knew, the more danger they were in. He scanned the road.

It was empty, and he heard nothing but the braying and shuffling of penned animals. A few of the homes now had lights appearing in the windows.

He stepped aside and indicated for Symes to lead. He needed to find out what else the priest knew.

* * *

I'Char followed Symes and the Pertise into the old man's hut. Satisfied that no one had followed them, I'Char told them to wait and went to get Win from the other hut. When they returned the old man had lit a few small lamps and was pouring wine.

The Pertise rose to greet Win. "I am Johearim. I have heard much about you."

Win sensed no nervousness or threat from the priest and took his hand. "How is that?"

"Symes told me a great deal. I have also been told of you by some of the disciples who bore witness to the times Jesus spoke to you. Very little that Jesus says goes unremembered."

The priest sat down, indicating a chair to Win. "Please, we have much to discuss and not much time. I must return to the city as soon as I can."

"You will not be taking us to the desert?" asked Win.

"No, that would be too risky. Nor can you go tonight. Crossing to the mountains at night would be most unusual and would likely be reported. But do not worry, we have a plan. There are mineral deposits in the desert that we use to preserve food. Miners go there frequently to gather this mineral. Jesus has many friends within the mining community. One of them will take you to him and your friend Prentiss first thing in the morning." The priest paused, looking from Win to I'Char. "I know you must have many questions, and I will answer them as best as I can in the little time we have."

Johearim was the first Pertise that Win had seen up close, other than the high priest Methurgem who had clashed with Jesus on the temple steps. Like Methurgem, Johearim was clad in a stylish robe, not overly ornate, but of a much finer material than what the other K'Turians wore. Though he was not young his hair had not turned gray. A neat beard highlighted his piercing blue eyes. For someone taking the risk to have this clandestine meeting, and hiding his beliefs from the other Pertise, he seemed remarkably at peace.

I'Char had resumed his post by the window. Without turning he asked, "How did you come to be a follower of Jesus?"

"It seems hard to believe, doesn't it?" responded Johearim. "After all, Jesus' teachings are a great threat to the Pertise. The Pertise, by being the translators of the Way, have held power over the people for countless generations through our place atop the Order. But the Way is supposed to be for all the people, not just those lower in the Order. We Pertise have lived comfortable lives at the expense of those below us. We've grown soft, since there has been no one to judge the judges."

"Until Jesus," said Win.

"Yes, this is the truth," said Johearim. "Jesus has exposed the hypocrisy in how some Pertise have translated the Way, and how they live. And he has openly confronted them. We knew that there had always been some who inwardly resented the easier lives of the Pertise, but until Jesus no one had voiced these sentiments.

"Yet I will tell you that many of us within the Pertise had already become uncomfortable with some of the interpretations of the laws. Jesus has shined a bright light on all of this—on us. I am ashamed of what I have been part of—what I am still part of. I know I am making the right choice in following Jesus, although it is not yet the time to fully break free." Johearim smiled slightly. "Or maybe that is what I tell myself, and it is really that I just do not have the strength yet."

The priest ran his hand along his fine robe. "Sometimes the flesh is weaker than the mind and the heart. I look to Jesus for strength. We priests had twisted the real meaning of the K'Turian Way, that of the sacrifice, to benefit ourselves. Jesus' message of sacrifice is really the very essence of what our Way should be, and perhaps was long ago. Sacrifice is not about providing things for those above you to give them an easier life. It is about helping others, no matter who they are. But that is something difficult for those at the top to see, let alone accept. The entire Order is an abomination. I am doing what I can from within to make things right, but I wonder if it can ever be enough. Even now Methurgem and other Pertise grow suspicious of my questions and challenges."

"So other priests have begun to follow Jesus because of his teachings?" asked Win.

"More within the Pertise than the general priesthood, though that may seem odd," said Johearim. "The younger priests are still intimidated and in awe of the Pertise, and do as they are told. And of course they aspire to be Pertise someday. And there are many, both priests and Pertise, who so firmly and honestly trust the accepted Way that they cannot step back and see how it is false. But some within the Pertise, especially those who study the ancient ways, have come to realize how far the laws have strayed, and how the current way we live is not what the Way should be."

"Do not forget the people!" said Symes. "Jesus has many followers amongst the people who have tired of the Order. They wonder why they should have to give almost all they have to those above them, and receive nothing in return."

"Methurgem is well aware of this," said Johearim. "And this is why he fears Jesus, for it threatens his authority. Methurgem is also very smart. He knows that the seeds of discontent have been sown. It is not just Jesus who is a threat, but the message he has spoken, for it undermines the very source of the Pertise's power. Even if he could put Jesus to death he could not kill the message."

"We left K'Turia just as Jesus was taken by the Pertise," said Win. "You must know he gave himself up in exchange for the release of Prentiss. What happened after that?"

"Methurgem planned on putting Jesus on trial, for heresy to the Way. But Methurgem realized that would cause a problem with the people. You saw how they reacted at the Temple. So we think he made a deal with the Lemians."

"What could Methurgem possibly offer the Lemians?" asked Win. "The Lemians can take whatever they want. They never hesitate to use their weapons, even on innocent people."

"He gave them Jesus," said Johearim. "Methurgem knew the Lemians do not abide troublemakers. He painted Jesus as an anarchist. The Lemians would take care of his Jesus problem, and he could blame it on them."

"Why did the Lemians let Jesus go?" asked I'Char.

"We do not know for sure. Of course Jesus knows what happened, but he has not told me. I can only hope that this is something that your friend Prentiss may discover, and record, so that we may all know it someday."

"Prentiss," said Win. "Do the Lemians know about her?"

"I do not know. But Methurgem thinks he can find Jesus through her and has ordered all the priests to be on the lookout for her. But we have hidden Prentiss well."

"Why didn't the Lemians give Jesus back to the Pertise?"

"We have wondered about this," said Johearim.

"To show them who was in charge," said I'Char. "The Lemians were demonstrating their power over the Pertise."

"Methurgem does not fear them," said Johearim.

"He should," said I'Char.

"Yes, I know. But he is arrogant and looks down on them as unbelievers. He is now obsessed with finding Jesus to put him on trial. Even though Jesus is no longer in the city, his following grows every day, and his teachings are repeated time and time again. In the past, the Order kept the peace; there was no real questioning. But now the Order has lost its purity, its blind acceptance. Fear of the Lemians keeps more order than the fear of the Pertise. I do not think that Methurgem has come to realize this."

"But the people still fear the threat of banishment by the Pertise," said Symes. "While some of us low in the Order secretly wondered if we could ever find Paradise, we always hoped. And reaching Paradise was our reward for a life lived according to the Order. It made all the payments of the sacrifices worthwhile. So while Jesus has many who follow him, most are still stuck in the old ways of the Order. The priests still have many supporters."

Johearim reached for Win's hand. "And so we must be very careful, as must you," said Johearim. His eyes moved briefly to I'Char. "Though I see that you travel with one who keeps great care."

"Is Prentiss in danger right now?" asked Win. "We came because we feared that she would be taken by the Lemians."

"Though she is well hidden, we cannot guarantee her safety," said Johearim. "We watch the Lemians carefully. But she may be in greater danger from Methurgem, who has more eyes and ears than do the Lemians."

"What if Jesus were to return?" asked I'Char.

"Then there will be a great reckoning," said Johearim. "And much as I want there to be a change in the way we live, I do not believe the people are yet ready for that. There would be bloodshed, and none of us want that. I pray that Jesus feels this way, and that is why he stays in hiding. But I have come to trust Jesus, and believe he knows what is best for all of us."

The Pertise stood up. "I must go, else I will be missed. I will only have the flimsiest of excuses if I am seen outside of the city by another Pertise, or my whereabouts reported to one."

Johearim once again took Win's hand. "Tomorrow, one named Coru Chiths will come to you. The miner I mentioned. Coru will take you to the desert. Even I do not know exactly where Jesus is now, for safety reasons. I pray for your safety as well, and for that of all our people." He pulled his hood back up over his head and went to the door.

"The roadway is clear," said I'Char.

"Thank you," said Johearim. "I hope someday all these suspicions will no longer be needed."

"Care is an eternal friend."

"As is trust," said Johearim.

"You sound like Jesus," said I'Char.

"Thank you, my friend," said Johearim, opening up the door and putting on his hat. "But what I really want is to be like him."

CHAPTER 6

WIN SLIPPED QUIETLY OUT OF THE HUT just before sunrise. He
had been on the second watch, and the night had passed
uneventfully.

He stepped carefully along the road, toward the hill from
which they had come, the city at his back. He needed as much
separation as could get from all other living beings. Though
everyone who lived on this road was probably still asleep, his
gheris still hummed with sensed emotions, as it always did. It was
something he lived with, like sight and sound, so much so that he
no longer thought about it; *gheris* was simply a part of how he
interacted with the world.

In the semi darkness he climbed the road until just before it
crested. Now he stood still, clearing his mind.

When he had arrived on K'Turia the first time, he had been
almost overcome with the powerful onslaught of his *gheris*, which
he had come to realize was the cumulative response of the people
to Jesus, and perhaps even emanations from Jesus himself.
During that time on the planet, Win's nervous system had auto-
matically muted that sensation for his own protection. This was a
normal Treb response to such a strong power, just as he might
involuntarily close his eyes when confronted with a blinding light.

But on this return trip to K'Turia, when he had first emerged
from the ship, he had not felt the strong emotions he remembered
from his earlier visit. All during the trek to the hut he had wondered if some remnant of his protective muting mechanism was

still in place, if he had been subconsciously blocking out the powerful impression of Jesus.

He took three slow, deep breaths, closing his eyes and letting his *gheris* flood over him. He sensed nothing amiss. In fact, he felt little emotional power at all.

That should have been a relief, but it actually made him feel even worse.

* * *

When Win returned to the hut I'Char was waiting for him outside. As was his wont, I'Char asked no questions about Win's disappearance.

"Someone is approaching from the city," said I'Char.

Win peered down the road, but the sun was about to rise, and he found himself looking directly into the light. He flicked his eyes away, and when he looked back he could see a lone figure, the sun at that moment just appearing, casting the figure in silhouette, an aura of light about its head.

"Our guide," said Win. For a brief moment his *gheris* whispered to him, a hint of the Jesus impression, and then it was gone.

The woman's hood was thrown back, showing short straw colored hair distinctly unlike most of the K'Turians they had seen. She carried a large pack on her back, making her look much taller than she was.

She stopped when she reached the hut, carefully set the pack down, and walked up to Win, staring into his face. Win was struck by her eyes, like her hair also much lighter than anyone else's he had seen on the planet. They seemed to hold the colors of the desert sand, almost as if he could look right through her to what was beyond, or as if she were part of the very land.

"You are the one called Win," she said, her voice confident and calm. "I would not mistake you." She looked at I'Char, and a flash of puzzlement crossed her face. "I know who you are, as well, for this I have been told, but you . . . "

"You feel you could not forget him, but you might not recognize him again," suggested Win.

She laughed. "Exactly. How did you know what I was thinking?"

"I'Char has that effect on people. Do not let it disturb you."

"I wasn't disturbed. Just surprised. I was told you were offworlders. I am Coru of the Chiths, the miners."

Symes appeared at the door. "Coru!"

"Hello, Symes, I am happy to see you again." Coru threw her arms around the old man and kissed his forehead. "You are looking well."

"Please come in, all of you," said Symes. "I will make some breakfast."

"We must be off quickly, I am afraid," said Coru.

"Cold porridge it is then," said Symes.

As they ate Coru explained the plan. "The only people who regularly go to the desert are the miners. We should draw little attention as long as it appears we are on a mining expedition. Even the Lemians are used to miners coming and going. Still, we must be on the lookout because they and the Pertise are searching for offworlders."

Win glanced over at I'Char but said nothing. As usual, I'Char's face did not reveal his thoughts.

Coru took a quick bite and continued. "The miners leave the city early in the morning to avoid the heat. We will be at some risk coming from this direction; most of the miners live in the north end of the city, closer to the mountains. From here, we will have to either return to the city to go from that way, or head north and circle around the Lemian camp, crossing the foothills, to reach the edge of the ridge. Both choices will be dangerous if anyone recognizes you."

"We were here before and no one seemed to notice us," said Win. "Or they thought we were pilgrims."

"Things have changed," said Coru. "While there is more support than ever for Jesus, the priests have more spies. There is great distrust all around. And we do not know what deals the

Pertise have with the Lemians. I understand that you would be of great interest to them."

"Which route will you take us on?" asked Win.

"Around the Lemians," she said. "It's faster. Hopefully they will simply ignore us, as they have in the past. To help with that, I have brought you new clothing." She opened her large pack and took out two sets of leggings, some odd looking pieces of sturdy leather with straps and buckles, hats, some other gear, and two smaller backpacks.

"You must dress like a miner on the way to gather halas, an important mineral we use. The miners wear these leggings, and their robes are specially made to fold up and out of the way when digging. I did not bring new robes for you, but hopefully you will not have to dig as part of our deception." She indicated the leather items. "These fit over your sandals to protect your feet in the mines. You don't have to wear them now, but if we are stopped and searched, they would be in any miner's pack." She gave the packs to Win and I'Char. "It is not my nature to be deceptive, but it is the safest way for everyone."

"Someone who comes within the guise of another is not necessarily bad," said Win.

Coru looked up in surprise. "I have heard Jesus say almost the same. He said, '*What one sees on the outside is not always what is within. It is only the truth which cannot be disguised.*'"

"That works both ways," said I'Char. "It is often necessary to be wary of someone or something that looks good."

"Like some of the Pertise," said Coru. "I understand." She touched her hair. "Unfortunately, you do not look like miners, your hair is too dark. She looked at Win. "Some of the miners keep their hair cropped. You might be okay. The halas, when handled over a long period of time, gets absorbed into the skin and lightens our hair and even our eyes."

"Like this?" said I'Char. When they turned to him, his hair had lightened considerably, and his eyes held the same flaxen hue of Coru's.

"How did you do that?" Coru asked.

"It doesn't matter," said I'Char. "If the Lemians see us this close, it won't be enough."

"Do you think we should go through the city instead?" asked Win.

I'Char shook his head. "No. Too many eyes. But let's make sure that our route is safely away from the camp."

"I have thought of that," said Coru. "Although it will add some time. Once we reach the hills we will be out of sight from the Lemians."

"From their eyes only," said I'Char. "Not their technology."

"We will be but three miners on the way to work," said Coru. "At least that is what we hope."

* * *

After only a few thousand paces away from the hut they were once again in the desert sands. To their right, the city shimmered in the sun, highlighted by the reflective buildings of the Lemian camp.

"This is when we are most vulnerable," said Coru. "We are in a place where very few have need to be. Those who live near Symes use the road to and from the city and the farmlands to the south. If we are discovered here it will be hard to explain, and there is nowhere to hide."

"Are the Lemians familiar enough about K'Turian ways to know that?" asked Win.

"I do not know," said Coru. "Actually I was thinking more of what our people would say. They would certainly find it odd for us to be out this way."

"Do you have a plan should that happen?" asked I'Char.

"If we meet someone who is sympathetic to Jesus, I will simply say that we were bringing something to Symes. We miners are quite high in the Order, and normally such a gift would not be a sacrifice of the traditional K'Turian Way. Those sacrifices only flow upward. But the message of Jesus is that each should help another as they are in need, no matter where they are in the Order. So a follower of Jesus would understand why we would be helping a poor man like Symes. If they are not a follower of Jesus, we will say we were here to collect a sacrifice. That would be unusual, but it has been done. A family debt, perhaps."

"How will you know if we meet a follower of Jesus?" asked Win.

"We have our ways," said Coru.

"What if we are seen by the Lemians?" asked Win.

"I'm afraid I'll have to leave that to you," said Coru. "Though my advice would be to simply stay out of their way and ignore them, which is what most of us do."

"Good advice," said I'Char.

* * *

As they walked Coru told them more about how she came to follow Jesus. "As I have said, we miners are high in the Order. We know where to find and how to quarry the halas and other minerals. As such, we provide. So we are not as high as those that create, like the builders and craftspeople, but we are above even the farmers.

"So we have really never been in need, receiving many sacrifices from those below us. But as we mine, we spend more time away from the city than anyone else. It gives us a different perspective. Have you ever known a person, and then are away from them for a long time, and when you return they seem very different, but those who were with them the entire time notice no change? It is like that. I would leave the city to work in the mines, and when I returned everything would be worse. Those at the top of the Order had more and more, those below, less and less. The priests had finer robes, the old people had only rags to wear. Yet no one questioned anything.

"Then Jesus came. I was away when it happened, but when I

returned to the city everything felt different. People were finally asking why things were the way they were. Some were worried, but most were hopeful, hopeful that things might change. When I heard Jesus speak he put into words what I had been feeling, he opened my eyes to what was right in front of us, that the Way that we had been taught was wrong. Perhaps it was easier for me to see, because I had a different perspective. But it did not take me long at all to realize the truth in his words.

"I have heard him say: *'Do you build your house on rock and solid ground, or on shifting sand? Just as your house must have a foundation, so too there must be a base beneath your beliefs.'* This is something that touches the heart of a miner. The old way was one of shifting sand; it was filled with laws that were being translated in a way that made things unstable. I wanted a real foundation, and the new Way of Jesus has given it to me."

* * *

It was late afternoon when they reached the edge of the foothills, where they stopped for a light meal. Coru told them to drink as much of their water as they wanted, for there was a spring in the foothills and more places ahead where they would find runoff from the mountains. They began to climb, slushing through the scree.

As usual, I'Char heard it first. "Get down!" he hissed.

Win heard the urgency in I'Char's voice but still hesitated. In one motion I'Char threw his pack off and roughly pulled both Win and Coru to the ground.

"Crawl apart from one another quickly and then stay still," I'Char ordered. "It's a Lemian scout ship."

They scrambled to separate themselves, freezing at the whine of a patrol ship, coming from the north beyond the foothills. It angled by their position, heading toward the Lemian base.

The sound died away and Coru began to move. "Not yet," I'Char warned.

The Lemian ship made a sharp banked turn, heading back their way. Win tensed, thinking they had been spotted. If they fell prey to the Lemians it would be more than their careers that would come to an end. He held his breath as the ship passed overhead.

They waited tensely, flattened amidst the dry scrub grasses as the ship briefly disappeared behind the mountain. The sound of the ship was hard to place, but then it suddenly cleared the mountain a little to the south in a wider circle, and Win exhaled only when I'Char motioned that it was safe to get up.

"That was close," said Coru. "Let's get higher into the mountains; we'll have more cover there."

* * *

As they ascended they stopped often, listening for more Lemian ships. But all was quiet. Soon there was some cover from pale white stunted trees which grew along the rock outcroppings of the hillside, and when they got higher the hill turned to full rock face. Coru was a strong climber and she set a fast pace, even though there was no trail and they had to scramble.

They reached the top of a small rise, putting them briefly in the open, but Coru led them quickly down the other side into a small hollow, a saddle between two ridges. At its base ran a small stream, with plenty of room to walk alongside.

"We'll make good time here," said Coru, "and we'll be completely out of sight except from above. Anything coming from the city we will hear, but if another ship comes over the mountain from the north as before we will have little warning. The good news is that we are now in a place where miners sometimes come; there are deposits of lesser ores here."

They followed the stream to the east, still in the saddle but the land always rising, the mountains looming to their left. Coru pointed. "There is a trail over the mountains in that small cleft. There are caves and abandoned mines on the other side. That is where Jesus is hiding."

When they reached the cleft they stopped briefly to rest. Behind them they could now see over the foothills they had climbed. It was past late afternoon, but the sun was still high enough that it was hard to gain a perspective on size; the city of Merculon could just as easily have been a large rock in a landscape. Far to the south the bright green of the farms cut a clean demarcation in the desert.

To the north the cleft appeared to lead directly into the wall of the mountain, but as they set off it was all just a deception of proportion; there were plenty of places to go. Here and there cairns marked the trail, leading them to the first of the abandoned caves.

They picked their way past the remnants of mining activity, a few small carts, some broken tools. When they reached the last of the caves the trail resumed, narrowing between another cleft. The trail turned yet again, and led straight into an opening that had been carved into the rock wall, a tunnel through the mountain.

"Miners cut this tunnel long ago," said Coru. "There is a newer trail and tunnel farther to the east, nearer the city, so this one is not used much these days."

"I would think the Lemians would have this area under surveillance," said Win.

"They do. The flyovers, and now and then a patrol. We're very careful."

When they emerged from the tunnel they were on a more north facing wall. Here, in the shadows, it was noticeably cooler. The trail continued along the rock face, dotted with caves. Coru led them up a small ledge and into an opening, a cave barely wide enough for the three of them. A few paces past the entrance it split into two. Coru entered the narrower opening, where they had to pass one at a time. The passageway turned sharply to the left, plunging Win and I'Char into darkness until they made the turn.

Here the passage was brighter, for it ended a few paces ahead and opened up into space. "When we leave this passageway we will be in view of some of our lookouts," said Coru. "You won't be able to see them, but they are in place to give early warning to Jesus and his disciples if someone unfriendly comes this way."

"You cut this passage so anyone approaching could only come through one at a time," said I'Char. "This is a good defense. But it won't stop the Lemians. They would blast their way through."

"They would get a few surprises if they did. We have weakened the walls above. Not enough to bring down the mountain, but enough to slow them down so we can get away."

Once outside they were on another ledge trail, and Coru paused only long enough to wave twice with her left hand, and then twice again with her right. The trail followed along the wall to a switchback, and when they cleared the turn a small part of the desert opened up before them, walled off by a ridge to the north, forming a sand filled cove.

Coru pointed to the smaller ridge ahead. "You can't see them from here, but there are more caves in that ridge. That is where Jesus is hiding. The caves have escape exits on the other side of the ridge."

"There are two lookouts," said I'Char.

"Yes, we always have —" She stopped. "You aren't supposed to be able to see them from here. I can't even see the cave entrances, and I know where they are."

"Five caves," said I'Char. "Four facing west, and probably a fifth somewhere in the middle, given how the trail leads. One lookout is in the second cave, and the other is in the last one."

"Your eyesight is extraordinary," said Coru. "Can the Lemians see this well?"

"No," said I'Char. "But their sensors would have no problem picking up the lookouts."

"What should we do instead?"

"Someone peering out of a cave looks suspicious," said I'Char. "You are miners, right? If there is any ore here, then mine. Just have everyone doing what they would normally do."

"Hide in full view," said Coru.

"Often it is the safest way."

"Too many miners might be suspicious. We'd have to plan for that. But I see your point and will tell Tthean. Come, we are expected."

She continued on, quickening her pace. "I have not been here for almost a month. I'll be happy to see Jesus once again!"

The first cave came into view, and when they reached the second one Coru waved again. A man emerged, slight of build, his hood pulled back. Win recognized him from their earlier visit, a trader who had initially been helping the Lemians but then fled to be with Jesus.

"Hello, Tsaph," said Coru. "I have brought the offworld friends of Jesus."

"Oh, Coru," said Tsaph. "I'm so glad you are here! Something terrible has happened!"

"What? What is it?" asked Coru.

"Jesus is gone!" Tsaph looked at Win and I'Char. "And so is Prentiss."

CHAPTER 7

"WHAT DO YOU MEAN, GONE?" asked Win.

"Come inside," said Tsaph. Wringing his hands, he led them out of the sunlight through a narrow passage into a larger room, partially lit from channels cut into the roof. They passed through that cave and into another passage. This opened up into a surprisingly large cavern, furnished with rugs and a wooden table.

A small group of K'Turians clustered in the middle of the room, most dressed in traditional K'Turian robes, a few in miner's gear. One of them stepped forward, a ruddy faced man with broad shoulders. "I am Tthean, one of the disciples of Jesus. He told us you would return."

"I remember you," said Win. "You were in the safe house with Jesus, before he was taken." He looked around. "Tsaph said Jesus and Prentiss are not here. Where are they?"

"We don't know exactly," said Tthean. He indicated one of the rugs. "Please sit, I will explain." When they were all seated, Tthean said, "A few weeks ago, Jesus told us he would be going off into the desert by himself. In spite of our objections, he would accept no companions, and said he would be back by nightfall. Three times he did this, returning safely each night. He then stayed here an entire week without returning to the desert." He looked at Win. "Your friend Prentiss was always with him during that time. She has become our scribe, saving his words so that his teachings will be fixed for all time. In another cave we have made copies of her writings, and have hidden them carefully."

One of the other disciples handed everyone drinks. Win accepted his and took a sip without looking at it, intent on Tthean's story.

"Last week Jesus told us he would be going into the desert again. We had received reports of the Pertise looking for him, and so we begged him not to go, but he said that he needed to prepare himself for a trial he must face. We thought he meant the trial that the Pertise wanted, but he said, *'That is but a trial of the flesh. I must face a trial of the spirit.'* He took no food, and when we asked him what he would eat, he said *'For our faith to remain strong, we must feed it with more than bread.'* Then he said he had to face the darkness. We took this to mean he would stay overnight. And this time he told Prentiss to remain here.

"When he did not come back on the second day we began to worry. We thought he had been taken by the Pertise. On the third day he still had not returned, and we went to look for him, but could not find him. I walked far into the desert but saw no evidence he had been there at all. Prentiss was especially worried. She said Jesus had been telling her about a great battle that would soon take place, for which he had to prepare not only himself, but help others to prepare for. At the time she didn't think it had anything to do with the Lemians or the Pertise, but now she was not so sure.

"So early this morning, Prentiss went to look for Jesus herself, taking Liall, one of the miners, as her guide. Liall knows the desert very well, and so we are not worried about Prentiss. But I should not have let Jesus go."

"You would not have been able to stop him," said Win, thinking of how he had failed in his own attempt to stop Jesus from turning himself over to the Pertise in exchange for Prentiss. "It was not your fault."

"I feel like it is," said Tthean. "I know that Jesus chooses his own path, as do we all. It is the very essence of his teaching. But I am worried. What if something bad happens? I could have done so much more, I could have . . . " His voice trailed off.

"It will be dark soon," said one of the other disciples. "Already the ridge trail to the north is in shadow. Liall and Prentiss will be back soon, and I'm sure they will be able to tell us where Jesus is."

Win heard the optimism in the man's voice, but his *gheris* sensed his fear, and the flood of it in the cavern. And for the first time since he arrived on K'Turia, he felt it too, starting as a doubt, and blossoming into a myriad of questions that had no answers.

* * *

Darkness came quickly, for the cave entrance faced away from the setting sun. Most of the disciples huddled in the small chamber near the entrance. Tthean had finally told them to go back to the main cave, promising to let them know as soon as Prentiss and Liall returned. Only Win, I'Char, and Tthean remained near the cave entrance.

By late evening Prentiss and Liall still had not come back. "It is very dangerous to walk the ridge trail in the dark," said Tthean. "They must have decided to spend the night below the ridge and will return in the early morning." His voice was flat in the darkness, for they had not risked a light so close to the mouth of the cave.

"Tell me about the trail," said I'Char.

"It is a continuation of the route you used to get here. It runs along this ridge, always on this side. The ridge, as you perhaps noticed from your approach, later curves around and then back toward us, forming a partial ring. The trail goes to the end of the ridge and then down into the desert on this side."

"Are there no trails to the desert before the end of the ridge?" asked I'Char.

"A few. But they are very narrow and are dangerous even during the day."

"What about on the other side of the ridge?"

"There is no real trail on that side, just some steep cuts down to the base. We can get to one of them through a few of these caves that cut clear through the mountain. That's our escape route."

"Which side of the ridge did Jesus go to?" asked Win.

"He left on this side, and always returned this way as well," said Tthean. "But if he followed the trail to the end, he could have gone around the ridge into the deep desert."

"Would Prentiss and Liall have gone that way?"

"Perhaps. But they were not planning on staying overnight. They should have been able to reach the end of the ridge, go down into the desert on this side, and have been back by now. If they did venture out around the ridge for any distance, it would explain why they are not back."

"Where would they stay overnight?" asked I'Char.

Tthean considered. "I don't know for sure. There are some rock overhangs and a few smaller caves. Liall might have been willing to try to return in the dark, but it would not be safe for Prentiss or anyone else not familiar with the trail." Tthean's voice changed. "First Jesus, and now them. I hope nothing bad has happened. If they are not back by late morning, we must go look for them."

"You should get some sleep then," said I'Char. "You can't do anything now. We will wait here."

"I am very tired," said Tthean. "I have not slept much since Jesus left."

"Go," said Win. "I'Char and I will take turns on watch here. We'll wake you if they return."

Tthean hesitated briefly, then nodded. "Thank you. We are grateful to have you with us."

When he was sure they were alone, Win said, "It could be as he hopes, that they are just waiting for the daylight."

"Only one way to find out," said I'Char. "I'll go look for them now."

"In the dark? He said the trail was dangerous," warned Win.

But there was no reply, and Win realized he was alone in the cave.

* * *

Win tried to stay awake, but it had been a long, difficult day. He dozed off, propped against the stone wall just behind the cave entrance. Now and again he would wake with a start, staring into the darkness, straining all his senses into the void. His *gheris* picked up the nervousness of the disciples in the next cavern, but his physical senses told him nothing.

The cave reminded him of the time of the Great Meet, the pilgrimage on his home planet to face the challenge at Braay, the challenge all Trebs had to overcome to reach *ana*, the plane of spiritual enlightenment. Twice he had failed that challenge, just as he was failing now, failing to feel anything, see anything, or find who he came to find.

He stirred, the failure turning to sadness, threatening depression. Then he awoke with a start as he saw a light from outside the cave.

The light grew brighter, and he somehow realized he was not really awake. His eyes followed the light as it moved toward him, just as another light had become his beacon at Braay, leading him not to enlightenment but to Sooni. The voice of Jesus seemed to fill the cave. *'The light of Truth you have now seen with your own eyes has always been with you. For how else could you have been shown that she was the one?'*

He opened his eyes. There was no light outside the cave, but the memory of it burned in his mind, and it so filled his thoughts that the impending sense of despair was pushed away. He felt warm, warmer than he should have against the cool rock. And, at last, he fell into a deep sleep.

* * *

When Win awoke the light of morning was filtering into the cave. Tthean, Coru, and I'Char were talking quietly near the entrance. Win immediately sensed that Prentiss had not returned.

He got up and joined the others.

"They are not on the ridge," said I'Char. "But I may have found something." He pointed down the ridge trail to where it curved back around toward the west. "Not far from where the ridge ends there are some small caves. Outside those caves I saw a cairn, which seemed out of place because it was in the middle of a clear part of the trail and I had passed no other cairns at all. On the wall next to one of the caves I found a symbol scratched into the rock, along with some K'Turian letters."

I'Char knelt and picked up a sharp stone. In a smooth part of the rocky ground he scratched out a symbol that looked like a compressed triangle, bisected by two vertical lines. Below it he drew two angular letters. "I could not see them clearly in the dark, so I had to feel them."

"Letters! Those are Liall's initials!" said Tthean. "As for the symbol, could it be this?" He took the stone from I'Char and redrew the symbol, so that there was a break in the triangle. It was now two separate mirrored symbols.

"Yes, it could have been," said I'Char.

"That's the symbol we use to refer to Jesus!" said Tthean. "Only his followers would know of it. It is the first and last letters of *alethiae,* the K'Turian word for 'Truth'."

"I could not tell if the scratches were fresh, or if anything else was there," said I'Char. "I went into the cave a short way. It appeared empty. Yet I felt air. It might go farther back and come out the other side of the ridge."

"It probably does," said Coru. "I would have to see which cave it is to be sure. That passage isn't used often; by the time you reach those caves you are almost to the end of the ridge."

"Have you seen markings there before?" asked I'Char.

"No," said Coru. "Although I have not been down to that end

of the ridge for quite some time. Miners sometimes do mark their passage on the rock though, for others to follow."

"Is there any reason Prentiss and Liall would have gone in that cave?" asked Win.

"Water," said Coru. "There are springs in most of the caves, or at least places where the water seeps through from above. They could have replenished their water bags there. But not food." She turned to Tthean. "I'm sure Liall had his miner's pack with him?"

"Yes. He gave one to Prentiss as well."

"That is good," said Coru. "A standard field pack has enough food for a few days, in case a miner is stuck in a cave or stranded by a storm."

"So they may have gone into the cave to look for Jesus there, or to try to reach the desert on the other side of the ridge," said Win.

"Or I missed some other marking," said I'Char.

"Only one way to find out," said Win, mimicking I'Char from the night before.

* * *

After rushing through a cold breakfast and filling their packs with food and water, Win, I'Char, Coru and Tthean were on the trail. The going was relatively easy, the trail wide and smooth, only here and again cutting back against the ridge. It was not yet noon when they reached the caves.

It was exactly as I'Char had described. Just outside one of the smaller caves they discovered a set of scratched letters on the rock wall.

"It is definitely the symbol for Jesus," said Tthean. "Liall and Prentiss must have left this for us."

"But why?" asked Coru. "Were they in such a hurry that they could not come for us? Or did they just want us to know that they went this way? And if they did, why have they not returned?"

"Maybe they got lost in the cave," said Win.

Coru shook her head. "I doubt it. The ridge is quite narrow here, the cave probably not so deep. Let's find out." She lit a lamp and led the way in.

The cave was actually quite wide, the light from Coru's lamp not nearly enough to show them the other side. I'Char lit his lamp as well, and they separated slightly to spread the light. The floor was uneven, the walls haphazard, rock jutting out at them from all angles.

"I have not been in this cave," said Coru. "But I feel some air. This way."

In about fifty paces they reached the back of the cavern. There were two cuts in the rock wall. From one they could feel the air flow, actually somewhat warm. No movement came from the other.

"The warmer air is probably from the desert, and it means it is quite close," said Coru. She shone her lamp on the wall near the openings. "No marks on either wall."

"Which way?" asked Tthean.

"Let's check this one first," said I'Char, indicating the opening that did not lead to the desert. "Just in case." He turned to the others. "I'll go, wait here." Without waiting for an answer he disappeared into the opening, his light quickly lost in the gloom.

"Shouldn't we go with him?" asked Coru.

"No," said Win. "He can take care of himself, better than you can imagine."

They did not have to wait long. I'Char came back and immediately headed for the other opening. "Nothing there," he said. "It just narrows and ends."

"Let me go first," said Coru. "I know this rock well, and will be able to tell if the footing is safe."

The passageway did not take a direct path, but wove its way amid large cuts in the rock. Twice it split, but both times it was clear which way the air was coming from. At one point they started to ascend, and had to climb over a short wall, bringing them onto a small ledge. Here they heard the first sound in the cave, the plinking of water. Their lamplight reflected back at them from the ceiling, wet with condensation, dripping into a small pool of clear water.

"This water would be fine to drink," said Coru. "It might be why they came this way."

Soon came a very narrow fissure they had to squeeze through. Once on the other side, the cave narrowed again, and the air flow became warmer.

Coru turned down her lamp. "It gets lighter ahead. We are almost there."

They made a final turn, opening to a wide gap in the wall. At the mouth of the cave they stopped and looked out. Here the ridge had turned slightly, and their view was blocked by the mountain. To the north they could just make out a narrow sliver of the desert. There was no sign of Prentiss or Liall.

* * *

"How can we get down from here, Coru?" asked Win.

The miner studied the ground around the cave entrance. She pointed to a cleft in the rocks. "I would go that way first."

She picked her way to the cleft. "This looks promising. Water has moved through here."

"So has something else," said I'Char, squatting near the cut. "Someone has come through this way." He indicated scuff marks in the hard ground.

"Fresh," said Coru, bending down to examine the markings. "At least not very old. Otherwise the wind would have covered that up." She looked up at I'Char. "You have a feel for the rock. You would make a great miner."

"Too enclosed for me," said I'Char.

"If Liall and Prentiss came this way, then why didn't they leave markings for us here?" asked Tthean.

"They could have been in a hurry," said Coru. "Or maybe

they just marked the cave entrance because they had never been there before, and wanted us to know where they went. Once out here, they might not have known the way down, and once at the bottom would not come back up to mark the route."

She stood up. "Be very careful. This is not a trail. Don't get too close together in case someone loses their footing." She began to ease her way down the cleft, dislodging scree which trickled down through the rocks out of sight. Just before they reached the bottom the cleft turned sharply to the left, the ridge forming a wall, and the mountain rising almost straight up on the other side.

At the bottom the rock quickly turned to a thin layer of sand. Cut off by the curving ridge and the full bulk of the mountain, they still could not see much of the desert.

They stopped only briefly to drink and eat, not even bothering to sit. Off again, they followed the cut to the north, the sand beneath their feet getting noticeably deeper and warmer. The cut widened, the ridge curving off, and the deep red of the desert came into view, spreading out into the north, far beyond the range of sight.

The desert was empty. There was nothing to tell them that Prentiss and Liall, or anyone else, had ever come this way.

CHAPTER 8

"NOW WE HAVE A DECISION TO MAKE," said Coru. "Should we follow the ridge, go straight ahead into the desert, or head east along the mountain?"

"When we went looking for Jesus the day before yesterday we went into the deep desert from the other side of the ridge," said Tthean. "We searched to about there." He pointed to where the ridge on their left started its curve. "Others went out through the ridge cove, west of that spot."

"So we should either go straight, or follow the mountain," said Coru. She looked up. "It will soon be the hottest part of the day. It will be a difficult walk in the desert."

"What would you have done if you were Liall?" asked I'Char.

"It depends on what time of day they reached this spot—if they even came down this way at all. I would have first gone along the mountain, staying in the shade, looking for signs of Jesus' passing through. Later in the day I would have turned north onto the sands."

"My thoughts as well," said I'Char. "And if I wanted to leave markings behind, it would be easier to do along the rock."

"Everyone agreed?" asked Coru.

"You three go ahead," said Win. "I'll catch up shortly."

Coru and Tthean looked puzzled. "A skill he has—he wants to try something," explained I'Char. He gestured ahead. "Come."

Win waited until they had disappeared around a bend in the mountain wall, then walked out into the desert until he felt no more rock beneath his feet. He picked up some of the sand and let it run between his fingers. He reached out with his *gheris*, not at the sand, for his sense only told him about emotions, but into the deep desert.

Something, very slight. *Worry.* Slowly weakening. He realized that was probably from Tthean, and perhaps Coru.

He sat in the sand, letting the heat of it engulf him, letting his physical and mental center sink into the ground, trying to use the desert as a sounding board for his sensations.

But he felt nothing.

Even if Jesus had passed by here, Win knew he was now far away.

* * *

They reached a spot where a large crevice rose up the mountain, filled with rock. At the bottom of the cleft Coru found more scratches on the wall. "Liall's initials again, followed by two lines, and an arrow," she said. The arrow pointed away from the cleft. "The two lines mean this is the second mark he made," she explained. "He is leaving us a trail, and the arrow tells us he did not go up the mountain."

"I still wonder why they kept going," said Tthean. "Did they have some idea that Jesus came this way?"

Win was thinking about Prentiss, and her tenacity. "Prentiss would have kept looking until they could go no farther," he said.

"With new water from the cave, they would have enough supplies for at least another day," said Coru. "Perhaps two, if they wanted to take the chance."

"But Liall would have known we would worry," said Tthean. "He would have insisted they come back."

"You don't know Prentiss," said Win. "She would have convinced him, or just gone on by herself."

"And Liall would not let her go alone," said Coru. "But if they run out of water they will come back. So we are no more than a day behind them. We may even meet them as they return."

They continued on along the wall. Here and again the face shifted, so they were sometimes walking toward a crevice, and other times facing almost directly into the desert. At one such curve they came upon the third set of markings.

There were no initials this time, just three vertical lines, and an arrow, pointing into the deep desert.

"It points just east of the end of the ridge," mused Coru. "They knew that Tthean and the others had searched just beyond the ridge from the other direction. So I think they angled toward that spot, to begin a new search area, deeper in the desert, with this as the easternmost edge."

"If we go that way, and they return using another route, we will miss them," said Tthean.

"Yet if we try to guess their return and get it wrong, we will also miss them. And we'd also miss any other markings they might have left," said Coru.

"Can you leave a marking in the desert?" asked Win.

Coru laughed. "We have lived with the desert for generations. There are ways. Of course, you can't just draw lines in the sand, the winds would scatter that within a day. But even a small pile of stones can be seen from some distance, as would this." She reached into her pack and pulled out a series of sticks, wrapped in a black cloth, and held together by leather strips. "Each of your packs has one of these to make flags."

She looked up at the sun. "If we leave now, we can be at a point even with the edge of the ridge by afternoon. From there we would still have time to explore deeper into the desert and be able to return by dark. Or if the weather holds we could stay a night in the desert."

"Let's go," said Win.

"Just one thing first," said Coru. She pulled her miner's pick from her belt and neatly added some letters below the markings on the rock. "My initials," she said. "If they come back this way they will know we have understood their message."

* * *

They trudged through the sand, the mountains still looming behind them. There was no other frame of reference, and so it did not seem they were making much progress. But sooner than Win expected they reached the spot where the ridge to their left started to curve back sharply to the west.

"We are not far from where I had searched the other day," said Tthean.

Coru, who was leading, suddenly stopped. "That's odd," she said, pointing ahead.

"I don't see anything," said Win.

"Look at the sand," said Coru, heading off.

Win still couldn't see anything out of the ordinary. Just the never ending sand, clear out to the horizon.

As they followed Coru they saw what she had discovered. Clearly laid out in the sand was a long narrow channel, like a trough. It ran toward the northwest, past the ridge. A clear set of footprints led directly into the trough.

"A trail?" asked Tthean.

Coru shook her head. "I can't imagine how it could be. Look how far it goes; it's too deep to have been made by hand." She knelt down, examining the trough. "And why isn't it filled in? Unless this was just made, the night winds would have obliterated it." She moved some of the sand along the edge and it cascaded into the small ditch, filling it.

"There is only one set of footprints," said I'Char.

"Sandals," said Coru. "Not the miner's boots that both Prentiss and Liall are wearing."

They followed the line of the trough, careful not to disturb it. The footprints ended, but there was no indication that whomever had made them had left the trough. Within a short distance they were surprised yet again, as a second line angled off from the first, which continued on. They chose a path between the lines so as to keep both in sight.

Coru was at the right side of the group. "It splits again! There is another line, to the north."

They found more lines, all heading generally to the north or northwest. At one point, six of the lines intersected, and just beside this point, there was another furrow, but this time in the shape of an arc, leading out too far for them to determine where it went.

"This must be very new," said Tthean. He knelt down and sighted along the line which passed just north of the ridge. "I went around that ridge just the other day. I would not have missed this."

"Could Liall have done this?" asked Win.

Coru was firm. "I don't see how."

"The Lemians, perhaps," said Tthean.

"But for what purpose?" asked Win. "They would have no reason to carve lines in the desert."

"I don't know why anyone would," said Coru. "I can't imagine what it might be."

They all looked out over the desert, following the lines, the soft desert winds accentuating the silence and emptiness of the landscape.

"I can," said I'Char.

They all looked at him, surprised. "It's a map," he said simply.

"A map?" asked Tthean. "What kind of map?"

"How would we ever read it?" Coru asked. "It's too big to see the whole thing."

I'Char pointed up. "Not from there it isn't. It's a geoglyph."

"A what?" asked Coru.

"A map to be read from above," said Win.

Suddenly the void in Win's *gheris* opened up, not with emotion, but as a bottomless pit would open. It wasn't the appearance of emotion, out here in the desert wilderness, rather, it was the realization of the very emptiness that surrounded him. In that moment Win finally understood what he had been missing.

Jesus hadn't just disappeared. He was no longer on K'Turia.

CHAPTER 9

CORU WAS UNCONVINCED. "How could it be a map? And who would have made it?"

"It doesn't have to be a map exactly," said Win. "Just some kind of giant drawing." He suddenly realized that his sense of Jesus no longer being on K'Turia had come to him just as they had discovered the geoglyph. A geoglyph that might be a map, a map that could only be seen from space.

"Perhaps," said I'Char. "I've heard of such things on other planets. Huge images of animals. Prentiss would have known about them."

"We need a better vantage point," said Coru. "We should go back to the mountain and climb up to get a better look."

"What about Prentiss and Liall?" said Tthean. "And Jesus?"

"If she found this, Prentiss might have come to the same conclusion we did," said I'Char. "She could have also wanted a better vantage point. As for Jesus —"

"Let's solve one problem at a time," interrupted Win. He was still reeling from his suspicion that it *was* a map, and it had something to do with Jesus. He wasn't sure if he wanted to believe that. "I think Jesus can take care of himself." But the emptiness he felt in the desert was crushing him. Had something happened to Jesus?

"But if Prentiss and Liall had found this and headed back to the mountain, we would have seen them, wouldn't we?" argued Tthean.

"Maybe not," said Coru. "They might have followed one of the lines deeper into the desert, and then returned another way. Although it looks like you can see far into the desert, it is something of an illusion. Once someone is more than a few thousand paces away, they become difficult to see."

"I think we should try to find out whether these do form some kind of image," said Win.

"Whatever we choose to do, we should do it quickly," said Coru. "The winds will obliterate these lines soon."

"I wonder," said Win. The lines, simple as they appeared, were a marvel, created by transient furrows in the one landscape that would easily destroy them. Win felt sure that even if they had come upon the lines in the midst of a windstorm, they would have still found them, indelibly etched in the sand. And the footsteps at the beginning of the trough, amazingly still there, a hint of where to go.

Win laughed at himself, thinking how self centered it was to think that these lines had been left for them. Yet Prentiss could not have made the markings, and he could not imagine why the Lemians would. Another offworld group perhaps? But who? And Tthean had said that the lines had not been there just two days ago.

Which meant they may have appeared just as Win and I'Char had reached K'Turia.

Win turned to the disciple. "Tthean, I can't explain how, but I think these markings have something to do with Jesus."

Win waited as Tthean studied his face, not needing his *gheris* to understand the emotions the K'Turian was struggling with.

Finally the K'Turian relaxed. "Jesus has said: *'Those who follow me must help those who are lost, for only with your help can they find the way, and only thus can you yourself find the way. Keep me in your heart and mind and I will be your guide.'*"

Tthean put his hand on Win's shoulder. "I sense that, in a way, you too are lost," he said. "I will help you as I can, with Jesus as our guide."

* * *

The climb up the mountain was steep and difficult, for there was no real trail, just a rocky course within a crevasse created by some ancient rock slide.

They had returned quickly from the desert, stopping only long enough for Coru to leave a few flags near where they had first seen the lines. On the way back they had taken a slightly different route, aiming for a place where Coru knew they could not only climb but have a good vantage point overlooking the desert.

Anxious to get higher up, they quickened their pace. Now and again Win turned toward the desert, but they were deep in the crevasse, and there was no clear view. At one such stop I'Char had said, "We aren't high enough anyway. Even if you could see the lines, they wouldn't tell you much."

After that Win kept his eyes focused on the terrain and tried to keep up. Coru and I'Char seemed to flow up the mountain, but he was not accustomed to this.

They stopped a few times, but briefly, mostly to drink, and, Win suspected, for the others to give him time to catch his breath.

At an especially difficult gap in the rock they had to carefully pull themselves up a nearly sheer wall. Once beyond that the way became somewhat easier.

"It's still a long way to the actual trail," said Coru. "But soon we will be able to skirt to the east, and find a place where we can see the desert."

A breeze brushed across the rock face, whistling slightly through the fissures, reminding them they had to hurry before the lines were lost. Yet Win still felt confident the geoglyphs would be there when they reached the top.

At last the crevasse widened, opening up to either side. Above them another sheer wall, impassable. Coru led them to the left, passing large boulders and chunks of broken slabs. Then they were out of the slide, edging their way carefully along a ledge against the mountainside, a steep drop only steps away.

The ledge turned away from the desert and soon they reached an open area, a large rock topping, almost flat, the desert spread out before them, shimmering in the heat.

There, below them and stretching as far as they could see, were the channels in the sand, looking like sharply etched lines from this height. It was now clear they had come upon only a small section of them; from this vantage point they could see many more lines, extending in multiple directions, some crossing, some extending far into the distance. The arc they had seen was actually part of a larger circle, one of a series. Even in part it was clear the lines were not a natural phenomenon.

"Incredible," said Tthean. He opened his arms and grinned wide. Then he looked at Win. "A miracle! It is a miracle!"

"What is it?" asked Coru.

"I don't know," said Win. "We still aren't high enough to see the whole thing. We have to climb some more."

Coru shook her head. "We won't be able to get high enough. It's just too big."

"There is another way," said I'Char, pointing skyward.

Win immediately understood what I'Char was suggesting. They would have to go back to the ship and ascend high enough to see the geoglyph from above. "Are you sure?" He looked up at the mountain. "Maybe there's a different vantage point where we can see enough of it to figure out what it is."

I'Char looked from the desert to the mountainside, calculating. "I'm sure," he said. "Only a flyover will tell us what it is."

"We can't leave now. We have to find Prentiss," argued Win.

I'Char turned back to Win. "You go back to the ship. I'll stay and find Prentiss. She is probably on this mountain right now. I'll find her, wherever she is."

"I don't know," said Win, staring into the desert. He understood I'Char's logic, but doubt had crept over him, a weakness that had engulfed him after the loss of Sooni. That weakness had been lifted for a time, thanks to Jesus. Now it was back, more foreboding than the shadow of the mountain.

"We came for Prentiss," he insisted.

"Yes," said I'Char. "But you also came for Jesus. And I think you are right; these markings are connected to him. The only way for you to find him is to discover what they mean."

"And then what?" said Win. He shook his head. "They probably have nothing to do with Jesus anyway." But in his heart he knew that they did.

"If you cannot determine what they mean, then come back. I'll meet you at Symes's hut with Prentiss."

Win knew that if anyone could find Prentiss, it would be I'Char. He trusted in I'Char's skills, and more importantly, in his tenacity and his word. Still, Win hesitated. "The geoglyph. What if *is* a map?"

"The you must follow it. No matter where it takes you."

"What about you?" asked Win. "How will you get off K'Turia?"

I'Char smiled, something he rarely did. "You were willing to steal a ship from the League to get here," he said. "Do you think I would hesitate to steal one from the Lemians?"

CHAPTER 10

THE SHIP WAS STILL THERE like a waiting pet. There was no indication that anyone had been near it. Win looked it over, from head to tail, looking for anything out of place, anything that might have been attached to it. But everything looked fine. He settled into the ship, and using every stealth maneuver he knew, lifted it into the sky.

He would risk only one flyover of the lines in the desert. Certainly the Lemians would be scanning K'Turia's skies with sensors and drones. But they would most likely be looking for something coming in from space, rather than taking off from the planet. The small Lemian cargo ship he was in would look harmless enough.

At least he hoped so.

He cleared the mountains, keeping as low as possible. The first of the creases in the dry land came into view almost immediately. Sharp and defined, the lines as straight as arrows. He again wondered how they kept their shape in the desert sand.

As he was gaining altitude to get a better perspective the ship received an incoming message. Though he could not understand all the words he recognized the harsh Lemian language. They were on to him.

He rose as fast as he could, taking pictures all the way, praying that they would capture what he needed. The Lemian voice crackled again, more insistent. A warning alarm blared in the cabin; the ship was being lit up, the Lemian ground forces were locking their weapons on him. Win punched at the communications board, opening the channel, knowing he could never fool the Lemians but trying to buy a little time. His eyes frantically searched for something loose that he could use to knock against the mic to create some static, but there was nothing.

Win dragged his fingernails across the transmitter while turning his head and mumbling something unintelligible. The Lemian voice asked a question in response. Win said, "What?" in Lemian, knowing the accent was all wrong, hoping that whomever was on the other end of the transmission would hesitate just a moment longer . . .

The voice squawked again, slightly less adamant. Win hit the thrusters, revectored, and shot out of the planet's atmosphere and into space.

* * *

As soon as Win was safely away from K'Turia he looked at the images of the geoglyphs. Surprisingly they were smaller than he thought they would be. A cursory deep space imaging of the planet could easily miss them.

Had they been wrong? Was this some local ritualistic marking and not a map at all?

He changed the magnification of the image again. It occurred to him that if the geoglyph had been larger, it *would* have been visible to anyone orbiting the planet, including the Lemians.

Large enough to need a small ship, just like the one he was in, but not so large as to be seen from orbit. A peculiar combination. Unless—

The footsteps in the stand, from a sandal. The first steps on a path. A new path.

Had Jesus somehow created these markings so that Win would know where he had gone?

Improbable as that seemed, Win somehow knew that the markings *were* a map, and they had been left for him.

He studied an image which showed a series of different sized groups of circles. Within the groups the circles were connected by lines, and some of the circle groupings were connected by wider lines. All the lines were angular except two sweeping swirls, one large, one small, which immediately made him think of spiral galaxies.

He knew there were countless spiral galaxies in the universe. Even if it were a map, how would he even know where to start looking?

In the very center of the geoglyph four of the thickest lines formed a square, and within it lay another set of circles and lines. Like a map inset. A star system?

He overlaid the image on the Sector Four map, where K'Turia lay. Nothing seemed to match up. If it was a star system, he needed to find what galaxy it belonged to.

He took the full image and separated out the larger pieces, the two spiral galaxies, then ran it through the ship's mapping program. Almost immediately the computer came back with a match, in the so called Sector Zero, League-speak for all regions of space not within League or Empire control. Sector Zero was not really a sector, but an amalgamation of widely scattered systems.

But this particular location was not far from Sector Four at all. And when he laid in what he thought of as the inset, a local system named Carth popped up on his screen. He lined up the inset with the star map.

It was a perfect fit.

* * *

The trip to the Carth system was long and lonely. Win's thoughts bounced between Jesus, I'Char, Prentiss. And Sooni. Always Sooni.

He tried not to think about whether he was on an absurd quest that would get him nowhere. He was committed now—there was no way he could return in time for his next mission. He was officially AWOL, and once the Military Council found out, they would presume he had gone to K'Turia against orders.

The same would be true for I'Char, unless he managed to rescue Prentiss and escape from K'Turia.

To keep his mind from its haphazard wandering, Win renewed his Treb exercise of *ru-ahkh shamah*, the meditative practice of spiritual breathing. This had been the foundation of his preparation for achieving *ana*. But after Sooni's death he had turned away from everything that had to do with that search for purpose. Yet here, alone in the depths of space, it gave him a way to anchor himself to something.

On K'Turia, Jesus had said to him, *"You must first awaken, and then commit yourself to your search. If you have inner conflict, you will never find your own self, and will never be able to take the first step on your path."*

He didn't know if his path would one day bring him back to his search for *ana*, but he was confident of his immediate goal. He had to find Jesus.

* * *

Win's meditations were often interrupted by vivid visions of Jesus, some of them memories from K'Turia, others totally new, coming to him in full blown scenes without any conscious thought creation on his part.

In one of them, Win watched as Jesus sat by a still lake, lowering himself slowly into the water, as if bearing a heavy burden. Jesus entered the water without raising a single ripple, the surface impossibly flat, pristine. Jesus stared into the lake, his eyes absorbing the sunlight reflecting off the water. "What do you think of this place?" Jesus asked.

"It is beautiful," said Win, knowing that did not come close to doing it justice.

"Yet this great beauty exists in the midst of an overwhelming darkness."

"Of what darkness are you speaking? I see only light."

"Can there be light without darkness? Or darkness without light? There are many levels of darkness, but there is only one light. The darkness here, which you will come to see, is the darkness of cravings. Of wants and desires, the likes of which drive beings into a single minded pursuit which overcomes their true purpose. For what they crave is not what they need."

"What is it they need?"

"To know the Truth. But there can be many perceived truths. What they need is to know what truth is real."

"What do you mean?" asked Win. "How can there be more than one truth?"

"For those who are not awake, truth can seem to appear in many different forms. Thus there can seem to be more than one truth." Jesus reached down, dipping his hand into the water.

"This is truth running through my fingers. It is felt but not held. It is known only as it is felt, only in that moment. And then it quickly falls away, giving it the appearance of change. But the one felt Truth does not change."

Jesus looked at Win. His eyes were as deep and as still as the lake.

"Absorb the one Truth as soon as you feel it. Though there is only one Truth, it will come to you in the way you will need to understand it. But you must reach for it on your own."

* * *

The star map brought Win to the very center of the Carth system, to a planet his data-map identified as Carthlana. Was there a chance Jesus had come to this planet? Or would Win find another clue here for him to follow?

He identified himself on an open frequency and received an immediate reply from Carthlana Spaceport Control. A suspicious voice speaking in simplistic but understandable Galactic demanded, "Why have you come here?"

Win thought about his vision of many truths. "I am a scientist from the planet Treb," he replied.

"We don't get many visitors. What do you want?"

"I have come to learn about your planet. I assure you, I mean no harm," said Win. "I am alone, and my ship has no weapons. Do you have scanning capability?"

"Yes. Hold on." There was a pause, and then the voice came back, less suspicious. "Your ship appears harmless. This is not a very good time to be visiting Carthlana, Treb scientist. It's not safe here. I won't forbid you to land but I advise against it." The voice sounded more like a recitation of a standard warning than a concern for Win's safety.

"Thank you," said Win. "I'll take my chances."

"I'm not sure what you want to study here, scientist, but you are cleared to land. Coordinates are being sent now."

* * *

Not much remained of the Carthlanian spaceport. What appeared to have once been a fairly large complex had been reduced to rubble. A small section had been haphazardly rebuilt, and even here the landing areas were littered with debris. Win set the ship down carefully in the spot he had been assigned.

Just as he emerged from his ship a klaxon split the air and loudspeakers blared warnings to take cover. Surprisingly, no one in the spaceport seemed to pay much attention. A loud blast shook the ground, followed by a distant pinging sound of high velocity weapons fire. Then silence.

Win caught the attention of one of the spaceport workers. "What was that?"

The Carthlanian looked at Win and his ship. "Offworlder, huh? That was the rebels. Or the militia. Or the government army. Who knows?"

"Is there a war going on now?"

"There is always a war going on," said the Carthlanian.

"Who is fighting?" asked Win.

"Everyone," said the man. "Only no one really knows why anymore."

* * *

At the edge of the landing area a crude handwritten sign had been propped up in a pile of dirt. In standard Galactic it read:

Devatus Center City—2000 paces
The Fields—10000 paces
Peace—too far to measure

As Win made his way toward the city center it began to rain. Not having to disguise himself here, he had left the flora based fabric garment he had worn on K'Turia back on the ship and had donned modern clothing. He pulled his hood up over his head. He saw a few offworlders mingled with the native Carthlanians. No one paid him any attention.

The rain came harder, making him feel uncharacteristically miserable; normally he enjoyed rain. But the war torn buildings cast a gloom over the entire city.

He wanted to get out of the rain and get some information. None of the buildings seemed very inviting. Many were nothing but empty shells, victims of the war and neglect. He reached a crossroad and here everything was a bit less derelict, as if some attempt had been made to recapture the city. One entrance was especially busy and a sign above it bore the universally recognizable icon of a tavern.

He dodged some small vehicle traffic as he made his way across the street. He entered the tavern and shook some of the wetness from his arms before passing through a standard weapons scanner and then into the bar. The room was large and dimly lit. Win studied the faces of the people eating and drinking at the bar and at the tables. Mostly he saw Carthlanians, their golden brown hued skin marked by deep colored veins. There was a smattering of other species, some of which he recognized: two rotund Berenese, a few hunchbacked Lapanesce, even a tripod Stanehon. No Lemians, thankfully, not that he expected any here. A line of motley looking patrons stood waiting in a cafeteria style food line.

Every spaceport in every galaxy Win had been to had bars like this one, another of the many commonalities across cultures. He waited for a place at the bar to open up, and when the barkeep looked at him Win pointed to what the Carthlanian next to him was drinking. It appeared to be some type of grain ale, another commodity available at any bar throughout the known universe.

Win held up a Universal Credit. "You take these?" he asked.

The barkeep took it and held it up to the light. His arms were covered in sunset yellow veins. "Sure. We don't see many of these anymore, but we can trade them with offworlders. Of course, we don't see many new offworld travelers for that matter." He jerked his arm down the bar. "Most of these are traders who come in every few turns, hoping things will be better. Things aren't, so they just drink." He shrugged and reached below the bar for Win's drink. "Won't be too cold, I'm afraid. Refrig unit failed. Just get here?"

"Yes. I'm a scientist, from a planet we call Treb. It's quite a ways off."

"A scientist, huh? Maybe you can fix my refrig unit. Can't get these old mechanical units fixed since the war, and no one trusts the new ones."

"There was some kind of attack near the spaceport."

"Crazies. Bad for business." The barkeep was pouring new drinks as he spoke. "The war—the big war—has been over for years. There is nothing really left to fight over, but that doesn't stop people from attacking anything and anyone. No one wants the unitary government back, but that doesn't stop what's left of them from trying to run things and get control again. There are rebel groups everywhere trying to stop them, or get control themselves. Or just causing trouble." He wiped at the bar with a rag he pulled from his belt. "Bad for business," he repeated.

"Maybe you could help me," said Win. "I'm researching—religions across different planets. I'm looking for an offworld spiritual teacher that I heard might be here."

"You study religions? I guess that means you won't be fixing my fridge unit!" The barkeep laughed. "Religion? I got no use. But religious types and teachers—you came to the right place. Ever since the war the planet's swarming with them. I don't know if any are from offworld though." He lowered his voice. "Be careful, friend, I think most of them are just phonies, out to swindle you."

Someone banged a mug on the bar, calling out to the barkeep in what Win assumed was a dialect of the local language, unmistakably demanding a refill. Like most planets that had achieved spaceflight and were frequented by offworld visitors, the primary local language had merged into a patois with Galactic. Some were easier to understand than others. The barkeep left Win to his drink.

Outside, the steady rain poured down on the dark and broken city.

Win moved to a seat by the window, the bar now packed with people waiting for the weather to clear. He tried some of the local food but he had no appetite. He closed his eyes and came close to falling asleep several times, his thoughts disappearing into the sound of nearby conversations. But he perked up when he felt people begin to stir. The rain had stopped.

Outside, the sun was beginning to cut through the cloud cover. It didn't make the city any more attractive.

There was a gap in the buildings off to his left, so he headed that way. He moved quickly across several streets, each one not much different than the other, empty buildings interspersed by a few rebuilt structures. There were a lot of bars.

The city was laid out in a traditional grid, but some of the streets were blocked by debris. He found himself being funneled into one direction, and suddenly came to an oddly open area, like a park, but so large he could not see across it. He remembered the sign in the spaceport, *The Fields*. There was an immediate change in the atmosphere, a cleaner smell, sharply contrasting with the ruin of the city.

A steady stream of people, some of them offworlders, were entering the field, following a narrow path through waist high grasses. A group of four improbably tall and skinny beings saw Win hesitate, and after conferring amongst themselves, approached him.

"I am Shali," one said, his hands slowly shifting, as if the movement had some meaning that coincided with his speech. With long, bony fingers, he pointed to the others around him. "We are all Shali. You are from Hahd? You look like Hahd."

Win was confused. "I am not sure I understand what you mean. I am Win of Treb."

The Shali repeated Win's name, turning to the other impossibly thin beings, skeletal outgrowths poking over their entire bodies.

"You are headed to the Core?"

Win gestured to the line of people. "Is that where everyone is going?"

"Yes. The Core is good. There are many answers at the Core."

"I need help," said Win. " I am looking for a preacher called Jesus. Do you know him?"

The Shali looked at each other again, repeating Jesus' name.

"We know of no such one. Who is the Jesus preacher?"

"He is also an offworlder, from the planet K'Turia. Do you know where I might find help in my search?" Win asked.

"The Core has much to offer. You may find help there."

"But beware of the tricksters," said another of the Shali. "The tricksters will smell your seeking. They will take you to the wrong place. They will take you and leave you lost and still seeking."

"Who are the tricksters?"

"Those who would lead you astray!" The Shali laughed in odd unison and continued on into the field, leaving Win standing at the edge of the path.

What am I doing here? Win thought. Jesus could be anywhere on the planet. Or not here at all.

Jesus, how will I ever find you?

Confused and suddenly uncertain, Win joined the procession.

CHAPTER 11

ARALYN HEARD THE OLD BUS as it slowly made its way up the barely cleared street. She was too tired to smile, even though the bus promised the end of her long work shift. Out of the corner of her eye she watched the bus edge past the bomb crater that her crew had just uncovered that morning; the bus driver, with no nav system, relying on feel alone to get safely through.

Most of the other workers glanced up, the cadence of the rock line slowing almost in unison, the expectation of relief. The line, mostly kids and teens her age, clearing the light rubble by hand, passing it from one to the other and then into a misshapen flat bed truck.

The arrival of the bus did nothing to lessen the harsh rattle of the drills, biting into the larger rocks and broken foundations. The drillers were older, on a different schedule, and would not be changing shifts now.

The bus stopped, the squeal of its brakes enough to be heard over the drills. The rock line slowed again, still moving, but in almost slow motion. Aralyn, at the front of the line today as the picker, deepest in the rubble, had a little control over the speed of the line, depending on how fast she picked up stones. She was the only one allowed to really look up for any length of time, to gauge whether the system was faltering. But there was a thin line between a slower speed to keep everything steady, and slacking off. The line drivers could tell, at least the smarter ones, and the picker would be the one to bear their wrath if they felt that everything wasn't moving fast enough. Some of the dumber line drivers couldn't tell, or didn't care, and would take it out on the pickers anyway.

Most of the workers hated being the picker, because of the pressure and the occasional smacking, but Aralyn often volunteered, especially when she knew who was on line driver duty. Not that any of them liked her, or did her any favors, but she knew with the smart ones she could manage things and even slow everything down when the younger kids needed a rest. Plus the picker job came not only with the day's rations that all the line workers got, but two credits as well. A pittance, but there was no other job she could get that would pay anything more than rations. Maybe when she was a little older she could get something better than rubble cleanup. But with the rebel unrest there was no stability, and there was a long wait for any kind of job.

And if she didn't eat much, two credits meant two entire days without having to work. Two days to do something else, to solve the new riddle that had thrust itself into her relentless life of repetition, of working to eat.

Today, though, she had been unlucky. The line driver was a brute. The workers, even the drillers, nicknamed him Cast Off for the way one of his eyes wandered. Cast Off would whack the picker with his hard staff whenever he thought the line was too slow, whether it was or not.

A few weeks ago Aralyn had borne his punishment, the memory of the beating hurting as much as the pain whenever her shirt rubbed against the raw skin. She had slowed the pace, but only because she had just sent an especially large slab down the line, and she knew it had to clear before speeding things up. But Cast Off was too stupid to see it, or didn't care. He rushed up to her, already swinging, the first blow catching her flush on the back. Aralyn saw it coming and relaxed as well as she could—soft bones didn't break. She saw the other workers in their desperate confusion of deciding to look or not look, some turning away, others staring in spite of themselves, all knowing it could be them in her place.

Beyond the line, the overseer had watched impassively, he had more to worry about than just the rubble cleanup. Even as the second blow came Aralyn was forming a plan, the overseer wasn't one of the bad ones, if she could just . . .

She was expecting three hits, and when the third one came she shifted her shoulders slightly in the direction of the blow. The staff had caught her in the shoulder, stinging. She let it spin her around, not having to fake much, because Cast Off had made a vicious swing. She fell to her knees, grabbing at her shoulder, the pain much worse than the shots to her back.

She thought about crying out, realizing it was too late, it would seem staged, and it wouldn't be her. They all knew how she reacted. She didn't cry, or whine, she just took it and stared. So that's what she did . . .

It had worked. The overseer yelled, freezing the line driver, who stood over Aralyn with his staff raised, breathing hard, his face a mask of hatred and surprise.

The overseer strode up to the driver and knocked the staff from his hand. "On the back only, you idiot," he snapped. "They're no good to us if you break their arms."

"She moved!" sputtered Cast Off.

The overseer eyed Aralyn. "Did you now?"

Aralyn hadn't responded, meeting the overseer's hard stare. It was the overseer who turned away first. He looked over the line, the workers all on edge, listening while trying not to appear interested. The overseer certainly wasn't afraid of any of them, but he had a quota to make. "Get back to work," he growled. He turned to Aralyn. "You lose one of your credits."

Aralyn had protested at that. "I ran a good line today!"

"That's the only reason why you aren't losing both credits. Don't be a problem, there are plenty of kids looking for rubble line jobs. You're a good picker but you've got an attitude I don't need." Cast Off snickered, and the overseer turned to him. "And you. You better learn to know the right line speed. There are plenty of people who would be happy with your job too."

He had strode off, Cast Off flicking him a rude gesture, and then when he realized that everyone was looking at him he spun on Aralyn. "I won't forget this."

And he hadn't. Aralyn had tried to avoid him, but she never knew who would be working the line, and today she had taken the picker job when she recognized one of the better line drivers. But that driver had been called away to another job, and had been replaced by Cast Off.

He watched her carefully the entire shift, and she was forced to keep the line moving faster than it should, mad at herself for giving in even this way. She stewed the entire day, on edge, only allowing herself to relax slightly when the bus had come. She'd be free in a few minutes.

But Cast Off was still on top of her, watching. "The shift isn't over! Keep moving!" He fingered his staff.

Aralyn looked up at him, knowing he was close to hitting her again. She didn't know if the overseer was watching or not. But she had taken enough from Cast Off. "You know," she said, "it takes more skill to be a picker than a line driver." She stood up, hands on her hips, and like a wave reaching the shore the line came to a stop as the last rock was passed.

Cast Off looked at her, incredulous. Before he had a chance to say anything, Aralyn said, "All *you* have to do is run around with a stick, yelling and hitting. A picker has to find the right rocks, and in the right order." She reached down and picked up a small stone, looked at it, and threw it over her shoulder. "Too small." She bent and grabbed a large boulder, and made a show of trying to move it. "Too big." She was speaking to the line driver as if he were a child.

Cast Off's arm started to lift, but he seemed unsure of what to do. His eyes filled with hatred, somehow realizing Aralyn was making a fool of him.

Aralyn reached for another rock, one that looked too big for her, but she lifted it easily, her muscles hardened from the long days of line work. She held the stone out toward Cast Off, and when his eyes slid to the stone she let it slip from her fingers. Cast Off yelped and jumped back to avoid the stone from crushing his foot, and he tripped, falling onto his backside. A titter of laughter went up along the line.

"Just right," said Aralyn.

* * *

The path was surprisingly narrow. The grass, still wet from the storm, glistened on Win's clothing before evaporating. Now and again he would make out movement ahead, but for the most part he could easily have imagined himself the only one in the vast field.

A figure appeared, seemingly out of the tall grass, and then another, moving away from him, and when he reached the spot where they had emerged Win saw that another path had joined the one he was on. Soon he came upon two more paths, and the trail widened considerably, becoming more packed down. He realized there must be many routes to the Core.

At the next crossing another group came onto the main walkway, three squat, red skinned offworlders in metallic coated garb. Win caught up to them and said, "Hello, are you going to the Core?" They responded in a language Win could not even connect to anything he had ever heard, and so he repeated his question in the other dialects of Galactic he knew, as well as in some of the more common languages. But nothing registered, and there was an awkward silence when both sides realized they could not communicate. One of them put out his hands in friendly frustration, and Win mimicked the gesture and continued on.

He hurried forward and was able to catch up to two Carthlanian women. The trail had widened enough so he could walk side by side with them. "Excuse me, may I ask you a question?" he said.

The two women glanced at Win but kept walking. "Don't give us any trouble," said the younger woman.

"I won't," said Win. "I'm just new here, and—"

"Never had any problems with offworlders," interrupted the much older of the two. Covered in layers of clothing, she was being helped along by her younger companion, but still managing to keep up a surprising pace. Only her hands and face were visible, her Carthlanian veins a faded pink. She glanced at Win, curious. "What do you want to know?"

"Thank you," said Win, trying to appear as non threatening as possible. "My name is Win. I have come to your planet looking for someone, an offworld preacher named Jesus. I was wondering if you have heard the name?"

"A preacher? I don't think so," said the old woman, yanking her arm away from her companion. "I can walk, Arca. Don't pull me." She turned back to Win. "But there are many preachers here on Carthlana, and some of them are from offworld. Arca, have you heard of this Jesus?"

The younger woman hesitated, cautiously scrutinizing Win. "You look harmless enough." Her voice softened. "I've never heard of that preacher. But if you are going to the Core you are going to the right place to find out. Everyone who is looking for someone starts there. It is why we are going. My brother went missing during the war, and I take my Grandmother here every month to see if there is any—news." She spoke without much emotion, giving Win the impression she didn't think they would learn anything.

"Can you tell me more about the Core?" asked Win.

"How much do you know about our war?" asked Arca.

"Nothing really," said Win. "I was told it ended, but that there is still fighting."

"Well, that's certainly true enough," said Arca. "To understand the Core, you have to know why the fighting started. Our planet was run by a single government, and for a long time, things were very peaceful." She stopped and looked around, as if worried that someone might be listening.

"Go on, girl," prodded the older woman. "Tell him. I doubt

the government has sent some offworlder to find out what we think. As if they care anyway."

Arca gave Win a half smile. "Sorry. Old habits die hard. The government grew as it took on more and more functions. In the beginning no one minded, because there always seemed to be some good reason, or some group that got something out of it."

"Like my new teeth!" the old woman blurted. "And that trip to the hot springs for my stiff joints."

"Yes, Grandma Lornay," said Arca. "Just like those things. Unfortunately, soon there wasn't enough money to pay for all these gifts, but we had all become so accustomed to them that no one could decide which ones to stop. Of course, the government agencies that ran all the programs did not want to end any of them either. The government had a massive amount of information about everyone—what people did for a living, what they liked, how much money they made, everything you can imagine."

"Damn bureaucrats!" said Lornay, spitting onto the trail. "They even knew how much I smoked."

Arca smiled at Win over her shorter grandmother. "Anyway, people began to complain about how much the government knew and wanted to know exactly what was being done with all this information. We didn't get very clear answers. Some protests started up, but nothing changed. As Grandma said, the data gathering was in the hands of the lifelong bureaucrats, answerable to no one."

"That was enough to start a war?" asked Win, surprised.

"Not at first," said Arca. "Hackers tried to find out exactly what the government knew. Every time they managed to leak some information the people became more suspicious of why all the data was being collected. A lot of us worried about how the data might be used against us. The hackers tried to destroy the databases. But they couldn't break them down fast enough, or get to enough of them—the data was everywhere, and well encrypted. Then someone blew up a datacenter. Then another one. Some people called them anarchists, some called them rebels. Or heroes. But no one knew exactly what to destroy, and soon it seemed somebody or other was trying to wipe out anything that might store data."

Win could imagine it. "And then no one wanted to risk storing data, either because they didn't want the government to have it, or because they thought the data wouldn't remain safe."

"That is exactly what happened," said Arca. "Even useful information got lost, or didn't get saved. You couldn't get records or get things fixed. And with all the corrupted data systems, the government lost track of who owed taxes, or who was supposed to get money, and pretty soon even the people who had supported the government weren't happy either. The rebel groups try to take advantage of all the discontent. Some people support them, some support the government. Most of us just try to keep our heads down and stay out of the way."

Win thought about the broken refrig unit at the bar, and it occurred to him that he had not seen any sign of mass transportation so far, odd for a planet with a spaceport. "Is that why everyone walks?"

"Yes," replied Arca. "No one trusts transports to work right or take them where they need to go. In fact no one trusts any technology that relies on stored data, which is just about everything. So whenever possible people avoid technology." She laughed. "We're purposely regressing."

"And the Core?" asked Win. "Is that a surviving database?"

"It is, but not in the way you might think. It's more of a real time information exchange. Nothing is stored electronically, everything is in writing, or oral. There are signs, bulletin boards, notes. There is nothing to hack. Occasionally it is raided by the government, but they consider it so primitive and disorganized that it is not a threat." She pointed. "We are almost there."

Win had been so intent on the conversation that he had not been looking ahead. The Fields ended at a high stone wall. The remnants of bombings and artillery attacks had left huge gaps in the wall, adding to what had probably once been evenly spaced passageways. The aqueduct like edifice curved away on either side and disappeared from sight.

Abruptly the high grasses stopped, and they came upon a large crowd emerging from other trails. The mass of people funneled through one of the large openings in the wall.

"This used to be an amphitheater, a park," explained Arca. "We would come for exhibitions and plays. It seemed the natural place for the Core."

They passed through the wall. Inside the amphitheater was mostly intact. Long stone benches lined the outer wall, rising up and forming a half circle around a large central pit which was filled with people. Beyond the pit were two more parallel walls, heading directly away from them. The walls were connected by a series of trellises, and here and there a roof, forming a partially covered roadway. The amphitheater amplified the buzz of people, but even with all the noise and activity it was remarkably calm inside.

Lornay was pulling at Arca's hand. "Let's go see," she said.

"You go, Grandmother, I'll catch up," said Arca. The old woman hobbled down toward the central area.

Arca sighed. "She is always excited to come here, hoping for good news. But I'm afraid it will be the same as always. We won't get any. He is my brother, and I love him, but he is gone, and I have accepted that. But Grandmother just can't let go."

"Maybe the hoping is good for her," said Win.

"So is acceptance, and moving on," said Arca. She shook her head. "I'm sorry, I know you are looking for someone too. I hope you have better luck."

Win's *gheris* picked up the complex emotions in the woman, the sadness, the unspoken hope, but also something else, a peace-fulness, an inner calm. *Acceptance,* she had said. Was this what acceptance felt like? He was so far from that. Where was her anger?

Arca was just like him, suffering the loss of someone, yet doing everything to hide the pain. Something else common across the galaxies.

The floor of the amphitheater was lined with tidy rows of small tables and easels. At each table people were poring over ledgers or looking at photographs. At one booth someone was reciting what sounded like poetry and then would pause, waiting for the listeners to repeat the words.

"The oral traditionalists," said Arca. "They don't believe anything will ever be safely stored again, even in writing, so they are memorizing poetry. Even books."

Arca explained some of the booths as they passed. "This one is for finding things that were lost. That one is for trading, mostly for repair parts. Out that way, along the walkway, is where the spiritualists are. That's where you should ask about your preacher." She pointed to a crowded booth. "And that is where Grandmother will be. It's the ledgers of the missing, and the found." She paused. "The ledger of the missing is much larger."

"I lost someone as well," said Win gently.

"The preacher you are looking for?"

"No, she was my —" There wasn't a word in the Galactic common language that carried all the nuances and weight of the Treb concept of mate. "She was my wife. She is dead."

"I'm so sorry," said Arca.

"Thank you," said Win. "I—I still grieve. I guess I haven't really accepted it yet." His voice trailed off, his mind on Sooni. He looked over at the table with the ledgers of the missing, where Lornay had just turned away, her stooped shoulders telling him what she had found, or not found. "I think your grandmother needs you now."

Arca turned to look for her. "Yes, you are right." She started off, but then stopped and softly touched Win's arm. "Acceptance doesn't mean you won't be sad," she said. "Maybe your preacher will help you understand this."

* * *

Win wound his way through the crowd. At the far end of the arena the amphitheater walls tapered downward on either side to the covered walkway. He joined the throng of people leaving the arena, passing under a lintel held up by stone pillars. Ahead of him, more pillars lined the walkway, and short walls ran perpendicular to it, connecting to the outer wall and forming uncovered rooms, reminding him of outdoor stalls.

To his left a small crowd was gathered just outside the walkway in one of the stalls, listening to a Carthlanian woman standing on a small platform.

"Why do our cities lie in heaps of ruin? Why is there sadness everywhere? Why have we turned on each other, brother against sister, family against kin, friend against friend?

"Destruction has fallen like rain from the heavens. You see the weapons, and you think it is the weapons that have caused this destruction, but that is not true. We operate those weapons! We have brought this upon ourselves, for we have lost our way, and have fallen into a trap laid for us by wickedness. This is what has brought our ruin!

"Do not fool yourselves and think the worst has passed. Unless we find our way to peace, the very pillars of this arena will be smashed, and the entire world made a wasteland. Such is the power of the evil which took root out of our loss of faith, and fed on our ever growing greed."

The woman paused, and her voice softened. "Yet all is not lost! Just as we let in this evil, so too can we drive it away. We must once again live our lives according to what is truly righteous, beginning with a love for each other. We must no longer strive for material things like technology and all it brings us. We must reject the temptations of greed and selfishness.

"I know you will say, how will we do this? Where should we begin? I tell you, you will have guidance and will receive strength. Not from me, I am but a messenger. I am here merely to tell you that there is a path that will take you there. Others who know the truth will guide you.

"But beware! There will be false guides who will try to lead you astray. The power of evil is great, and can come in many attractive forms. These forms are illusions.

"Yet the vigilant will be able to tell the illusion from the reality, the reflection from the truth. You will be challenged, for the power of evil does not want you to find the truth, and will block you at every turn. But if you hold to your faith you will succeed, one at a time, until we are all walking in the light."

The woman's words reminded Win of his vision of Jesus, when Jesus had warned of what could keep Win from discovering the truth he needed to learn.

The woman stepped down. Three of the listeners near Win began an animated argument.

"She says everything bad that has happened is all our fault!"

"Not just ours. She said that it is whoever succumbs to evil ways."

A third man interjected, "I don't think she understands the problem at all. None of this is my fault. Her flowery words aren't going to help people." His voice was skeptical.

"So what are we supposed to do?" asked the first man.

"First we must make sure things don't get worse; we have to force out the evil that got us here."

"Is she saying the government is evil? Or the rebels?"

"Neither. Or both."

"How will we know?"

"She says someone will guide us."

"And who will be this guide?" asked the skeptical man, sarcastically.

The woman who had been speaking on the platform had come up behind them. "If you are ready, you will know him when he comes," she said quietly.

"And just how will we do that?"

"You must prepare by knowing yourselves," said the woman.

"You must know why you choose to do one thing and not another. Next, you must believe. You must believe that there is a way to peace."

"You mean an end to the war?"

"Before that can happen, you must first come to your own inner peace. Inner peace is the seed that grows into the peace of the world."

The crowd began to disperse. As the woman passed by Win she turned and added, "Remember what I said about false prophets, even if they display wondrous powers. The true guide does not need to perform miracles, while the pretenders will be eager to show you their tricks. Those who are ready to walk the path of enlightenment will not need proof." She was speaking to the three Carthlanians, but she was looking right at Win.

Win was going to ask her what she meant, but she turned and quickly disappeared into the crowd.

* * *

Win continued on through the walkway, stopping now and again to listen to other speakers. The themes were varied. One prophesized the end of the world. One blamed offworlders for the planet's problems. An offworld speaker blamed unnamed secret sects within the government. The only commonality seemed to be the need to blame someone. Anyone.

Win thought about the first speaker. Her audience seemed to think she was blaming them for the planet's problems. Yet he had heard a different message. It had nothing to do with blame, but with personal responsibility.

He knew he was guilty of this same mistake. When Sooni died he blamed himself, and he also blamed the supervisors who instructed her to perform the experiment, the manufacturers of the equipment, and even Sooni herself. It was difficult not to find something or someone to blame. His rational side knew that placing blame was one of the things that caused his suffering. But knowing it and not doing it were two different things. He could not convince himself not to be angry; his anger wasn't some logic he could dispel. He needed another way.

He stopped to listen to an offworlder preacher, speaking to the largest gathering he had yet seen in the Core. Win didn't recognize the offworlder's race. The speaker was a tall, very light skinned biped, with a very long graceful neck and large eyes. He was addressing the crowd in perfect Galactic, in a voice that was melodiously enticing.

"It is not my place to criticize the people of Carthlana," he said. "Yet you must see that your planet had become too dependent on technology. Surely there is nothing wrong with technology, it can do things that beings cannot, and thus it is wondrous. It became so addictive that everyone relied on it, allowing it to achieve a power of its own. Yes, the technology had power, as did those who wielded it over you.

"Your response was to break the power of this technology by eliminating it. Yet look where this has led you. You lack many of the basic necessities of life. You have lost much of what you had learned, much of your art and wisdom. You are forced to do so many things by hand that you have no time for anything else. You have captured one freedom, only to lose another."

The preacher continued on smoothly. "Now, I do not say you should return to the old ways. But there is another answer. Instead of looking to machines to solve your problems, you must allow a new force in your life. There are beings who possess the power to alter the course of your world's journey. If you accept their power, they can accomplish much more than what your machines did for you. Yes, such beings exist.

"And who are these powerful beings? Surely they are not of your people. Your people only have the power that produced this world. See where it ended up! No, you require the help of offworlders. I am not one of them, and not all offworlders have such power. But some do."

What kind of power?" a voice called out from the crowd.

"We don't need offworlders telling us how to live!" yelled another.

"You are an offworlder!" shouted a woman in the back. "Are you going to save us?" Her voice was filled with both disbelief and hope.

The preacher's voice became reverent. "Let me tell you of some of the powers they have. Some of them can travel great distances with no means of propulsion. Some can create and change energy, such as fire. Others can know what you are thinking."

The preacher held out his arms in a welcoming embrace to the crowd. "Now, I know you may say, 'No one can do these things!' Let me tell you. I have seen these miracles and can tell you they are true! They are not miracles of technology, but miracles of power. Just as one of you may have more physical power than another, so too do these beings have great powers.

"Now others may ask, 'Even if they do have such power, what good does it do us?' I tell you, these beings can help you! You can regain your way of living without having to rely on technology. You will not need technology! Those with the power I speak of will give you everything you want!"

The speaker paused, extending his long neck, his eyes opened wide. "I know you must have many questions. Who will ask of me?"

Someone in the front row said, "Why would someone so powerful help us? What would they want in return?"

"They would help for the same reason you might help a friend who is in need. You would do it because of the need, and because you can. So too those of power are willing to help."

"But they must want something!"

"Only that you listen to them, and follow their counsel, so that you do not get led astray by technology once again."

Another called out. "I don't believe someone can do those things, even an offworlder. I'd have to see proof."

"Of course! I did not believe it either until I saw it. This is not something you have to take my word for, or take on blind faith. I assure you, once you see these miraculous things performed, you will certainly believe."

Win's *gheris* was picking up the intense mixed emotion of the crowd. Belief and disbelief, but also a longing hope. The Carthlanians wanted this to be true. They wanted a savior, someone of great and obvious power to come along and instantly solve all their problems.

The charming offworlder pointed to different people in the crowd. "You, and you, and you. All of you, soon you will see these miracles for yourselves. For one such offworlder is already here, on Carthlana! I have seen him, and soon you will also!"

Win was struck by some of the similarities in the messages of this speaker and the first woman he had listened to. Both were promising the people a way out of their misery. And both had spoken of someone who would bring them guidance. Either of them could be referring to Jesus.

Yet their descriptions of the savior were very different. The woman spoke of someone who would set an example, instead of doing everything for them. This speaker told of someone who could perform great feats, who would solve their problems with some unknown power.

And why had the woman warned of false prophets? Had she been speaking specifically to him? Or was that something she said to everyone?

The slender speaker was coming down off the dais, being quickly surrounded by the excited audience.

"Tell us more about his powers!"

"He has many. For one, he can harness the power of emotion, converting it to energy. And he has great physical strength, and can move large heavy objects with ease. He can see into the future, and by knowing what might happen can help you prepare for the worst and even avoid it."

This was sounding less like Jesus and more like some offworlder race with different abilities, thought Win. Still, this could be just an exuberant follower, misunderstanding the abilities and the message of Jesus. It was the best clue Win had that there was a powerful offworlder on the planet, a description that could certainly apply to Jesus.

"When can we see this offworlder?" Win asked.

"Soon, very soon. In fact he is in this city right now, and his following grows every day."

"Where is he?"

"That I cannot tell you. He is preparing for the great battle that will be coming, where he will help all of you to recapture your world."

Someone in the crowd said, "A great battle? Is he with the rebels?"

Win felt a hand on his shoulder. He turned to face a handsome Carthlanian man who wore a long silky garment that was the most luxurious clothing Win had seen on the planet. His skin was porcelain ivory, his veins mere whispers. His eyes, though clearly not offworld, bore an odd similarity to the speaker, large and welcoming.

"Excuse me," he said. "I am Drason. I could not help overhearing your question. I believe I can help you. I know where to find the powerful one of which he speaks. That is, if you are interested."

"I am," said Win. "But why tell me, and not all these people?"

"I am not sure they are ready," said Drason. "But you are not of this world, and so you might understand. What is your name?"

"I am Win. Is the offworlder named Jesus?" Win's felt his heart racing.

"He has many names," said Drason. "The name Jesus does sound familiar."

"You have seen him?"

"Yes. He is in the city, not far from the Core."

"Are you a follower of his? I have come a long way to find him."

Drason smiled, his voice soothing, without the wild exuberance of the speaker. "You have just a little way left to go."

Without waiting for a response Drason turned and headed into the walkway. Win hesitated briefly, then followed. It seemed unlikely he would find Jesus so quickly after arriving on Carthlana such a short time ago. Yet people on K'Turia had known about Jesus, and there was no reason to assume that he would not be known here. Though Drason's answers were vague, perhaps there was some reason for the secrecy. Perhaps Jesus had been forced to hide. He had to find out.

As Win entered the swarm of people, his *gheris* picked up a new emotion, something that felt like fear. Or worry. It was acute but not widespread, as if it were shared not by many but overwhelmingly by one person. He looked around but could not identify the source.

He caught up to Drason just as he reached the end of the walkway. Here at the back of the amphitheater there were fewer people. Beyond an open space the Fields began again.

The worry continued to impinge on Win's *gheris* sense, and now he was better able to focus on it. As he turned to look back at everyone leaving the walkway, he caught a glimpse of a young Carthlanian woman staring at him.

"Are you coming?" asked Drason.

Win turned back toward the Fields. "Yes." After a few steps he glanced back again The young woman had moved in their direction and she quickly looked away.

They were being watched.

CHAPTER 12

WIN FOLLOWED DRASON THROUGH the outskirts of the Core, in the opposite direction from which he had entered the amphitheater. On this side, the stones of the original structure had fallen into even greater ruin, in places the walkway all but obliterated, forcing them to step carefully. Giant slabs had collapsed haphazardly, forming a myriad of dark cave-like openings. Haggard and wary faces peered out, quickly disappearing whenever Win looked their way. The walkway was nearly deserted, and no one was entering the Core from this direction.

"Where are we going?" asked Win.

"Back into the city," said Drason.

"I thought all the preachers were at the Core?"

"Most are pretenders. The last one you heard was one of the few real ones, one who knows about who has the true power, the One. But most of the people of Carthlana are not really ready to see him."

Win looked over his shoulder. No one was behind them. He wasn't sure who Drason was leading him to, but it was the first real hint of an offworlder who might be Jesus, so he kept going. He could always come back to the Core later.

The grasses of the Fields on this side of the Core were wild and weedy, in places overrunning the path. They passed a rusted hulk of a transport, some crash from long ago, now almost lost in the tangle of weeds. Now and again what looked like connecting trails crossed the path, quickly disappearing into the jungle of growth.

Across the Fields ahead of them, the city looked dead, the buildings broken, roofless, no glassy reflections to break up the monotony of ruin. The path seemed to be heading towards the most desolate part of the city. When Win looked back again the path was hard to see, the grasses tall and dense. It would be hard to know if someone were following them. He took his bearings, scanning past the Core to the city beyond it where he had started. From this distance the buildings there did not look as bad. His eyes followed the cityscape around the Fields, the buildings becoming shorter, a blackened trail of destruction. Maybe at one time the Fields would have seemed a refuge, a circle of grass holding back the stone and chrome and metal. Now it looked more like the frenzied overgrowth would threaten the remains of the city.

Drason had disappeared, only a hint of bent grass telling of his direction. Win hurried to catch up.

"Drason, wait!" When he reached the Carthlanian he felt a little foolish. He certainly could not get lost here, with the city all around him. "Why is this path to the Core so unlike the one on the other side?"

"Fewer come this way," said Drason. "If we had gone out the other path we would have had to walk all the way around the Fields. We'd be late."

"Late for what?"

"You'll see. You have a chance to see the One invoke some of the powers I told you about. This will be something very special for you."

"What do you mean by powers? Some ability your people do not have?"

Drason kept walking, and Win had to hurry to hear his response. "Powers that no one has. The One can change people, transform them. He can make things happen, things others could not make happen. Miracles even."

"Calling something a miracle is how some people keep from

being frightened of what they don't understand," said Win. "Nothing more."

Drason stopped so suddenly that Win almost ran into him. The Carthlanian seemed almost angry for an instant, his eyes darkening, sharply contrasted against his refined features. But his smile quickly returned. "No matter what I tell you, you won't believe me, so why don't you just wait and see for yourself? We are almost there. What do you have to lose? Besides, you have come all this way."

Win was torn between his curiosity and his stubborn dislike of going into something blind. The stubbornness had gotten him into a lot of trouble in the past. But curiosity had not, so that won out. "Let's go," he said.

* * *

The Fields did not end cleanly; the growth crept out into the city, weeds and spindly brush filling gaps in the streets. Potholes served as giant plant containers, filled with slimy water and algae, smelling of both decay and growth, the combination a sickly mix of sweetness and rot. Blackened moss edged up anything standing. Entire buildings had collapsed, gaping holes staring at them like eyes in an unending series of skulls.

"Watch your step," warned Drason, as he glided effortlessly around the rubble. "And follow my path closely. There are many unexploded bombs here."

"Is there no other way?" Win asked, carefully picking his way along.

"The other way is worse. You'll be safe with me. It is not far now."

They passed a small group huddled around a sooty fire in a barrel, squinted eyes watching them warily. One of them bent over to pick up a board, tapping it in his hand, a warning. Out of nowhere the others all suddenly brandished some kind of weapon.

Two of the vagabonds broke and ran, their footsteps unusually loud in the eerie stillness.

"Why are they running?" asked Win.

"They fear you because you are an offworlder. As I told you, they are not ready. They must be brought into the fold."

A twisted sign, the lettering long obliterated, hung precariously over a set of stairs leading downward. "An old subway station," explained Drason, making his way down the steps. "Come."

A damp, musky smell emanated from the opening. Win hesitated at the top, watching Drason descend into the semi darkness. Win was struck by the incongruity of Drason's fine clothing and the ashy rubble, an odd flare of elegance amidst the trash and decay.

"This is a strange place for a powerful offworlder," said Win.

Drason turned to look at him. "The unready not only fear what they do not understand, but they are threatened by it. Who knows what they might do in their fear? You saw how they watched you, how they took up arms. You might have been attacked if you were not with me. The One is very powerful, but he does not want to waste time with the unready. So until enough are prepared, it is best he stays hidden."

Win thought about Jesus on K'Turia, having to hide from the priests, spirited away into the caves. Maybe it wasn't so hard to believe the same could be happening here.

Still, he was cautious. He could not imagine why Drason would try to harm him, and if that had been the intent, certainly the Fields would have been an easy place to do it. Why drag him all the way here?

Drason saw him hesitate. "Perhaps I was wrong about you. Maybe you are not that interested in finding out about the One. Why did you bother to come all this way?"

Win looked down into the dank stairway, the steps littered with debris. Dark and dubious as it was, it paled in comparison to the risks he had taken on K'Turia, the risks he had taken in coming here. He shrugged and descended into the ground.

* * *

Aralyn emerged from the Fields just in time to see the offworlder and his guide cross the street. She darted after them, trying to follow their path exactly, fully aware of the danger of unexploded ordinance.

She kept way back, but her quarry did not turn around. If they had, she thought they would have seen nothing but another bedraggled Carthlanian, a young woman with short hair and dark eyes. She had plenty of practice blending in, hiding from soldiers, rebels, thieves, anyone who might want to harm her. So even if they had looked right at her, she would have been invisible, blending into the very background.

Still, it was rare for her to do anything to bring attention to herself, and following someone certainly risked that. But she had something that needed to be done, and that meant following the offworlder and the well dressed Carthlanian, whom she had been suspicious of since she had first spotted him. Few walked around the city in finery these days, a slap in the face of all those going without. What was the offworlder doing with him?

She gave the destitute group near the barrel fire as wide a berth as she could, not because she was afraid, but to let them know she wasn't any kind of threat to them. She let her eyes move freely past them, not staring, but not ignoring them either. She could feel them watching her.

She hesitated at the top of the stairway. She had been in the subways before; they could be a good place to hide or even sleep. But she didn't know this station. Some of them were fine, actually dry once you got past the open stairways, but others were a mess, collapsed and dangerous.

A brief echo of conversation drifted up out of the opening, growing fainter. That got her moving. She wasn't going to let the offworlder get away.

* * *

The steps ended, opening up onto a wide subway platform. Water dripped from the steps and from above, plinking Win on the head, and pooling at his feet. Huge archways formed the roof, the tiles cracked and broken, forming gaps which let in shafts of dirty light, ashen motes drifting in the beams. The platform was relatively intact, but the trackbed was flooded, clogged with debris, the water barely moving. Dark moss ran along the base of the walls. To the left the platform ended at a wall, the tracks disappearing into blackness. To the right the platform continued on, surprisingly well lit from the holes in the roof.

"This way," said Drason, as he walked along the deserted platform.

Win followed him, past an unreadable tiled sign on the wall, his feet slapping on the wet pavement. Another staircase ran upwards, closed off with rusted bars, the stairs a jumble of trash.

A low murmur of voices floated toward them, echoing in the tunnel. The platform curved, following the tracks, and opened up into a vast room, arched entranceways over staircases leading in many directions.

In the center of the room a group of people were arrayed in three concentric circles, gathered around a tall solitary figure in a black hooded robe who was facing away from Win. The outermost circle was chanting, swaying along with their incantation, a deep, slow vocalization that reverberated and fed on itself.

"Azael, Zagam a Abaddan." The chant was repeated, the outside circle continuing to move side to side, the other two rings of people rigid, mostly Carthlanians, but some offworlders as well, a mix of ages and races, men and women, intent on the hooded figure in the center. Win did not recognize the language but it reminded him of something very old, the guttural sound entwined with the litany.

The outer ring fell silent and the middle ring began to chant, now two groups swaying to the sound, "Allu, Moloch, a Abaddan."

"Do you feel it?" whispered Drason. "Do you feel the power?"

The middle ring stopped chanting and now the inner ring began, the seven closest to the center figure, now all three circles moving to the cadence. "Abaddan Gihenna . . . Abaddan Hinnom."

Win glanced at Drason, whose eyes were transfixed on the hooded figure, and the Carthlanian was mouthing the words along with the group, swaying with them, his eyes wide.

The entire group took up the chant. "Abaddan Gihenna . . . Abaddan Hinnom!" The chant grew louder, louder, joining with its echo to fill the massive room.

Win took an involuntary step back. His *gheris* was telling him nothing, an eerie void in the midst of the visceral emotion in the room. Something was pulling at him, trying to drag him into the group, and he fought back instinctively, not even knowing what he was resisting.

The chanters raised their arms, shaking them, the cadence unwavering.

"This has nothing to do with Jesus," said Win. He could barely hear his own voice. "I'm leaving."

Drason pulled his attention away and grabbed Win's arm, his fingers digging into Win's flesh. "You cannot leave now! All is about to be revealed!"

Win tried to pull away but Drason spun him about to face the group. The hooded leader of the ritual had raised his arm and the chanting stopped, the sound cleaved. Win could not see the face hidden within the deep hood. But Win's eyes were drawn to the figure's hand and the large knife it held. The knife stabbed down, violently, and the crowd lurched, whimpering. The knife rose again, but now it looked different somehow, as if it had transformed into another knife, and again it fell.

Once again the crowd responded, edging forward, sighing in approval. Win could not help himself, he stepped closer, trying to see what was in the circle being stabbed, watching the knife come up again and quickly down, each time shifting, slipping into something else, leaving a trail not of blood but of change, as if the movement was telling some history of the blade.

The group could hold back no longer, it broke into a heinous moan, primal, enthusiastic. Again the knife came down, but now it was no longer a knife, it became a black smolder in the shape of a blade, leaving a trail of thick viscous smoke.

"What is happening?" yelled Win, trying once again to free himself from Drason, who clung to his arm with unbelievable strength.

"It is the maskah!" Drason's voice was filled with awe and reverence. "It is the path to power! If you accept it, it will take you to the One!"

"This is not Jesus!"

"Open your mind! Do you think Jesus is the only power?"

"I have come for Jesus, not for this!"

"You cannot have one power without the other!"

The black smoke twisted and formed into a solid shape, rising from the central figure, moving outward. It hovered over a Carthlanian woman in the inner circle. Her arms raised up, welcoming the image, the veins on her arms turning a blood red. The maskah spun, shifting into the semblance of the woman, a shadow copy, red veins pulsing out of the blackness, looking down on her. The woman's body rose up, joining with the smoke, the shadow absorbing her face, then absorbing her whole body, which wracked at the joining, and fell back to the ground, shaking.

The maskah moved to the next person, a young girl, who raised her arms, becoming one with the dark mass. Next an offworlder, a squat tailed triped, the maskah once again forming into a perfect duplicate, a shadow twin, merging into the triped.

The maskah spun from one to another, faster and faster, completing the circle, now moving on to the next row of worshippers. Win was hopelessly transfixed, unable to take his mind off the ritual, the transformations, feeling the power. Drason pushed him forward toward the outer group, and Win was unable to resist.

The maskah was upon a Carthlanian woman right in front of Win. For a brief instant it wavered, then split into two, a twin within a twin. One of the shadows joined with the Carthlanian, but the other hovered, a tendril of blackness reaching out toward Win. He stood frozen, helpless.

The tendril spun back on its core, forming the outlines of a new body, a new face, and for the briefest heartbeat Win saw a Treb, himself, and no sooner had that impression registered it was replaced by another Treb, a woman.

The maskah shook violently, the two pieces rejoined, and it spun around the rest of the circle, bypassing them, their arms raised in expectation.

The moaning wavered, the sounds now confused, angry.

The maskah slid to the center of the circle, above the hooded figure, who had turned to stare at Win. The figure raised his arms and pointed, then pushed out with his hands, as if ordering the maskah toward Win. A deep voice blew from the hooded figure, commanding. The maskah flew toward Win, shifting as it came.

It twisted to a stop just out of his reach, reforming, a shape defined by its shadow. The edges darkened even more, making the inside seem lighter, outlining and then filling into the form of a woman, becoming distinct for the merest blink, but one that was unmistakable to Win.

Sooni.

CHAPTER 13

"SOONI!" WIN'S VOICE CRACKED. At the sound of his yell the solid black smoke of the maskah once again rearranged into the image of Sooni, a look of pleading across her face, a mix of agony and hope. Win reached out, but the edges of the maskah tore into her, sucking her back from him, the entity jumping back out of reach.

Win tore away from Drason, stumbling forward, his arms outstretched, his eyes on the maskah that was Sooni, and he crashed into the outermost ring. The maskah stopped, hovering. Win pushed through the worshippers, feeling wild eyes on him, and as he moved the maskah slid back, now over the inner ring, just in front of the central figure.

Hands shoved him from behind, pushing him into the circle of people. A woman in the second ring grabbed at him, pulling him. With each step he took the maskah slid back, drawing him in.

The maskah flitted over the central figure, and now it grew blacker, denser, wisps of darkness reaching down to the ritual leader. The hooded figure reached up to it, his arm swirling, and the maskah responded, spinning, reforming, becoming Sooni once again, her face in agony every time it rotated toward Win. The crowd kept pulling and prodding, manipulating him toward the center of the circle.

The leader of the ritual began to speak, the voice deep, resonant, chilling, the words incomprehensible to Win. The being gracefully slid aside, his arm still held above, controlling the maskah, where the face should be nothing but blackness, impossibly dark. Win was shoved into the circle, surrounded by the seven, who crowded in on him, smothering him with their presence.

The hooded figure barked a command and they stopped, and then he pointed at the maskah and swept his hand toward the far side of the circle. The maskah slipped away from Win, over the circle and beyond it. Win was frozen in fear, shaking uncontrollably, his eyes darting from the hooded figure to the threatening circle and to the maskah.

The maskah waited. Win was pushed forward, toward the maskah, and as he moved the maskah did as well, sliding away from him, out into the room beyond the worshippers. Another shove and Win fell into the first ring, arms grabbing at him, keeping him from falling, pushing him on. With each step the maskah slipped farther away.

Hands tore at his clothing, the crowd now moaning, a rising tide of excitement tied to Win's movements. He fought his way through, desperately shoving the hands and arms away, coming face to face with a wide eyed Carthlanian, a wild grin on his face, leering into Win. Win pushed by him, finally breaking free of the outer circle. The maskah hesitated briefly, once more appearing as Sooni, and then it sped away, across the huge room.

Win stumbled after it, knowing it could not be Sooni but needing to get away from the crowd, who had begun their chant once again, the sound itself pushing him forward. He began to run.

At the far side of the room lay two arched openings. One was brighter, a grated exit showing a stairway beyond, leading up. The maskah flew by, disappearing into the other opening, dark.

Win skidded to a halt, torn. Through the grate he could see the stairway, relatively intact, and at its top the clear opening of the surface. An escape. He grabbed the grate but it would not budge, rust scaling his hands. Behind him, the chanting grew louder, the threatening crowd was steadily coming toward him.

Win ran to the other opening, a dark staircase heading down, only the first few steps visible. He spun around, the crowd was closer, spreading out to block off the room, wide frenzied eyes boring into him.

Cold air blew from the staircase, and then came a wailing, like someone calling to him. He turned to the staircase, listening. It came again, a woman's voice, he could imagine it was Sooni, calling his name.

The cold air blew at him, blending with the wail, covering it, melding with the chanting. Win took one more look at the other staircase, the crowd steps away, the hooded figure behind them, exhorting them.

Win reached back and felt for the wall, his hands feeling for a handrail. He started down the steps, taking the first few quickly, and then gingerly reaching out with his feet into the darkness. The wail came again from below. He thought he saw a slight breach in the darkness ahead, a small hint of light.

Three more steps and the handrail gave way. He stumbled and fell, the stairs coming up to cut into his outstretched hands, and he tumbled, falling down the staircase. He came to rest in a shallow pool of water, the surprise scaring him more than the pain of his fall, and he jumped to his feet.

Above him the worshippers crowded around the top of the staircase, a black silhouette of swaying bodies.

He heard a swish of water, the air damp, and he took a careful step away from the staircase. He sensed he was on another platform, a lower level. It was so dark his eyes struggled to adjust. One direction was definitely a little lighter than the other, and the breeze blew from there.

He put his hand on the wall, slick with moss, and moved slowly that way, stepping on things he could not see, pieces of broken tile sliding underfoot, then something soft and yielding. He jumped, jerking his foot up in terror. After a few steps the wall gave way, a reeking odor from an opening, Win's hands feeling the grate. He passed it by, the smell of decay, finding the wall again on the other side of the opening. Total blackness now, the light from the stairway he had fallen down completely lost, the slight lessening of the darkness ahead too far away to help him.

He crept forward, passing another grated opening, the bars unyielding. He had no choice but to go on. At the end of the platform a solid wall blocked his path. He edged to his right, feeling for the end of the platform. To his dismay the tiny lightness he had been heading toward was not a way up but was beyond the wall, somewhere along where he expected the trackbed. He stuck his head out around the wall, and thought he could see, far ahead, the tunnel leading toward some light, perhaps emerging into a higher chamber or outside.

He was breathing hard, his adrenaline flowing. What he had experienced he could not comprehend, nor the reason. Who here could know of Sooni, what she looked like, what she sounded like? It had to be a trick, some power of the hooded figure or even Drason, making him see and hear something he wanted to imagine. But why?

The siren call came again, from the trackbed, sounding more like Sooni, making him wonder if he was imaging it was her after having seen her image.

There was only one other explanation. Inherent within the Treb concept of *ana* was the resurgence of the spirit into an indestructible form, the connection of the living being with the everlasting spirit.

Could she be calling to him from beyond the grave, the *ana* connection of eternity? Win had never achieved *ana*, so he could not truly understand this connection, he could not even imagine what was possible.

Could someone who had achieved *ana* and had died be able to take on some semblance of a physical body, or even return to the corporal world? To come back to him, to rejoin him forever?

Or even just to help him find a way out?

He looked down the tunnel again. The lightness seemed

real, but so had the image of Sooni. He crouched and lowered himself off the platform, feeling for the trackbed. His feet touched water and he slowly let himself down, feeling for the bottom.

The water was not deep but the trackbed was slippery, filled with muck and debris. He started forward, heading along the tunnel toward the light, trying not to think of what might be in the water. The trackbed rose perceptibly.

The light ahead sharper now, the tunnel leading up to the surface. He began to run, tripping again and again, desperate to get out. At the entrance to the tunnel a rusted hulk of a train car partially blocked the way, a dark gray sky beyond. He squeezed past the twisted metal and staggered out, the overcast sky still bright enough to momentarily blind him.

Someone screamed, a cry of despair. A woman was bent over the body of a young boy, cradling him in her arms, his head bent back, his face a wash of blood. Beyond her, two more bodies, unmoving.

A squad of armed soldiers, their backs to him, were heading up the street, shouting, pointing their weapons, ordering people back inside. A group of men hesitated, and the soldiers opened fire. One fell and the others ran off, away from the soldiers, towards Win.

Someone stopped to help the woman, urging her to get up, but she was screaming, not letting go of the boy. Another stopped, and together they finally pulled the woman away.

A man yanked at Win's arm as he raced by. "You'd better run, offworlder!"

Win stood, bewildered, watching as the street filled with running people, intent on distancing themselves from the soldiers. Another series of shots split the air, breaking Win out of his trance.

Everyone now running except for one woman, wearing a black shawl, her back to him, but her steady gait unmistakable.

Sooni.

He ran after her, joining the crowd, and as soon as he did so the woman in the black shawl started to run as well. Another squad of soldiers was coming up the street, yelling to prod the crowd. Some ran into buildings, but most continued on, splitting around the soldiers, racing away. Win followed the fleeing crowd, trying to keep the woman who looked like Sooni in view.

The soldiers stopped in the middle of the street, firing in the air. Win heard one of the soldiers laugh. Bullets ripped at the pavement, spurring the crowd faster. Glass shattered behind him.

The crowd twisted around a corner, the street jammed with people trying to get away. Win had lost sight of the woman in the shawl. Was he imagining her as well? Or was it some kind of trick, a twin created by the maskah?

The crowd surged forward with each gunshot. Win's breathing labored, he could not keep up this pace much longer. But every time he caught sight of the Sooni look-alike he forced himself onward.

A door slammed, then another. People ran into buildings, mere shells, bombed out foundations, blackened with soot, offering little protection. The few who were left on the street kept running.

At the corner Win stopped, trying to decide which way to go. He had seen some Carthlanians go straight, while others had turned onto the cross street. Walking calmly away from him to his left was the woman in the black shawl.

"Sooni!" He ran after her, and once again she quickened her pace, disappearing around the next corner.

When Win got there the cross street was deserted. He walked slowly along the street, peering into buildings cluttered with rubble. One large entranceway stood intact, and when he looked in he saw two Carthlanian women huddled in the corner of the debris strewn room, watching him fearfully. He moved on. A door slammed somewhere ahead. He ran up the street but could not tell where the sound had come from.

Stymied, he stopped and surveyed the area. Where had

everyone gone? He could see ahead a few blocks, no one was in the street. He guessed that the civilians had gone into hiding, or had turned on some of the side streets ahead. There was no sign of the woman in the shawl, the woman he knew could not be Sooni but who still managed to pull him along.

He followed the deserted street, the buildings devastated, now mostly just walls. The cross streets were empty, barely passable, filled with rubble. Far ahead he thought he saw a brief movement, a piece of fabric blowing in the wind. Thinking it might be her shawl Win sprinted ahead, but when he got there all he found was a tattered curtain flapping in a gaping window well.

Win tore at the curtain, frustrated and confused. In the silence he heard voices somewhere ahead. He moved carefully to the next corner, remembering the soldiers, and risked a quick peek around the edge of a shattered wall. The side street was a little wider. At first he saw no one, and then far ahead, another flutter of dark fabric, someone walking away from him. It was too far away to see who it was but his mind filled in the image, the woman in the shawl.

The voices grew louder. Four men emerged from an alley just ahead, between him and the woman. Two of the men carried what looked like some kind of mortar tube. The other two had rifles, scanning the area. None of them wore uniforms like the soldiers he had seen earlier. Win ducked quickly back around the corner when he saw one of them start to turn his way.

"You're late. You don't have much time to get that launcher to the rendezvous point." The voice was urgent.

"We ran into a government squad and had to go around," someone replied.

"We'll run point for you, let's go."

Win heard them heading away from him and risked a quick look around the building. The four he assumed were rebels were trotting down the street. Beyond them came a quick movement, a man cutting across the street, falling in a short burst of rifle fire from one of the rebels..

The rebels stopped, guns ready, but no one else appeared. Voices drifted back to Win.

"It was just some civilian!"

We don't have time to stop for anyone, soldiers or civilians. Shoot anything that moves. Keep going."

The rebels ignored the body and kept on down the street. Win considered turning around and going back, but he wasn't sure whether that would be any safer. He was caught between the soldiers and the rebels.

And the woman in the shawl was ahead of the soldiers. He had to find out who she was.

Win followed along behind, impotent, ducking from doorway to doorway, keeping out of sight. The rebels were in a hurry and rarely looked back.

The street ended, opening into a small plaza. Win slipped into a building and peered out an open window, staying in the shadows. The rebels raced across the open area, jumping over a low wall. Behind the wall other rebels took the mortar and hastily began setting it up in a battery. A few guards lined the walls, but seemed intent on the activity inside the perimeter.

One of the rebels raised his arm and yelled. The mortars coughed as one, firing somewhere high to Win's left. The rebels quickly reloaded and the barrage continued. Over the swoosh of the firing Win heard explosions off somewhere, the rockets finding their targets.

Streams of smoke gathered in the rebel staging area, floating wisps punctuated by the red flames of the mortars. The smoke drifted beyond the far wall, twisting, solidifying. And she was there again, the woman in the shawl, emerging from the smoke. She looked right at Win, raising her arm, beckoning to him. The smoke spun, clearing, and Win could see her clearly.

It was Sooni, or someone who could be her twin. Though her head was partially covered by the shawl, Win could see her face, her arms. Again she beckoned to him, and then was partially lost in the smoke.

Win looked on hopelessly. The guards had turned their attention back to the perimeter. Win measured the distance across the open space; he could never cross it without being seen. He glanced around the partial room he was in. The far wall had fallen, open to the next building. He crossed over into it, again peering out a window opening, the glass long gone. Like the other building, the walls here were full of holes.

Four more buildings lined the plaza. If he could pass through each of them the same way, he might be able to make his way to the other side and get beyond the rebels. The mortars fell silent. Win heard the unmistakable sound of an argument, but could not make out the words. One of the rebels was trying to scale the wall to leave, but someone pulled him back, gesturing toward the mortars.

The man who was trying to leave threw down his gun and picked up a shell, and the rebels began to reload. The smoke dissipated slightly and Win saw the woman in the shawl again. She had moved partially up the far street, out of sight from the rebels. She waved again, beckoning, pointing to the rebels, as if pleading for Win to go *now*, this was his chance.

The mortar barrage started anew. Win made his way into the next building, then one more. But in the third there was no opening in the wall, and though it had no roof the wall was too high to climb. He would have to chance the street, at least until the next doorway.

He waited for the smoke to build, the acrid smell of powder filling the air. With one last glance he thought he saw the woman again but he could not be sure. He slipped out to the street and then quickly into the last building but to his dismay there was no way through. To reach the woman he would have to cross the open street.

He braced himself, then raced from the building. He had only taken a few steps when he was suddenly pushed from behind, arms around him, shoving him to the ground, his face slamming onto the hard street.

A high pitched whine split the air, a whistle of death screaming overhead. A massive explosion, the ground heaving. The pavement clawed at him, hot debris raining on his back. His head twisted, one eye blocked by a chunk of stone.

His other eye was clouded by dirt, his vision obscured by haze. But he could see well enough to know that the entire rebel group had been wiped out, the walls flattened, the mortars silenced.

Beyond that, where the shawled woman had been, there was nothing. Not a building or even a wall. The entire street had been obliterated.

CHAPTER 14

WIN STRUGGLED TO GET UP, fighting the hands that still held him. He twisted free and spun around to face a strangely familiar Carthlanian, a girl with dark eyes. Her face was smudged with soot, making it hard to tell her age. Not a child, but not a full grown woman either. A teenager.

"Stay down!" she shouted. Another bomb hit, pellets raining down, stinging. Win turned back toward the sound. What was left of the rebel staging area was shrouded in a dense curtain of dust.

He took a few steps and stumbled as another blast hit, the sound deafening. The young woman grabbed at him, her fear pulsing through her arms, something he would have felt even without his *gheris*.

"We have to get out of here!" she warned, the blue veins on her arms and neck quivering.

"I can't—I saw someone I know over there. I have to go look!"

"It's too dangerous. They'll keep up the shelling until nothing stands. You'll be killed." Her voice was sharp, intense. Mature.

Two more explosions rocked the building next to them, flinging chunks of debris into the street. Win flinched. He could not see anyone in the rubble.

The girl had not let go of his arm. "The government forces will be here soon to make sure everyone is dead. If they find us they'll think we are with the rebels."

Win took one last look at the destruction and reluctantly allowed himself to be pulled away.

* * *

Win had to run to keep up with her. When she turned to make sure he was still there, he realized why she had seemed familiar. She was the one he had spotted watching him as he left the Core. Turning a corner they almost tripped over a man crawling in the street, his leg grotesquely twisted.

The girl ran past the injured man, then stopped in indecision as Win caught up. Howling in pain, the man had stopped crawling, seemingly unaware of their presence.

The girl bent over the injured man. "Shh, try to be quiet, they'll hear you!"

The man looked up at her, wild eyed. As he shifted they could see a piece of shrapnel sticking out of his torso.

"We can't leave him here," she said. "If the army finds him they'll just kill him. If he's one of the rebels it doesn't look like any of his friends are coming to help."

"Maybe they are all dead," said Win.

"Or just too busy looking out for themselves," she said. "Let's try to get him off the street."

As they bent to pick him up the man coughed, a mass of blood coming from his mouth. He coughed again, a deep rattle, and slumped down, his eyes vacant.

She put her hand to his neck, checking for a pulse, then shook her head. "He's dead. Let's go." Her voiced betrayed no emotion, as if she were accustomed to seeing death.

She set off again at a run, nimbly sidestepping debris. Only when they had not heard any more mortars for quite some time did the girl visibly relax and slow down. She led Win into a vacant building.

"This will do for now," she said, peering out the shattered doorway. "But be ready to move if the army comes."

The girl wore a ragged jacket with a lot of pockets and dark leggings, her feet covered with low boots. Her dark hair was haphazardly cropped, sharp edged, so short Win could see the Carthlanian veins on her scalp. A small pack hung at her waist.

"You've been following me," said Win.

"Not really," she said.

"Yes you were," said Win. "I—I can tell."

"So what if I was?" she responded, a little defensively. "I belong here. You don't. Besides, I saved your life so it was a good thing I was."

"That is true enough. And I am very grateful. But why don't you tell me what's going on?"

She turned back to him. "I heard you asking about Jesus at the Core."

"That doesn't explain why you are following me."

"I need help finding him and I thought you might be able to lead me to where he is."

"Who are you? Why do you want to find Jesus?"

"My name is Aralyn. I've—heard about Jesus but have never seen him." She studied Win while trying to appear disinterested. "Now it's your turn. Who are you and what are you doing here?"

Win was trying to decide how much to tell her. She seemed honest enough, but he had already been misled by Drason.

"My name is Trebor Win. I came here to find Jesus."

A spark of interest flashed in her eye. "So he does exist?"

"I assure you, he is real. But I don't know for sure if he is here. Do you?"

"I've heard that he is." Her eyes darted away briefly. "Will you help me find him?"

"Perhaps. But not right now. I saw someone else here, someone that really can't be here. I need to try to find her first."

"Who is she? Does she have something to do with Jesus?"

Win's first though was *of course not,* what could Sooni—or the apparition or whatever he saw—have to do with Jesus? But why had he seen Sooni, in just the place he came looking for Jesus?

He'd never had such an experience before, seeing someone in the flesh who looked like Sooni.

"I don't think so," he said. He searched the girl's eyes. Though she looked tough he sensed nothing threatening, but then he had not felt anything from Drason either. Had Drason been trying to harm him, or was he just some kind of cult fanatic? "Did you follow me down into the old station?"

"Yes. I got there just in time to see you running out the other side."

"Do you know what all those people were doing there?"

"People? What people?"

"In the station. They were chanting, some kind of rite. And someone in a robe. Their leader, I think."

Aralyn's brow wrinkled in confusion. "I didn't see anyone. Just you, running off through the station."

"That's impossible," said Win. "I had to force my way through them."

"There was no one there," said Aralyn, insistent.

"When you followed me from the Core, you must have seen me with someone else. He said his name was Drason and that he'd be taking me to Jesus."

"Yes. I saw you with him. The one with the fancy clothes."

"He was at the ritual as well."

Aralyn's eyes flared. "I tell you there was no one there!"

Win was baffled. "I believe you. But something is going on. There were people in the subway, a lot of them. And I saw —" What exactly had he seen? "I saw something, not really a person—I can't explain it. It looked like someone I knew. She led me to where you found me."

"Whoever it was almost got you killed. If I hadn't come after you, you would have followed her right into that attack."

Win shook his head. "No. The woman I saw, she would never hurt me."

"Your story reminds me of something Jesus said: *'Look to me for guidance, but beware, for evil can masquerade as a messenger of light.'*"

Win's eyes narrowed. "I thought you said you had never seen Jesus?"

"I haven't." She took another look out the window, then reached into her pack and pulled out a small device. It was visibly damaged, dented and charred. "But I have this."

"What is it?"

"Some kind of recorder. Let me show you." She pressed on it, but nothing happened. She pressed again, then shook it. "It's damaged. It doesn't always work."

Win held out his hand. "Let me try. I have some experience with devices like this."

She hesitated, as if unwilling to part with it, then slowly handed it to Win. It was surprisingly light, clearly an advanced technology. It was hard to discern its exact purpose, it certainly could be some kind of recorder. He felt the indentations of some controls and pressed.

A crystal clear voice began speaking. It didn't seem to emanate from the device but rather surrounded his head.

"Guidance comes in many forms. My words can be a guide to you. Yet some need to see as well as hear; they must walk a physical path to find their spiritual path. It is for this reason I have come, to walk such a path before you. I will show you what you must learn. Follow me, in my footsteps, and in my example."

Win nearly dropped the recorder. It was the voice of Jesus.

CHAPTER 15

WIN WAS IN SHOCK, his mind fixed on the voice that had emanated from the recorder. The voice he had first heard on K'Turia and would never forget.

Jesus.

The recording had stopped, and no matter how he tried to manipulate the device it would not work again. Just as he was about to ask Aralyn more about it, they heard the sound of marching footsteps in the street. Aralyn pushed him to the back of the room. "The army!" she whispered. "We need to find another way out!" They followed a maze of deserted corridors, dark and filled with debris, finally emerging into a smaller street behind the building. They froze, listening for any sound of pursuit, but the dim sounds from the main street faded away.

In the silence Win thought about the recording. Just hearing the voice of Jesus stirred Win's heart. Whenever he had heard Jesus speak, it always had seemed that the words were meant for Win alone. It was no different this time. *'I will show you what you must learn.'*

Certainly he had much to learn.

He had come here looking for Jesus, and instead had found the ghost of Sooni. He didn't understand why. Certainly no one on Carthlana would know about Sooni.

On K'Turia, he had a vision which connected Sooni and Jesus in some way. Both had tried to guide him. Could the

Sooni image here on Carthlana have something to do with Jesus?

The Sooni he had seen in the ritual was clearly some kind of phantom. Yet the Sooni he had chased after had seemed real. Could even that one have been an illusion? Who was perpetrating this?

"I think they're gone," said Aralyn. "This way."

She led Win along the alley, dodging puddles and rubble. Once they crossed a main street again, at a run, into another set of back alleys. Finally they reached an area of the city that appeared to be quiet, people walking calmly in the street.

"These people don't seem very worried," said Win.

"You get used to it," said Aralyn. "The fighting."

"Shouldn't you be getting back to your family? They'll be worried about you."

"I don't have any family," she said stoically.

"You seem pretty young not to have anyone."

"It's like that for a lot of us. The war —." Aralyn finally slowed down. "We should be safe around here," she said. "I need to get something to eat. Are you hungry?"

Win hadn't thought about food. "I want to know more about the recorder, and what else you heard on it. It could help us find Jesus."

Aralyn looked around cautiously. "Not now—not here, anyway. I still don't know who to trust. Let's get some food and go someplace quiet to talk."

Win waited impatiently while she stopped at an outdoor food stand. She turned to him and asked, "What do you eat?"

"I'm not very hungry."

"Well, I am. I haven't eaten all day." She paused. "I don't have a lot of money."

Win dug into his pocket. "I have these."

Aralyn snickered. "Good at the spaceport maybe. Not here. But I'll take it and trade it in." She snatched the credit from Win.

"Anything then. There isn't much I can't eat."

As Aralyn filled a bag Win had his eyes on the crowd,

searching for the woman who looked like Sooni. But all he saw were Carthlanians.

"Let's go." Aralyn led them a few blocks before speaking again. "I know a place we can hole up."

"Where do you live?" asked Win.

"Here and there. My home was destroyed."

"I'm sorry," said Win.

"It's not just me. This war, all the fighting. It's ruining everyone's lives. Soon there'll be nothing left." She handed the bag of food to Win. "Here, make yourself useful."

After a few more blocks the cross streets became farther apart and less crowded. Aralyn turned into a side street relatively clean of debris.

"Here." She pushed open a gate and led Win into a small courtyard ringed by a series of interior structures. A few Carthlanians sitting on a stoop silently watched them pass. Aralyn crossed the courtyard and exited another gate, where a walkway led to more small buildings.

"This used to be a hotel," she explained. "It's not in business anymore. People come and go. It's pretty quiet and no one should bother us."

She pointed to a mark on one of the doors. "This means someone is using it." On the third door the mark had been rubbed out. Aralyn opened the door and gave one last look around. She picked up a soft stone on the stoop and drew a mark on the door.

The simple room was surprisingly clean and tidy. Two beds lined the side walls. Just inside the entrance was a small table and some unmatched woven chairs. An open doorway led into a second room.

Aralyn took the bag from Win and sat at the table. "I'm sorry, there are no plates to eat off of." From the bag she took out some vegetables, dried meat, and two large containers of water. She ripped the bag to make a placemat, then took a knife from her pack and began cutting the food.

"It's hard to believe," Aralyn said as she cut, "but there has been one small benefit of the war. People have had to learn to farm again." She held up a soft looking spotted tuber. "These taste better than when the government ran the farms. Here, try it."

Win dropped into the chair across from her, suddenly feeling very tired. He bit into the tuber and chewed mechanically. Aralyn ignored him, intent on her food.

After a bit she looked up. "Don't you like it?"

"It's fine," said Win, dropping the tuber on the table. "I'm just anxious to hear more about Jesus. And where you got the recorder."

Aralyn gulped a long drink. "What do you know about what is going on here? The fighting?"

"A little. I just arrived. Some kind of rebellion against the central government."

"It's more complicated than that, but I guess you're right, that is what it amounts to. Except that 'rebellion' implies the people fighting against the government are doing something wrong."

Win recalled the group he had seen killing people indiscriminately in the street. "Whose side are you on?"

"No one's. I just want it to stop. Most of us do."

Win thought about the trouble on K'Turia. "Are people fighting because of Jesus?"

Aralyn frowned. "What makes you say that?"

"Nothing really."

Aralyn hesitated. "Actually, it's the other way around. Some people think Jesus will help stop the fighting."

"How about you?"

She shrugged and dug back into her food. "I'm not sure what to believe. There are a lot of preachers making promises, but not many of them come right out and say what they mean. Some of the preachers have spoken about a—savior, someone who will bring peace. Maybe it is Jesus. But how could one person help us? How could anyone help us?"

She looked up at Win. "You said he is real. Have you seen

him? *Can* he help us?" Her voice was full of skepticism, tinged with just a bit of hope.

"I can't answer that," said Win. He didn't want to dishearten her. On K'Turia, Jesus had caused the fighting, not ended it. Or rather, people had started fighting because he was there, because of his message. *Was that Jesus' fault?*

"What's so special about him?"

"It's a long story," said Win.

Aralyn wiped her mouth with her sleeve and leaned back in her chair. "It will be dark soon and it's not safe to move at night. We should stay here. So we've got time."

Win bit off another piece of the tuber. Where to begin?

"I saw Jesus on another planet, a place called K'Turia. A very different place than this one. The people there are very religious, their religion defines them and everything they do. People are born into castes —"

"Castes?" asked Aralyn.

"A hierarchy of power and status," explained Win. "The priests are at the top of the castes, and they used their power to keep it that way. They had perverted the religious rules to benefit themselves. Jesus was teaching the people of another way, a different path. It would have changed the entire social order."

"So he's a rebel?"

Win considered. "I hadn't thought of him as such, but it is one way to look at it."

"What happened there? Did the people believe him?"

"Many did. Some did not. I had to leave, and when I went back to look for him he was gone. It's kind of complicated to explain, but I have some evidence that he came here."

"Does he preach violence? We don't need more fighting."

"No, he is very peaceful." Win was thinking of the sacrifice Jesus had made to avoid bloodshed, a sacrifice that saved the life of his friend Prentiss, a sacrifice that probably had saved Win's life as well. But on K'Turia there had been bloodshed nonetheless.

"Then how does he get the people to change?"

"I think you know the answer to that, otherwise you would not be looking for him," said Win. "It's his words, what he says."

Aralyn shrugged. "Maybe." She looked away, as if not wanting to admit to a breach in her skepticism. "Things I've heard on the recordings, they make me feel—hopeful. That there is another way, a way to peace." She looked back at Win, the hardness back in her eyes. "But it's probably all just another false promise."

Win leaned forward. "What have you heard him say?"

"It's all bits and pieces. Some of it repeats. Much of it is like what we heard today. Something about a path. I thought it meant I was to follow some clues to where Jesus is, that maybe he was hiding for some reason, maybe because he was afraid of the government. And if I could figure out the hidden meaning in the recordings, I could find him."

"What makes you think Jesus needs to be hiding? Are there people who are after him?"

"I don't think many people even know he exists. Just those who go to hear the spiritualists at the Core. If the government thought he was a threat, they would certainly not let him stir up trouble. The same goes for the rebel groups. They might want to use Jesus for their own purposes."

"One thing I am sure of," said Win, "is that Jesus won't let himself be used by anyone."

"Why are you even on Carthlana?" asked Aralyn. "Why are *you* looking for Jesus, and why here?"

"That too is a long story. And I don't want to burden you with my troubles, you have enough of them here already. I am looking for Jesus for rather selfish reasons, to help me—to help me get on a new path. Not to save a world, just to help myself. I went back to find him on K'Turia, but he wasn't there. Some signs led me here. I have no idea how Jesus would have made it to this planet. And now you tell me you have heard he *is* here. And his voice is on the recorder. It's all pretty amazing." Win thought about the impossible odds. "Have you met anyone who has actually seen him?"

"No, but maybe the old man did."

"What old man?"

Aralyn took the recorder out of her pack and placed it on the table. "I was in the city of Nalry when one of the rebel groups launched an attack. They fired at everyone and everything. I thought I would die that day. I was trying to escape when an old man lying on the ground grabbed onto me. He had been injured real bad. His head was a bloody mess. I wanted to help, I really did, but I—I just wanted to get away. I told the man I was sorry, I couldn't help him."

Her voice broke, the first crack in her tough demeanor. "What had I become, that I couldn't help someone who was hurt? That's what this war had done to us, to me. But the man just smiled at me and said, 'But I can help *you*.' And he pulled me down onto the ground and rolled over me, covering me with his body just as the rebels rushed into the street. I tried to get up, but the man whispered in my ear to pretend I was dead. The rebels walked right past us, they must have seen the blood on him. When everything was quiet I said, 'I think it is okay now, we can get up.' He said, 'I'm afraid I can't move. I think my legs are broken.' I offered to get help but he said, 'There is no time. Please, you must take this.' "

She picked up the recorder. "He gave me this device and told me to keep it safe. I asked him what it was. He looked up at me, his eyes were so bright! He said, 'It is the word of Jesus!' She paused. "And then he died."

Aralyn rubbed at her eyes. "I don't know if he had ever seen Jesus. But when he said those words . . . there was a look on his face that's hard to describe. He looked . . . *healed*. Even though he was bleeding and dying, he looked healed. He wasn't afraid."

Win could imagine it, he could understand how someone would have felt the power in the words of Jesus, just as the people on K'Turia had, just as Prentiss had, just as he had.

"People here might listen to him," he said.

Aralyn shrugged. "Maybe. Nothing else is working." She took another drink. "We could use some help."

Win was looking for help too, but just for himself. And if he found Jesus, maybe he would understand why he was seeing visions of Sooni. But if Jesus could stop this war, certainly that was more important than what Win needed. "I'll do what I can to help you find him," he said. "Where do we start?"

"The recordings keep speaking of a path," she said. "If we could find it, that might help."

"Maybe you are being too literal," said Win gently. "Jesus may be speaking of a spiritual path."

"I'm not sure what that is," said Aralyn. "In any event, we can't find the spiritual path without finding Jesus, can we?"

Win felt a jolt, a clarity of thought. He had been assuming he had to physically find Jesus to resolve his own uncertainties, to support him in his quest for his spiritual journey, to free him from his torments over Sooni. Maybe —

Aralyn had been toying with the recorder. Suddenly the voice of Jesus once again enveloped them.

"Just as a shift in the wind portends the weather, and tells you how to prepare, so too can you be guided in the preparations for your spiritual journey. Yet you have to first open your mind to my guidance, not only by sight, but by feelings, feelings that go beyond emotion. And no matter how many physical senses you have, you must be ready and willing to consider that which comes to you from outside of your normal way of connecting with what is around you. No matter where you are from, no matter what race you belong to, no matter what kind of being, you have one sense beyond all that is embodied in you physically, and that is the spirit. Listen to what your inner spirit tells you, for it is far more aware of what lies beneath the superficial, no matter how real that may seem.

"The guidance I speak of is knowledge, but this knowledge is very different from what you might learn in a book. It is the knowledge of yourself, of who and what you are, of your place in the universe, of your connection to the universe and everything in it. Once everyone recognizes that this knowledge is something already within them, and accepts it, they will look differently on themselves, on others, on the

world, on the universe. Once this knowledge is revealed as the Truth there will be everlasting acceptance and the peace that comes with it.

"You must be open to the guidance I bring to you. It is not only in my deeds and my voice, but in all that is around you. My guidance may come in many forms, in what you see as reality, in dreams, in visions.

"Yet you must beware and be vigilant, for there is a darkness, a power of evil that will try to mislead you and take you astray, away from the path of knowledge and truth. Evil may masquerade as good, even presenting itself as a beacon of light. Evil is real, but it is not true. Evil will try to trick you into believing it will serve you, but this is a false promise. So you cannot ignore evil; you must face it and overcome it. But you can only do this by accepting the Truth, which will bring you to a place of inner strength. If you do not, you will be overwhelmed and succumb to the force of evil. Once overcome, evil will show its true self, its hollowness. It will be but a wisp for you to pass through."

Aralyn smiled, a tinge of hope in her voice. "He's talking about peace. Maybe he *is* here to help us."

Win was staring at the recorder, the inanimate object that had managed to capture Jesus' essence like a sacred relic.

Maybe Aralyn was right, but Win had heard something very different. Jesus was talking about evil. He seemed to be warning Win about being misled.

Misled by visions.

Misled by Sooni.

CHAPTER 16

UNABLE TO QUIET HIS MIND, Win had not fallen into a deep sleep. The disturbing ritual, the dark man, the ghost-like image of Sooni kept vividly returning, unsettling. And the words of Jesus, sometimes mystifying but always ultimately enlightening, bringing Win hope that he had come to the right place in his search.

He got up and quietly crossed the room to peer out the shuttered window. It was just beginning to lighten outside.

Behind him, Aralyn said, "We can't do anything until the sun is up, no one will be on the streets."

"I can't sleep," said Win.

"Why don't you finish up some of that food."

"I'm not hungry."

"On Carthlana, you should always eat when you can. You never know what is going to happen or when you might not be able to find food."

Win turned to her. "Don't you have anyone to be with?"

"No. It's just me."

"You are all alone?"

"Aren't we all?" She got up and disappeared into the back room, emerging with a bucket. At the door she turned to him. "I'll be right back, there is no running water in the rooms. Don't go anywhere."

Win sat at the table. She didn't have to worry about that. He had no idea where to go.

* * *

During breakfast, Aralyn barely paused between mouthfuls of food, only slowing when she noticed Win watching her.

"You seem to know this area well," Win said.

"I've moved around a lot to stay clear of the fighting. Right now this place is pretty safe."

"How old are you?"

Aralyn wiped her mouth. "Old enough. I saved you, didn't I?"

"You aren't comfortable talking about yourself," said Win.

"There is really nothing to tell. Like everyone else, I'm just trying to stay alive. I mind my own business. If you are going to stay around here, you should too."

"I think there is more to it than that. You are also looking for Jesus."

"Not the way you are. People talk as if Jesus will save the world. I'm not sure the world can be saved."

"But you are still willing to try. You may not believe now, but I think you would like to."

"You sound like my mother."

"Your mother? Why?"

"She was convinced that if you believed something hard enough, it would be true."

"Where is she?" Win asked.

Aralyn pushed back from the table. "You asked a lot of questions. Why don't you answer one for me? Who was that I saw you with leaving the Core?"

"I only know what I told you. He said his name was Drason. I thought he would help me find Jesus. I was wrong."

"He reminded me of someone. I really didn't get a good look at him, but I think I may have seen him somewhere before. I'm not sure."

"At the Core?"

"No. It was the day I—the day my parents . . . I was on my way home from school. I passed a man coming from the direction of our house. He had this strange smile on his face. I didn't think much of it at the time, just that he looked creepy. I remember turning my head as I walked by him, thinking he might follow me or something, I don't know, sneak up behind me. But he just kept walking away. When I turned back there was this loud whoosh, and our house exploded. I mean it was gone."

She got up and turned from Win, reaching for the bucket to splash water on her face, rubbing her eyes. Win looked away as she untucked her shirt to dry herself.

After a moment Win said, "I'm sorry."

The girl smoothed down her shirt and tucked it back in. "I had forgotten all about that guy until I saw you at the Core. The one you were with, Drason? I think it was the same man I saw on our street that day."

"You think he had something to do with the bombing?"

"I didn't at the time. But now I'm not so sure."

* * *

After breakfast Aralyn cleaned up the table. "It's probably safe to go out now."

"Where do we start?"

"There might be a few people around here who will recognize me. I can try asking them a few questions. I think they'll trust that I'm not after something, at least as much as you can trust anyone these days."

On the way out Aralyn rubbed the mark off the door. The walkway was deserted. The sky had brightened, already warm in the courtyard.

In the outer courtyard, a man was sweeping the area in front of an open doorway. "Wait here," said Aralyn. She approached the man and held a quiet conversation, the man pointing off into the distance.

Aralyn beckoned to Win and led him out of the courtyard into the street. "He told me some of the religious groups take their meals in the marketplace down the street when they are not at the Core. They might know something about Jesus. And about Drason. I'd like to find out what he is all about."

"I don't trust him—he's dangerous," said Win.

"You went with him, didn't you? Besides, I can take care of myself." She tightened her waist pack and headed off down the street.

Within two blocks the street ended at a large open area clear of the rubble that littered the rest of the city. A cross street led to open pavilions on both sides, packed with people. Sellers called out the names of different foods, the smell of spices permeating the air.

Tables ringed the pavilions, filled with local Carthlanians and a scattering of offworlders. A Carthlanian man in a ragged jacket pushed past them, his wispy white hair covering half his face. He smacked his hands down on one of the tables, freezing the conversation.

"Listen to me, all of you! Don't pretend you don't know what is going on here! You know what our leaders have done to us and you know what we are fighting for. But what are you doing? Nothing! It is time to stand up. No more letting them dig into your personal affairs. No more should you let them take whatever they want without your consent. They do not own you. You are not their slaves! But you let them treat you as slaves. We must fight them. This is what the rebellion is about!"

Win looked at Aralyn. "Do you know this man?"

"No. But there are many like him. Rebel supporters. They wander around trying to stir up the people."

"Shut up, you troublemaker," said one well dressed man who sat at the head of the table. "This area has been spared so far. You'll bring the fighting here."

The ragged Carthlanian pointed at him. "You think if you ignore the problem it will go away? The fighting will come here too. Your homes will be under attack. You will see friends, family, children lying in the streets. It is only a matter of time."

A woman grabbed her food and got up from the table. "I

don't need to listen to this. The fighting is bad enough. We don't need to be lectured by you." She moved off toward another table. Two others followed her.

The white haired man turned his eyes on the remaining people at the table. "If we do not stand up to them, the government will rule our lives until we die. They will tax us, invade our privacy, mislead us!"

"They have already done these things!" someone hissed. "We cannot stop them. Now leave us alone with what little peace we have."

The ragged man stared at him, then deflated and shuffled away.

"Crazy fool!" The table erupted in nervous laughter.

Aralyn pulled Win away. "He may be crazy, but he is right. This area is peaceful now, but it will change. It always does." She scanned the crowd. "Come on. You start with the offworlders. I'll mingle with the Carths and see if they know anything."

* * *

Aralyn made her way across the common, immediately shifting back into what she thought of as her safety mode. Not trying to hide, but not drawing attention either. It was a demeanor she had learned after carefully watching what drew the attention of the government forces. Slink around and they think you are up to something, act all brazen and they needed to take you down a peg.

She looked back to where she had left Win. She hoped he would listen to her warning about not being too nosy. She still hadn't made up her mind about him. He seemed harmless, but walking around asking questions about an offworlder might get them noticed by the wrong people. Better to split up. If he got picked up, it was no skin off her back.

But she had to admit, she was more interested in finding Jesus since she met Win. It was refreshing to meet someone who was focused on something more than just survival. Win had come all the way to Carthlana to find Jesus. Certainly she could walk around a little and ask a few questions.

* * *

Win watched Aralyn wind her way through the tables before approaching the nearest group of offworlders, heads bent over their food. He waited politely by the table until one of them noticed him and looked up.

The man looked very much like the large eyed, smooth talking preacher Win had seen in the Core, the one who had extolled the virtues of the powerful offworlders who would help the Carthlanians. Certainly the same species, but Win couldn't be sure it was the same man.

"Can I help you?" the man asked, his voice a silky tenor.

Something about him bothered Win. "Sorry to interrupt," mumbled Win. "I was just wondering what is good to eat?"

The man gave Win a practiced smile. "That's what you want to know?" When Win didn't reply, the man said, "As you wish. Try the local vegetables, any of them. They are very good."

"Thanks." Win walked away, feeling the eyes of everyone at the table on his back.

He passed a few more tables, looking across the plaza for Aralyn. He spotted her in an animated conversation with another woman whose back was to him. Something about her was familiar, a strange sensation of déjà vu tugging at him.

Maybe it was just the dark green cape she was wearing, something he had seen before. Or—

He waved to get Aralyn's attention as the woman began walking away, the very manner in which she carried herself screaming out a recognizable cadence. He staggered. "This just isn't possible."

Yet for just an instant he felt so sure. He locked his eyes on her, stunned. The woman turned a corner and was gone.

It was Sooni.

CHAPTER 17

WIN RACED THROUGH THE FOOD COURT, drawing startled looks, people backing away. He barreled past Aralyn, her eyes wide. Around the corner he found himself on a broad street which led into an even larger square, teeming with people. He sought in vain for the woman with the green cape.

Aralyn came running up behind him. "What's the matter?"

Win didn't take his eyes off the crowd. "That woman you were talking to, did you see where she went?"

"I've been too busy trying to keep up with you. Who is she?"

"It looked like Sooni—the woman I told you I was looking for, the one I had seen in the underground."

"You mean the one who almost got you killed?"

"I told you she wouldn't do that."

"Who is she, anyway?"

Win glanced at her. "She is—was—my wife. But it can't be her."

"Why not? I thought you were looking for her."

"Because she's dead." He grabbed her arm. "Let's go."

Win prodded her down the street, almost at a run. The street ran into another plaza surrounding a crumbling fountain barely trickling water.

"There!" said Win. "I think I see her—near the fountain."

"I don't like this," said Aralyn. "We're drawing a lot of attention. This could be some kind of trick."

Win forced himself to slow down. Maybe Aralyn was right. Could the woman they were following be trying to harm him, leading him into more danger? Had she really looked like Sooni, or was that what he wanted to believe?

The first woman he had seen was dressed in black. This woman wore green. Her cape fluttered in the breeze, the woman halfway across the plaza. She appeared to be in no hurry.

Win took a deep breath. "What did she look like?"

"She's an offworlder. She looked—she can't be your wife. She doesn't look anything like you. Her color, her features are all different." Aralyn looked at Win's almost bald head. "She has hair too."

"We Trebs are very diverse." He dodged a family cutting across their path, his eyes never leaving the green cape. "What did she say to you?"

"I asked her about Jesus. She said he was at the Core. I told her we had just come from the Core, he wasn't there. She told me he was always at the Core, I was just looking in the wrong place, he was inside. I thought she was crazy. We only have one Core. And there isn't any *inside* there, it's all open."

"What else did she say?"

"I wasn't paying much attention because she wasn't making any sense. She was pointing to my chest. She said something about not being disheartened, because I had come so far."

Win spun and grabbed Aralyn's shoulders. "Are you sure that is what she said? About not being disheartened?" His heart was racing.

Aralyn stared at him. "I think those were her exact words. Why?"

Win let her go and broke into a run. *Do not be disheartened. You have come so far.* The very words Sooni had spoken to him in their first contact, on Treb at the Great Meet, during his search for *ana*.

* * *

The green caped woman had just entered the thoroughfare at

the far end of the square. Though the street was wide, it was still much smaller than the plaza, and while it was just as crowded Win had no problem keeping her in sight.

Whomever he was following was very different from the ghost-like being he had chased out of the underground, the being who had nearly led him directly into the bombing of the rebels. That one hadn't always seemed corporal, yet it had looked like Sooni. The woman he now followed seemed very different from that earlier image; this woman looked real. Aralyn had spoken to her.

"Hey, Win! Slow down! I can't keep up with you!"

"Sorry," Win muttered, but he barely slowed.

The recorded message of Jesus had said: *You have to open your mind to the guidance, and not only see, but feel the signs.*

Win had a much different feeling now. He was excited, but less out of control than when he had seen the ghost-Sooni. That one he had blindly followed into a path of destruction, almost to his death. Now his eyes were open. He wanted to see where this Sooni was leading him. And why.

* * *

Every time they got close to the woman she would turn a corner, and when they reached it she would be well ahead, as if magically keeping them at the same distance apart. The buildings became shabbier; no one had bothered to clear the rubble here. No crowds now, just a few people quickly passing through.

Aralyn didn't know this part of the city very well. What was she doing here, following an obsessed offworlder with visions of his dead wife?

She'd worked hard to stay out of trouble, to stay alive. She couldn't throw it all away on a fool's errand. Finding Jesus suddenly didn't seem so important. Even Drason could wait.

"Win! Stop. Stop! I don't know where we are. It might not be safe."

Win half turned to her, jogging, still focused on the woman in the cape. "I appreciate your help. I really do. But I have to find out what this is all about. Go back to that marketplace, I'll meet you there. If it gets too late, I'll go back to that room."

"You can't just go running around the city. It's too dangerous, you've seen what it's like."

Win stopped and finally turned to look right at her. "I'll be careful, I promise." Then he ran off.

Aralyn reluctantly let him go. She didn't believe him. Maybe he would think he was being more careful, but no doubt he'd just run into another attack. Or the woman would lead him into one.

A sudden image of her mother came to her, warning her not to hang around with strange men. 'As you get older, you'll be drawn to the ones who are different,' her mother had said. 'They always seem more interesting. But be careful. Interesting doesn't necessarily mean good.'

Win certainly was different. But she had a feeling her mother would not have minded if she didn't leave him just yet.

He was just a few blocks ahead. Sighing, she began to run after him.

She didn't think anything she said would change his mind. This offworlder had to learn things the hard way, by getting it shoved in his face.

She just had to make sure she wouldn't be too close if the lessons were hard ones to learn.

* * *

Soot floated in the air. A plume of smoke drifted up a few blocks away. Win wasn't surprised when the woman he was following headed in that direction.

The years since Sooni's death had not blurred Win's memory; he needed no photos to recall every detail of how she looked. He didn't need to create visions to remember her. So why was he seeing Sooni now?

Even in his plague of nightmares, his only-if dreams of how things might have been, no Sooni like this had ever appeared. He refused to believe his mind was playing tricks on him, that he was creating some escape from his pain, with Sooni leading him to peace. He didn't deserve that, and he would not let himself off so easily.

The woman had reached another corner, smoke massing behind her. This time she turned, looking right at him. Win was so surprised he stopped. Still too far away to make out her features, yet the unmistakable familiarity pulled at him, the recognition just as he would have known her in a crowd of Trebs. As anyone would recognize someone well known to them.

She beckoned to him, then she slipped into the smoke.

Win heard someone behind him. He glanced back and saw Aralyn. He didn't have time to argue with her, so he kept going.

Around the corner it was as if he had entered a different city. The woman in the green cape was gone. Smoke billowed from the doors and windows of a building across the street. On the sidewalk a man was crouched over a small boy, shielding him from the heat. The man caught sight of Win and Aralyn.

"Help me! My daughter's in there!"

Win rushed to the man. "Let's get out of here!" He had to shout over the resonance of the fire.

"I have to get to her! Please, can you watch my son?" The man's eyes were pleading.

Win instinctively reached for the boy, who shrunk back in fear. Aralyn was suddenly there, pushing past him, whispering, "The kid is scared enough, I'm not sure he's going to deal well with an offworlder."

Aralyn knelt down in front of the boy. "What's your name?" The boy was still staring at Win.

"His name is Breal," said the man. "Please, just watch him for a little while. Breal, go with this nice girl. I'll be right back." He hugged the boy.

Aralyn looked up at the building. "You can't go in there."

"I have to try."

"You can't just leave your son here. What if —." Aralyn pushed away from the boy. "You can't ask us to do this. I can't be responsible for him." Her voice was hard.

The man looked at Win. "Do you have children? Please, I have to go."

The heat pushed at Win, a finger of guilt, reminding him of Sooni's death, a fire there too. A fire Win had not braved, thinking Sooni was dead. But this man, knowing his daughter was likely dead, was going in anyway. Was that love, or just foolishness?

Win put his hand on Aralyn's shoulder. "Watch the boy." To the man he said, "I'll come with you."

"No!" shouted Aralyn, her eyes wild, looking back and forth from Win to the boy.

"I have to," said Win. "Please, just wait here."

Win followed the man toward the building, more than just smoke visible now in the windows, red tendrils of flame snaking out into the dingy gray sky. A spray of water appeared, dim figures operating a manual tank truck, the stream pulsing with each pump.

The man rushed up the steps. Win yelled after him to wait, but he disappeared into the smoke, another specter in Win's life.

Win sprinted to the people running the pumper, pointing to his robe. They ignored him, so he ran into the stream of water, trying to stay on his feet as it blasted him.

Soaking wet, he half covered his eyes with his sleeve and edged up the stairs and into what was left of the doorway. He couldn't see the man, but even if he had been just a few steps away it wouldn't have mattered, the room was black with smoke.

A wail from somewhere above him. The girl?

"Sela! I'm coming!" The voice of the man, not far ahead.

Win stumbled forward. Another muffled explosion, the vibrations in the floor buckling Win's legs as chunks of ceiling came crashing down. Something cracked behind him, fresh air rushing in, followed by an eerie silence which lingered, the silence powerful enough to hide the roar of the flames. Then a fireball, more intense than any fire Win had ever seen. He could not close his eyes, the fireball came at him, a mass of pure white light, surrounding him until he could see nothing except whiteness, utterly untainted by the darkness of the smoke.

From all around him, from the whiteness itself, there came a voice, a voice Win could never forget, the voice of Jesus: *'Pain leads to guilt, because you confuse that which you can change from what you cannot. Guilt is an excuse for dwelling on something you cannot change instead of freeing yourself to face the challenges ahead of you and within you. I ask of you: if you have not even raised your sword, then what is there to be guilty of?'*

The whiteness enveloped Win, cradling him. The building shook, the walls collapsing, and just as Win lost consciousness he swore that the very stonework which rushed at him bounced harmlessly off of his safe white cocoon.

CHAPTER 18

"WIN! WAKE UP!"

Win opened his eyes to find Aralyn anxiously peering at him. Overhead, the sky, still dark with floating ash, the hard pavement of the street against his back.

He sat up, Aralyn cradling his shoulders. "Slow," she said. "You might be injured."

"I'm alright," said Win, rubbing dirt from his eyes. He was still dripping wet, covered in soot. "What happened? Where's —"

"He's right over there. He's hurt, I think, but he won't let anyone near him." Her voice dropped to a whisper. "His daughter didn't make it out."

Win followed her eyes to the building, or what was left of it. A small crowd was still trying to get the fire under control. A few steps away the Carthlanian man was sitting on the ground, his arms wrapped around his son, the boy crying in convulsive sobs.

"It's a miracle you got out," said Aralyn. "The building collapsed all at once. There was so much stuff in the air I couldn't see a thing. Then here you were, in the street. You must have managed to get out just before it all came down."

Win let her help him stand up. He didn't feel any pain. "Really, I'm fine. We were still inside when it came down. I saw the ceiling fall."

"That's impossible," said Aralyn. "No one could have survived that. It's all on fire too."

Win decided he wouldn't tell her about the white light, the protective embrace. Or about hearing the voice of Jesus. Not now, anyway. "We should go look for his daughter," he said.

"People looked. They didn't find anyone."

"Still —." He approached the man slowly, not wanting to scare the child again. A gaping leg wound oozed blood over the man's torn clothing, and his face was black with soot.

"Let me help you," said Win. The boy heard his voice and turned. His eyes settled on Win and all at once he stopped crying. Without thinking Win held out his arms and the boy came to his embrace.

Aralyn knelt by the man, helping him to lie down. His eyes were dazed, unfocused. She glanced up at Win, shaking her head.

"Where did the white ball of light go?" asked the boy.

"You saw it too?" said Win.

"It was so bright!" The boy looked over at the ruins. "My sister is dead, isn't she?"

"I don't know. I'll go look again, okay?"

The boy tightened his embrace. "Please don't leave!"

"I won't. I'll be right over there, you'll be able to see me. Stay with your father, don't let him worry about you. And my friend Aralyn is right here."

Aralyn was compressing the man's wound. She looked up at the boy. "Your name is Breal, right? Listen, do you want to help your father?"

"You think that is a good idea?" asked Win.

"He has to learn sometime. Come here, Breal, your father needs your help. Just hold this tight. You're not afraid of a little blood are you?" She jerked her head at Win, telling him to go.

Win made his way through the pieces of the fallen building, joining others combing the rubble. The fire was not completely under control, but it had at least been contained to one area, where it still burned, intense.

"Any survivors?" Win asked one of the searchers.

The man wiped a dirty hand across his brow. "None yet. I don't think there will be any. We've looked through what was thrown clear. The rest of everything is right there." He indicated the fire.

"You didn't happen to see an offworlder with a green cape, did you?"

"No, why? Was she inside?"

"I don't know," said Win. "Probably not." He stared into the flames. No hint of white now. There would be no refuge in that inferno.

* * *

Win jerked his head around.

"What?" asked Aralyn.

"Shh." He focused on the sound. "Gunshots."

"I can't hear —" A pop, pop, followed by a larger bang. "It might be government forces. We've got to go."

Win looked at the man's leg, wrapped with a crude bandage made out of a piece of torn clothing. He was unconscious. "Can he be moved?"

"He doesn't have any choice, we've got to get him out of here."

"We don't even know his name," said Win.

The boy spoke up. "Varshan. My father is Varshan."

"The government won't care what his name is," said Aralyn. She held up the man's arm, indicating a rough tattoo on the inside of his bicep. "See this mark? He's a rebel."

"It doesn't matter. Let's get him out of here."

"You realize what will happen to us if we get caught helping a rebel?"

"Then I'll do it," said Win.

"That's not what I meant," said Aralyn. "We'll argue about this later. Come on, let's get him up."

As they lifted him Varshan's eyes popped open. Very lucidly he said, "I won't let them hurt you," and then he collapsed into their arms, unconscious.

They dragged the man, dead weight, as far as they could, a few long blocks. The boy followed stoically, never far from Win's side.

"Let's rest in here," said Aralyn. They squeezed through the doorway of one of the many empty buildings, Aralyn pushing the rusted door shut with her hip. The sound of gunfire had died down.

As they set Varshan down he groaned. "Careful," said Win.

"No, that's good," said Aralyn. "It means he's coming out of shock."

"How do you know all this?"

"You'd be surprised what you learn in a war." Aralyn probed the wound. "I can wash it out and put on a clean bandage, if I can find one. But he'll need some medical attention soon."

She got up and went to the door, opening it carefully. "It looks okay." Turning to Win, she said, "Keep them quiet while I'm gone."

Win didn't know what to do. He had had some basic medical training, but he never had any use for it on his research ship. Varshan's breathing was shallow but steady.

Win turned his attention to the boy. "Are you all right?"

"Yes." But Breal's voice quivered. "I want my sister."

"I'm so sorry," said Win. He spoke as calmly as he could, smothering the frustration and sadness he felt from not being able to help save the girl. It wouldn't help to lose control in front of the boy.

"It wasn't your fault," said Breal, looking down, trying to hide his tears.

"No, I guess not," said Win.

"Where are you from?" asked the boy.

"A planet called Treb. It's very far away."

"Why are you here?"

"I came to find someone."

"Why?"

"Because—the person I'm looking for—he helps people. And I need some help."

"Will he help you?"

"Maybe he will," said Win. He thought about the woman in the green cape, leading him to these people, leading him to the white light, the cocoon of safety. "Maybe he already has."

* * *

Aralyn had somehow found a clean cloth and rebandaged Varshan's leg. He had slipped in and out of consciousness, sometimes wide-eyed, other times just dazed. The boy had fallen asleep against his father.

"We have to figure out what to do with him," said Aralyn.

"Can we get some help from the rebels?"

"If I could find the rebels, so could the government. You really don't know much about war, do you?"

"No, I guess not." Win actually had been part of a war mission, but even with the danger he had faced it was nothing like what was going on here. He watched Aralyn checking Varshan's leg, grown beyond her years, sadness tugging at him. She had endured so much.

"How long do you think we'll be safe here?" he asked.

"I looked around, it's pretty deserted. For now anyway. But he needs a doctor." She glanced at the boy. "He could lose the leg," she whispered.

"Can we get him back to the marketplace?"

"Maybe. But people will ask questions. And if anyone sees his mark . . ."

"We could cover it up. We don't even know if the building fire had anything to do with the rebels. We've got to get him help."

She shook her head. "It's too risky. The government has spies everywhere. Someone is sure to report a wounded man who's with an offworlder, especially after a fire."

"There aren't any offworlders helping the rebels, are there?" argued Win. "I could just say I was only trying to help someone who was hurt."

"No one does that here. Everyone minds their own business. I told you."

Win slumped against the wall and closed his eyes, trying to regain some strength. His skin still felt warm, not from the fire, which had not touched him, but from the protective embrace of the brilliant white light.

"What's your name?" The voice, a dry croak.

"You're awake, good." said Aralyn. She held a bottle to the man's lips. "Have some water. Just a little."

"I'm Trebor Win. She's Aralyn. Your son told us you are Varshan?"

Varshan nodded. He reached out for his son, gently stroking his hair, the boy moaning in his sleep. "Is he all right?"

"No injuries," said Win. "He—he misses his sister. He knows."

Varshan closed his eyes. Win thought he had fallen asleep again, but then realized the man was quietly sobbing. After a long time the Carthlanian opened his eyes and said, "You helped us get away?"

"It was the least we could do," said Win.

"Not many would have bothered." Varshan coughed, spitting up some blood. "I have to tell you something." He fell back again, his eyes squeezing shut in pain.

Aralyn looked at Win. "No, really, you don't. We don't need to know anything."

His eyes still closed, Varshan said, "That tells me you already know. You should go. If the government catches you helping me, you know what will happen."

"We can't just leave you," said Win.

Varshan opened his eyes and looked at Aralyn. "He's an offworlder, he doesn't understand. You need to explain it to him."

Aralyn got up, busying herself with her pack. Without facing Varshan she said, "I tried, he won't listen."

"I need to be alone anyway," said Varshan. "My daughter—I failed her."

"What happened?" asked Win.

"We used to live in that building. After my wife died I—I joined the rebels. A week ago I had to do something—something dangerous, so I left Breal and Sela with relatives. I came back to get them, to take them to a place where I have friends, someplace safer. Sela begged me to stop at our old apartment, she wanted to see if some of her mother's things were still there."

Varshan shifted his position, grimacing. "Breal didn't want to go in—too many memories, I guess. So I waited outside with him. The building had been damaged, but it looked deserted and safe enough. Sela was only in there a few minutes when it started to come down. I wanted to go after her, but couldn't leave Breal. Then the fire started. That's when I saw you."

"It wasn't your fault," said Aralyn. "It happens, old fuel tanks, old wires. It was an accident."

"It *is* my fault. I brought her there. I let her go in." Varshan's voice cracked, he was crying again, trying not to wake the boy. "It's my fault."

Win saw the torment in Varshan's eyes. He had been told so many times that he had not been responsible for Sooni's death. Yet he had never accepted that; he always felt that he should have been able to do *something*. Yet the voice of Jesus had said: *Pain leads to guilt, because you confuse that which you can change from what you cannot.* In this moment, he truly understood the pain of self imposed guilt.

"Punishing yourself won't help you," said Win. "Or Breal."

"You don't know what it feels like," said Varshan.

Win and Aralyn spoke at the same time. "Yes, I do."

* * *

Win and Aralyn had argued in whispers while Varshan and Breal slept. "He said he knows a place where some of his friends are," said Win. "They'll be able to help him."

"He means rebel friends," said Aralyn. "I told you—*he*

even told you—we can't get involved in all that. I won't do it."

"I'll take him," said Win.

"He's lost a lot of blood. What happens if he passes out along the way? You have no idea where to go, which areas are safe."

"Look at me," said Win, pointing to his face. "No one will bother me. I'll just tell them I'm lost."

"Let's say you make it there. Then what? It must be some kind of hideout. Do you think the rebels will just let you leave once you know where it is?"

From across the room, Varshan said, "I promised I won't let them hurt you."

Aralyn stared at him, her voice flat. "I don't know you."

"What you mean," said Varshan, "is that you don't trust me."

"I don't trust anyone," said Aralyn.

Varshan nodded toward Win. "Then what are you doing with him?"

"That's none of your business," said Aralyn.

"Aralyn, I understand your concern, but what do you want us to do?" said Win. "Arguing without an alternative isn't very helpful. Besides," he looked at Breal, "we can't just leave the boy."

She had stomped off, out the door, not coming back for so long Win had thought she had abandoned them.

When she returned, she ignored Varshan and came to stand before Win, hands on her hips, petulant. "I'll go under one condition. We'll get them close to where he wants to go, then leave them. I don't want to know exactly where it is. He can crawl the rest of the way."

"It will work out," said Win.

"I told you, you sound like my mother. Just because you believe something doesn't mean it is true."

"Sometimes it does," said Win. "Maybe she was right."

"Look what happened to her," said Aralyn. Her voice was defiant, but her lip quivered. "For all I know the rebels blew up our house."

"We don't do that," said Varshan.

Aralyn spun on him. "Don't give me that. I'm no fan of the government, but you rebels are just as responsible for this war, for all this death. You want to feel guilty for losing your daughter. Maybe you should feel guilty for what you are doing in the war."

"Aralyn! That's not necessary," said Win.

Varshan slumped back against the wall. "Let her be. She's right. I'm certainly guilty of something."

* * *

I'll check the street," said Aralyn, and disappeared out the door. She still sounded angry.

Varshan leaned on Win. He had practiced taking a few steps and claimed he was fine, but Win felt him tense every time he put weight on his leg.

"I can help, too," said Breal.

"Stay close, my son. Don't let our new friends worry about you wandering off. We'll be somewhere safe by tonight."

Aralyn's head appeared in the doorway. "Let's go."

The street was deserted for as far as they could see in both directions. Dense white clouds now filled the sky. "That way," said Varshan. "We need to head toward the river."

Aralyn looked up sharply. "I should have guessed."

"Yes, it's pretty deserted," said Varshan. "If we turn north near the old power plant we'll avoid most people the entire route."

"No one will be on those streets because that area isn't safe," said Aralyn.

"Better for us," said Varshan.

Aralyn stared at him, then stomped off down the street. Over her shoulder she said, "We need to hurry if we are going to get there before dark."

Win was surprised at the progress they made given Varshan's condition. After a short time they established a rhythm, Aralyn would scout ahead while Varshan rested, and then Win would help him make it to where Aralyn waited.

"The power plant is just a few blocks ahead," said Varshan. "There might be some people using it for shelter, so we should turn here. This next section we'll need to move through quickly."

"Let's take a short rest," said Win. "Do we have any food left?"

"A little," said Aralyn. She unwrapped some dried fruit from her bag and gave it to Varshan and Breal.

"What about you?" asked Varshan.

"You need your strength," said Aralyn. "I'm not going through all this so you can faint on the way."

Varshan offered the food to Win, who shook his head. "I'm fine."

When Varshan tried to stand his leg gave out; Win could barely hold him. "It stiffened up," said Varshan.

Aralyn took his other shoulder and between them they half dragged Varshan along the street. His injured leg could hardly take any weight.

"It will take too long if we have to keep checking ahead," said Win. "We'll have to chance it."

They had just made the next corner when two men appeared out of a doorway a block ahead. For a moment the two groups eyed one another, and then the two men headed off away from them.

"Probably okay," said Varshan. "Let's go."

But the cross street at the next intersection was not empty. A group was heading toward them. They'd been seen.

Aralyn tensed, but Varshan said, "Don't try to hurry, it will only draw attention. If anyone asks, just say I fell and cut myself on something rusty. But no one will ask, not around here."

"I know how to blend in," snapped Aralyn. "But I'm better at it when I'm alone."

From the direction of the power plant came the sound they had been dreading, a heavy vehicle. The people in the street scattered. Breal hid behind his father.

Varshan cocked his ear. "Sounds like a troop carrier." He looked at Win. "There's no good place to hide around here. It's decision time. You either have to leave me or we have to make a run for it."

"We're not leaving you," gritted Win. He was already surging ahead, not giving Aralyn a chance to argue. People pushed by them, but everyone seemed intent on their own escape. The sound of the truck grew louder.

A drop of water hit the pavement, and without warning the rain was coming down in torrents, as if turned on by a switch. Within moments they were soaked, the rain bouncing off the pavement, the buildings barely visible, the people now wraiths flitting through the sheets of water.

Aralyn started to laugh.

"What's the matter?" asked Win, bewildered.

"You must be blessed!" she said. "No one will be able to see us now!"

CHAPTER 19

THE RAIN STOPPED as quickly as it had begun. A thick fog settled in almost immediately, the air cold and wet.

The rain and Varshan's injury had forced them to seek shelter and rest. There were few options; they settled for a rusty over-hang over the doorway of a partially collapsed building. Once on the move again, their pace was much slower, punctuated by frequent stops.

Varshan was slipping in and out of deliriousness, groaning when awake, thankfully silent otherwise. Aralyn had washed his wound yet again, using the last clean wrap and rainwater she had captured in a plastic sheet from her pack.

"Remember your promise," she reminded Win. "We get as close to the river as we can and leave them. I want to be back well past the power plant by dark."

"I didn't promise anything," said Win.

"But —"

"Let's just see how things turn out."

"I thought you wanted to find the woman you said looked like your wife," Aralyn said, her voice hard.

"I will. After I help these people."

"And you seem to have forgotten about finding Jesus."

"I have not," said Win, sensing Aralyn's fear. He tried not to sound argumentative. "One of the reasons I want to find him is to learn more from him. And one of his teachings is to help others to the best of our ability. What good is finding him if I'm going to ignore what he is teaching?"

They shouldered on. The boy had gone increasingly quiet and now barely spoke, but gave them no trouble. With his father supported on both sides, there was no room for him to hold onto Varshan, and instead he kept his hand pressed against Win's leg. Win tried to talk to him but Breal's responses were limited to nods.

The clouds had darkened to a near black. The heavy fog stayed throughout the rest of the day, the hint of sun not enough to burn it off. Win kept expecting Aralyn to argue about turning back, but she kept going, amazing him with her strength and determination. Or stubbornness, he could not be sure.

The rubble filled streets were broken only by pools of water collecting in the fissured pavement. They had seen no one for many blocks, though the fog was so thick they had no idea how many people they might have passed.

Tired, Win tripped on a rock, stumbling, jolting Varshan awake. "Where are we?" he asked, his voice parched.

"I don't know exactly," said Aralyn. "Still heading north of the power plant, mostly. But the streets here are not in a grid."

"There will be —" Varshan's eyes rolled back, fluttering, and he was unconscious yet again.

What did he say?" asked Aralyn. "There will be what?"

"I don't know," said Win.

They let him down as gently as possible and Aralyn checked the wound. "The bandage is holding. He might be getting an infection, or it could be just the blood loss."

"It would be better if we could elevate his leg," said Win. "Let's look again for something to make a stretcher."

"We should keep moving to take advantage of the fog."

"We'll move faster if we aren't trying to drag him."

Aralyn sighed. "I'll see what I can find."

"Don't get lost," cautioned Win.

"Do you want me to go look for something or not?"

"Sorry," said Win.

"I'll follow the buildings on this side of the street," said Aralyn. "I'll find my way back."

While she was gone Win tried again to talk to the boy, who collapsed in his lap. But Breal's eyes were half closed, either out of exhaustion or shock.

A scraping sound snapped Win's head around. Aralyn, emerging out of the fog, dragging a long flat plank, held together by a jagged metal brace.

"It's a piece of wall I found in one of the buildings," she said. "It's plenty strong. If we wrap the end here with some rags we should be able to keep from getting cut."

They rolled Varshan onto the makeshift stretcher and headed off again. Although now bearing his full weight they moved much more quickly. The streets narrowed, the grid long since gone, alleys constantly crossing their path. Aralyn thought they were heading in the right direction.

They came to a very wide fork, the street they were on splitting, both directions leading very wide of their route. The murkiness still kept them from seeing far enough ahead to determine if either path would swing around again to the north.

"I've never seen a late day fog last this long," said Aralyn.

"Which way?" asked Win.

"I don't know. I've never been around here. I'll go look."

"Let me go," said Win. He was afraid if he sat he'd fall asleep. "Don't worry, I won't get lost."

"We probably already are," said Aralyn.

Win chose the left fork, running his hand along the buildings, counting steps. Within a block the fog, still dark, had begun to lift off the ground, allowing him to see much farther ahead. The street was clearer, the buildings still decayed and empty, but there was much less debris. After the second block the road began to shift to the right, back to their original northerly course.

A sound ahead startled him. A voice? No, more than one voice, in unison, reminding him of the chant in the underground.

It hummed in his head, the pressure building, pulling him forward. He reached out for the wall to keep from toppling, his balance awry. He closed his eyes to center himself.

The chanting stopped. When he opened his eyes the fog seemed even darker, a black hood, but it had risen higher off the street. A slight breeze blew, shifting the miasma, pulsating. He took a few steps forward, giving into the pressure which urged him on, and as he passed a windowless building the wind sucked by him, drawn inside, the sound cutting through the quietude. Had he imagined the chanting?

One more block, he thought. Slowly he edged ahead, the pressure lessening, and now he was sure he was going the right way, the street straightening back out directly north. And the road, in much better shape here, as if swept clean.

Aralyn would be happy, it would be easy going.

* * *

He returned to find Aralyn fiddling with the recorder. "I thought you had gotten lost," she said.

"It's all good," said Win. "We should go left here, the road turns back to the way we were originally heading. And the streets are really clear. We'll make good time." He didn't say anything about the sound he had heard.

"No," said Aralyn. "Varshan awoke for a bit while you were gone. I told him about the fork, where we are. He said we had to go right, the left fork is mostly blocked, and it turns back toward the center of the city."

"No it doesn't," said Win. "I was just there."

"He was pretty adamant."

"He must be confused," said Win. "The left choice is the easy way."

They both jumped at the sound, the voice from the recorder. *'Be vigilant, for the forces of evil will try to keep you from the true path. The way to enlightenment is not always easy. Sacrifice requires work. Beware the promise of success without effort. The true path is one of light, not just a break in the darkness.'*

The memory of the street flooded over Win, the clear path, the break in the blackness of the fog. That way had seemed so . . . easy. He wanted to think it was some kind of payback for all his hard work, trying to help Varshan. Now he wondered if something, or someone, was trying to lead him astray.

Win stared at the recorder, hoping it would give him more guidance. It's silence demanded his decision.

"Let's go the other way," said Win.

They had barely begun to move again when they felt a change in the breeze and glimpsed the first wash of real light in the sky. But the visibility was still limited, they could barely see a block ahead.

They went on as before, stopping now and then to rest, Varshan moaning. The street turned abruptly, and from what they could tell they were again heading in the right direction.

"We must be getting close to the river," said Aralyn. "We need to decide where to leave them —"

"Leave who?" A commanding voice, from behind them. Aralyn, holding the front of the stretcher, turned so quickly Win almost dropped his end.

"Quick!" whispered Aralyn. "This way!"

She started down the street, pulling on the stretcher, forcing Win to follow, Breal grabbing at his belt. They had taken only a few steps before three Carthlanians emerged out of the fog, brandishing some kind of pistols. They wore makeshift, unmatched uniforms of fatigue type shirts and pants.

"Stop right there," said one of the men, keeping a distance, his pistol pointing at them. "Where are you going?"

Aralyn shot a warning glance at Win. "There was a fire, and we found this man and his son. He's hurt. We were trying to get him some help."

"Where was this fire?" the man asked suspiciously.

"On the other side of the old power plant," said Aralyn.

"And you came this way? Why didn't you go back to the center of the city?"

"We—we got turned around," said Aralyn. "The fog."

Win heard footsteps behind them. No escape that way. "Please," said Win. "We were just trying to help. Can you get this man some medical attention?"

"No one just tries to help," said the man. He took a few steps closer, his entire bearing intimidating.

"So I've heard," said Win. "Where I come from we do."

"And where is that?"

"A planet called Treb."

"And why are you here? Who's side are you on?"

"I'm not on anyone's side," said Win.

"If you stay here, you'll have to pick a side."

"Who's side are *you* on?" demanded Aralyn.

The large man eyed Aralyn. "What's your story, girl?"

Aralyn stared at him, defiant. "I don't have one. Just trying to survive, like everyone else."

"Careful, Kesh, they could be spies."

Kesh came closer, looming over Win. A line of fresh scars ran across his forehead, forming a crisscross pattern with his distinctive Carthlanian veins. "I never heard of an offworld spy before." He looked down at the stretcher. "Varshan!" Kesh glared at Win, his eyes hard. "Put the stretcher down," he ordered, "and back away." Over his shoulder he said, "Watch them."

Kesh put a hand to Varshan's forehead, then examined his leg, expertly probing. He looked up at Win. "What happened?"

"It's just what I told you," said Aralyn, interrupting. "We found him near a fire. With the boy. You obviously know him, so take him and let us be on our way."

Kesh motioned to the other two men to take the stretcher. He reached out for Breal, who slunk behind Win.

"You'll have to come with us," said Kesh. "You'll never make it back before dark."

"We can't take them Kesh. They'll find out where —"

"Shut up," said Kesh. "I need to think. But Varshan obviously trusted them enough to tell them where to go. Blindfold them. If they are lying we'll find out soon enough."

* * *

Rough hands pushed and pulled Win along. He heard a door open, the hands prodding him ahead. The door closed and a lock snapped.

"Keep them here, don't let them see anyone else yet." Kesh's voice. "Give them food and water. I'll see to Varshan and the boy and then return to question them."

Win's blindfold was yanked off. "This is for your protection as well as ours," said Kesh. The rebel disappeared down some steps into the gloom.

Win's eyes slowly adjusted to the dim light of the windowless room. One of the guards prodded them down the steps, Aralyn shaking off his arm. At the bottom of the stairs they emerged into a basement, its expanse spreading off into the darkness. In the distance the echoed murmur of voices. The guard motioned to a nearby table with food and water.

"Where are we?" Win asked the guards.

Aralyn cut in. "We don't need to know." She sat down at the table and began to eat, studiously avoiding eye contact with the guards. After a while they drifted off a bit, yet still watchful.

Win sat down and leaned back in the chair, closing his eyes. It had been a very long day. His muscles ached from carrying the stretcher.

"Win?" Aralyn said.

"Yes?"

"Why did you go into that building to help Varshan, anyway?"

Win tried to think of how to explain his actions. "Because if I hadn't I'd be asking myself why not."

"You must've known there was no way to save his daughter."

"I had to try."

"Had to? You didn't even know those people."

"Should that make a difference?"

"The reason we are all in this mess," she waved her arms, "the war, everything, is because people were minding everyone else's business but their own. Telling each other what they could and couldn't do. If everyone had just kept to their own affairs, none of this would have happened."

Win opened his eyes. Gently he asked, "Isn't that what's happening now? Everyone looking out just for themselves, the rule of the wild? No one's helping each other, you said so yourself."

Aralyn would not meet his gaze, casually taking a sip of water, a mannerism Win had come to realize was her way of admitting she had nowhere else to go in her argument. "Sometimes I think you say things just to get a reaction," he said. "Like you want to connect. Seems odd for someone who doesn't want to be noticed."

Aralyn's eyes flashed briefly, then she shook her head. "I just hate everything that's going on." She lowered her voice. "It's all their fault, the government, the rebels."

Win leaned toward her. "Everything isn't always so clear cut."

"Even if people are dying? Someone needs to be held accountable."

"Even if you could place blame, that doesn't always solve the problem. Not every bad thing that happens is someone's fault."

"You said your wife was dead. How did she die?"

The sadness swept over him. It was always there, but now and again, at a certain word, a certain memory, it engulfed him, the pain piercing. "She was killed in an accident."

"An accident? So *you* don't blame anyone?"

Win needed to say no. For Aralyn's sake, so she would not blame herself for the loss of her parents. Even if she didn't now, at some point as she grew older she would start to wonder what she might have done differently that day.

And for himself as well. He had seen the futility of guilt when

Varshan couldn't save his daughter, just as he could not save Sooni.

"I was not there when it happened," he said. "Others tried to save her, but they could not reach her."

"Is that why you tried to save Varshan's daughter? Because you could not save your wife?"

"It's hard to explain," he said, trying to stay in control, the grief threatening to conquer him. "What I know and what I feel are . . . two different things. I've been blaming myself for a long time."

"Didn't you just say that placing blame doesn't always solve the problem?"

Win smiled sadly. "You listen pretty carefully, don't you?"

"Maybe you should too," said Aralyn, taking another drink of water, trying hard to act nonchalant. "You also told Varshan that punishing himself wouldn't help. Maybe you need to take your own advice."

* * *

"Come with me," ordered Kesh.

Win got up, glad to be able to move, but Aralyn said, "Where are you taking us?"

"Don't worry," said Kesh. "Varshan has confirmed your story. No one is going to harm you."

"You mean harm me anymore than you rebels have already."

"I appreciate your anger, child," said Kesh. "But we are fighting this war precisely to help people like you. A bit of understanding will go a long way."

"I'm no child. And I think you should let people decide for themselves whose help they need," said Aralyn.

"Something we both agree on," said Kesh. "And speaking of help, we want to thank both of you for what you did for Varshan and the boy. Varshan would not have survived without you. Our medic says he is already improving and will be able to get up soon."

"We did what we could," said Win. "But we couldn't save his daughter."

"He told me," said Kesh. "I had actually never met her, but Varshan spoke of her and the boy often. He was trying to keep them out of his—his activities. He's done his part. I've told him he should step back, so he can take care of his son."

"Like retire?" said Aralyn. "Can you just quit a war?"

"You can," said Win. "It's called peace."

Kesh gave Win a cool look. "If only it were that easy, offworlder. You're an interesting man. Come, I'd like to learn more of why you are here." He turned to Aralyn. "It is almost dark. You understand it would be unsafe for you to be on the streets now, and I can't spare anyone to get you home at night."

"I don't have a home," said Aralyn, bitterly.

"None of us do," said Kesh. "You can stay here tonight. We'll be leaving soon and won't be using this hideout anymore, so it doesn't matter if you know where it is."

He led them through the basement room, lighting a small flash to show the way. Empty crates lined the walls. Passing through a rusty door they found themselves in a much smaller, well lit room. Ten sets of large Carthlanian eyes fell on them, men and women, most of them dressed in the same military style fatigues. The room smelled of food and sweat. Varshan lay sleeping on a cot, Breal sitting by him. At the sight of Win the boy came running up and threw his arms around Win's legs.

"He seems to have taken a liking to you," said Kesh.

"He was afraid of me at first," said Win.

"You're his savior," said Kesh. "That will overcome any fear of the unknown."

* * *

Win's *gheris* sense was picking up a confused mix of emotions. A combination of celebration and excitement, as if in expectation for a momentous event. But underlying it, or perhaps from different people, a sense of anger, and finality. His *gheris* did not have the capability to distinguish between individuals in a crowd. And a very strong feeling, held by a few, or even one, could overcome lesser emotions of an entire group.

He had learned that anger was one emotion he should never ignore.

The evening meal had ended in drinking, a foul smelling distillation Win sipped at to be polite. During dinner the rebels had barely spoken, perhaps still suspicious of their guests. Sensing their discomfort, Win and Aralyn retreated to a dark corner. But as the night wore on the volume of conversation gradually increased.

From the shadows Win watched a woman at the far side of the room, the only one not taking part in the carousing. She wore the same clothing as the rest of the group, but somehow seemed to be separate, detached. Now and again she would look over at the other rebels with a look of what Win took to be disapproval. He still had not figured out all the Carthlanian expressions.

Win, still sensing the suffused anger, couldn't shake the sense of foreboding he was getting from his *gheris*. "I'm going to see if I can find out something," he told Aralyn. "Stay here."

"Don't ask too many questions. I don't trust these people."

Win got up and casually walked over to the quiet woman, focusing his *gheris*. His sense was right on target, she reeked of disapproval, combined with repressed anger.

"Mind if I join you? I'm really not much of a drinker," he said.

The woman looked him up and down, then returned her stare to the rest of the rebels. Her eyes were hard, tense. "Suit yourself," she said. "But I'm not going to be much company."

"My name is Win."

"So I've heard. What's an offworlder doing with that young girl?" She jerked her head toward Aralyn.

"Nothing. We just happen to be looking for the same thing."

"Oh? What's that?"

"I'm not trying to be secretive, but I don't think either of us know for sure." He nodded toward the boisterous table. "You seem unhappy with your friends." The woman gave him a sharp look. Win spread his hands. "I don't want to cause trouble," he said. "I just meant that you must not like the drinking."

"It's not that," she said. "I like the drink myself, most times. I just don't think this is a time for celebrating."

"Because of Varshan's daughter?" said Win.

"He's not the only one who lost someone," said the woman, bitterly. "My husband is also dead."

"I'm sorry to hear that," said Win. "Did this just happen?"

"Why should that matter?" the woman snapped. "My pain is the same."

"I understand," said Win.

"How could you? You're not even from this planet."

"I too have lost a mate. Not here, and a long time ago. It makes no difference where you are from, the pain is the same."

The woman's voice was filled with anger. "No one was more important to me than my husband."

"That is how I feel too," said Win. "Some people say that time heals the pain, but it doesn't really. All that changes is that instead of thinking about it every second, other things become more immediate, crowding out your memories for a short time, but then something happens to remind you of what you lost, and with that memory whatever was masking your senses is pierced, the pain sharper than you ever remember, even right after the loss."

The woman's voice shook. "You do understand."

Win sat down. "I wish I could tell you it would get better," he said. "But it hasn't for me."

"You left something out," said the woman. "The anger. The government killed my husband. And now I have this anger. It will give me the strength to do what I must do."

"And what is that?"

"To avenge my husband's death." Her voice was harsh.

"That won't bring him back," said Win, as gently as he could.

"I know that, I'm not stupid." She frowned at Win. "You

sound like Varshan. His wife died in a government bombing, did you know that? That's why he came to us. But he doesn't have the strength to do what needs to be done. He's always looking for a different solution. Look where that got him." Her voice hardened. "I'm not like him. I will not sit and do nothing. Someone must pay for my husband's death, and I can make that happen."

"Do you know who was responsible?"

"Anyone with the government shares the blame. Any I strike down will be fitting punishment."

"And so you would choose at random? Someone completely innocent of your husband's death could be killed."

"No one was more innocent than my husband," she said, the anger rising to the surface. "We were not part of the rebels. I only joined up after he died, so I could make them pay."

Win indicated the rowdy group. "With their help?"

The woman scoffed. "They think they are committed, but they don't go far enough. They don't understand what it means to totally sacrifice yourself, as I'm willing to do."

Gently, Win said, "I met someone who taught me the meaning and importance of sacrifice, not necessarily to give yourself up, but to give what you can to help others."

"That's what I'm going to do," said the woman. "I'm going to help everyone who suffered at the hands of the government. And at the same time, I'm going to end my pain." She looked over at the other rebels. "And whether they know it or not, they are going to give me the means." The fire blazed in her eyes, and Win's *gheris* sense was awash with her anger.

He got up to leave her with her thoughts, knowing he was not the one who would be able to allay her pain. "You didn't tell me your name."

"It doesn't matter, but it's Listra." She stared at Win, her veins almost invisible in the dim light. "Let me ask you something, offworlder. You don't seem angry. It's all that keeps me going. What do you have?"

Win thought about his journey of lost time and empty space

since the loss of Sooni, his escape to find solace amongst the stars, and now his search for Jesus.

"I'm trying to find that out," he said. "I think I'm learning to have faith. Faith that there is something that will explain all of this, something to make sense of the pain, the suffering. Something to explain why bad things happen to the innocent."

CHAPTER 20

THE AFTER DINNER DRINKING went well into the evening. After briefly checking on Varshan, who was resting comfortably, Win and Aralyn had retreated back to their corner of the common room. Listra, the woman Win had spoken with, had disappeared.

"They seem pretty happy for a group that is at war," said Aralyn.

"Sometimes people hide their fears and sadness behind a smile," said Win. "Or they deaden themselves with drink."

"What about you?" asked Aralyn.

"There are other ways to try to escape pain," said Win.

"Do they work?"

"Not really. They just change the way the sadness hits you."

For a while they sat in silence, the sounds of laughter echoing off the hard walls, doing nothing to lighten their moods.

Aralyn nodded toward Kesh and another man sitting at the far end of the other table, their heads huddled together in conversation. "Those two don't seem to be celebrating. I wonder what they are up to?"

"Are you always this suspicious?" asked Win. But his curiosity was aroused. His *gheris* was picking up a new intensity, a seriousness apart from the merriment.

Kesh pulled a piece of paper out of his pocket, and the two Carthlanians bent over it, Kesh tracing his finger over the paper. "I think they are looking at a map," said Win. "I can make out a few of their words, although I can't follow what they are talking about."

"You can hear them from here? Over that racket?"

"We Trebs have a keen sense of hearing."

"If they are planning something, then I don't want to be anywhere near when it happens," said Aralyn. "Maybe all this drinking is to get their courage up for some kind of attack. I'm going to go see if I can hear what they are saying."

She got up but Win put a hand on her arm. "Let me. They are probably even more suspicious than you are, and I have an excuse to be over there." He held up his drinking cup.

He crossed the room and filled his cup, pretending to listen to a humorous story one of the rebels was trying to tell over the constant interruption of her audience. The woman spoke in a particularly sharp Carthlanian patois but one that Win could mostly follow.

Half listening to the story, Win focused his attention on Kesh and the other man. After briefly looking up at Win, Kesh went back to his conversation, probably comfortable his voice would be lost in the din of the rest of the group.

Win managed to pick up on quite a bit of their exchange, and when the story ended he joined in the laughter before drifting back to his seat.

"Did you hear anything?" said Aralyn, looking over at Kesh.

"If you keep staring at them they'll wonder about you," said Win. "Let's just not say anything for a bit in case anyone is watching us."

Win sipped at his drink; it didn't taste any better than it had the first time he tried it. Not looking toward the rebels, he said, "You were right. They are planning something. Some kind of attack, I think. I heard them mention something about setting charges."

"Did they say where?"

"I don't know. I heard a lot of words I didn't understand. One of them was Azotus."

"That's a city down the river from here. It's not as big as Devatus. A lot of older people live there, pensioners who used to work for the government. There's a big government data complex there. I've heard the city is pretty peaceful."

Win glanced over at Kesh and the other man, still deep in conversation, Kesh forcefully pointing to a spot on the map.

"That might be about to change," said Win.

* * *

The rebel group broke up in twos and threes. Kesh finished his conversation and approached Win and Aralyn.

"Let me show you where you can get some sleep," said Kesh. "I'm afraid we don't have much in the way of comfort here." He led them out of the common room into a long corridor, lined with doorways. "These used to be storage rooms," he explained. "Most of them still have doors. The first one on the left has some blankets. Take what you need and pick whatever rooms you want. There is a wash basin in the third room on the right. The pipe over it brings in water from the river. It's clean enough."

Kesh gave Aralyn a hard look. "Don't try to leave during the night. We have guards outside, and they may mistake you in the dark."

"When can we go?" said Aralyn.

"We'll talk about that tomorrow. Soon though. Don't worry, you are safe here." Kesh left them, the door to the common room closing with a dull thud.

"Safe? Who's he kidding?" muttered Aralyn. "Nothing safe about being with a bunch of rebels. You saw what the government forces do to them."

"It's still better to stay here tonight," said Win.

"I know. But let's get out first thing tomorrow."

Win went into the storage room and picked up a few blankets. As he handed one to Aralyn he said, "Do you mind if I try to get something on your recorder?"

Aralyn shrugged and dug it out of her bag. "For some reason I'm not really tired. Let's give it a try."

The next room was dry and clean. "This looks good," said Win.

Aralyn kept walking. "It's too small. I don't like small spaces. They make me feel trapped."

The next few rooms were larger but filled with trash. Down the hall they found something better, a big room with a few crates to sit on. Aralyn placed the recorder down between them. "I've tried to keep track of the sequence of buttons I hit," she said. "In case that had something to do with making it work. But nothing seems to matter. It either works or it doesn't."

"I wonder," said Win. He was thinking about the last message, the one warning of evil, evil that would waylay one from the true path. The message coming right after he had seen—or thought he had seen—another path, an easy route through the confusing streets and the troubles they were facing.

Maybe the messages weren't so random after all.

The recorder came alive. *'Two neighbors argued over a plot of land, with each man claiming it was part of his property. On the land grew some trees of great value. They contained a rare extract which could be made into a medicine that could cure a deadly disease. The neighbors could not reach an agreement and their arguments over the land grew and grew. Out of anger one of the men set fire to the other's home. In retaliation, that man set fire to the other's farm. The fires spread and destroyed the special trees. In the end neither man had anything; no homes, no crop. Still they fought on, their battles becoming ever more violent, even though the cause of their discontent had long since vanished.*

'You will all face difficulties and battles in your lives. These are the hills and mountains of your worldly journey. You should not read too much into these events, no matter how painful, no matter how personal they seem. They are just there, the experiences of life. People will get sick, they will have accidents, they will die. These things do not happen because of what you have done. Thinking so is self

centered; you are not the cause of all that happens in the universe, nor do you have some power to stop these events. You cannot be angry at the universe for being itself. Instead you must think of what you have to offer the world, so that in your way you will help create a freedom from anger and hatred. And in turn you will be creating unity and peace.'

Aralyn stared at the recorder. "He's talking about the war. Here on Carthlana."

No he's not, thought Win. *He's talking about me.* About how I've reacted to the loss of Sooni. My guilt. My anger.

And then a sudden realization: *And he's talking about Aralyn. Her* loss. *Her* anger.

As if responding to his thoughts came the voice of Jesus once again:

'You may say, "I am right to be angry. The wrong that has happened to me, it is not fair. Something wicked must be causing this anger and pain, something evil must be at work." I say to you, evil does exist, but not all bad things are caused by evil. Difficulty and challenge are part of your worldly journey; the universe will be what it is. But anger is the doorway which allows evil an entrance. Anger, guilt, self pity; these are all ways in which evil can invade. They weaken you to the point where evil can creep into your inner self. If you are so self absorbed in your anger you will be oblivious to this invasion.

'This is the nexus of the spiritual and the corporal world. Only the power of your spirit and your faith will help you overcome the pain and challenges of the worldly plane to keep you free of the influence of evil.

'What is important is how you deal with the events of life. How can you ever progress on your spiritual journey if you cannot handle the simple challenges of the worldly plane? If you blame others for your plight, if you are consumed by anger? Your spiritual journey cannot begin until you have released your anger and are at peace with yourself and what goes on around you.

'I have told you of the path you must take, the path of acceptance,

the path of sacrifice. The force of evil will try to keep you from this path, but once you are upon it, evil will fall, overcome by your faith. If you allow your spirit to embrace my path you will be able to walk through evil itself as you would walk through a cloud of smoke.'

"What does it mean?" asked Aralyn. "What is he saying?"

"I think you know," said Win, as gently as he could. "He's telling you—he's showing you—how to understand the loss of your parents. How to go on. How to get past your anger."

"But how could he know?" said Aralyn, incredulous. "He doesn't know anything about me."

"Now maybe you will understand why I am looking for him," said Win.

"But how? It's just a recording."

"Jesus has this power to tell each of us what we need to hear. You and I can both hear the same words, yet they apply to each of us differently. I don't know how the words are reaching us. That's not important. The message is."

Win watched Aralyn's puzzled look shift to one of understanding, hearing but not yet believing that the message could apply not just to the war, but to her, the words clearly about the unfairness of her loss. About her trying to place blame. About her anger.

'You must not live in the past. Rethinking everything that has happened is a waste of energy and spirit; it makes you miss what is right in front of you, of even the very lessons of how to get past your pain.'

And with this Win fully realized why he was hearing this message at just this time. Jesus was once again showing Win a path, a way forward. But the path required work and dedication. He would have to learn difficult lessons to overcome his inner obstacles, *his* anger, *his* guilt. And whatever else was keeping him from finally achieving peace.

* * *

Aralyn lay awake long into the night. At least she thought it was night, there were no windows. She had stayed in the large room with the crates even though it didn't have a bed. The other rooms were too small, suffocating. She had told Win she didn't like small rooms. In fact she was terrified of them, terrified of any tight space she could not see out of. She had spent too much time hiding in small cubbyholes.

After her parents had died she had crawled through the remains of the smoldering house looking for them, still thinking that somehow they might have survived. Squeezing through the debris she found bits and pieces of their lives, her father's shoes, her mother's books. No one came to help. She looked for the entire day, and only the fire kept her from staying there overnight. The house next door had been long abandoned, and she slipped inside through a window, staring out all night at her own house, still stupidly hoping that her parents would emerge. The next morning she searched again, but the fire had taken hold, and there was not much left. She squeezed in to the only section that had survived the fire, a tiny gap between the collapsed walls of the foundation, and hid there until her hunger finally forced her out.

While searching for food she almost ran into another battle between the rebels and the government soldiers. She raced into the nearest building as mortars exploded behind her. Again she was forced into a cubbyhole, the only protection from the shelling. A part of the roof fell, trapping her, and she screamed, no longer caring if someone heard her. She tore at the debris blocking the opening, crying, cutting a gash in her leg as she finally crawled out and ran into the street. She still didn't know how she had escaped without being shot.

Those were her memories of small spaces, places of pain, places of terror, traps. Since then she had avoided any small space, any place where she could not see an exit. Her worst nightmare was that she would die like that, trapped in a tight space with no way out, or even worse, seeing the hint of an exit she could not reach.

She also didn't trust the rebels. She sat against the wall by the door, holding the only thing she could find that would serve as a weapon, a sharp edged piece of crate. It would not do much good if they wanted to harm her, but she would not go down without a fight. She knew the rebels could still kill her and Win, especially if they changed their minds about needing the hideout. The rebels would not trust her and Win to keep it a secret. Especially her.

Win. She barely knew him, but she already trusted him more than anyone she had met since she had been alone. She wasn't particularly fond of offworlders, but she liked this one. Maybe it was because he spoke to her like an adult. He also seemed to have a genuine interest in helping people, something her parents had always preached, and taught her to do when she was younger. Their death and the war had hardened her; she had tried at first, but she had seen too many people die trying to help others. She still remembered the first time she had walked by someone who needed help. Actually she remembered every time, and felt guilty about them all. When Win had put himself in danger to help Varshan it hit her—that was exactly what her mother or father would have done.

And Win knew about Jesus. Her wild idea about finding Jesus, about him somehow having the answer to how to end the war, maybe that wasn't so crazy after all. She had searched the city for clues of Jesus, allowing herself to think she was working hard to learn about him. Suddenly here was an offworlder, of all people, who had come all the way across the galaxy to find him, making her efforts seem half hearted and puny in comparison.

She didn't want to allow herself too much hope; she had been disappointed too many times. But Win obviously believed that Jesus could help. She wasn't sure exactly what he could help with, but it wouldn't hurt to find out.

And then there were the recordings. Win had recognized the voice of Jesus. With Win's help, the recordings were starting to make sense. The words, which before seemed rather general, now took on a new meaning; the more she thought about it the more she understood Win's claim that Jesus' words were meant for them. For *her*. She still didn't know how that was possible.

Certainly she was angry, just as Jesus said. He also said that she should not be angry at the things that just happened in life, like people dying. Like her parents dying. That she should accept it.

How could she just decide to make her anger disappear? She didn't *try* to be angry. It just happened.

Jesus also said that evil existed, but not every bad thing that happened was caused by evil. But that meant *some* bad things could be caused by evil. How was she to tell?

The image of the man walking away from her house before the explosion, the chill she had felt as he passed her, almost forgotten as she was overwhelmed by what had happened next. Seeing someone who reminded him of that, this Drason. And the soldiers and rebels, killing for no reason.

Evil. It certainly existed here on Carthlana. Maybe it wasn't so hard to tell after all.

She clutched her sharpened stake and tried to stay awake, vowing not to take her eyes off the doorway for the rest of the night.

* * *

Win twisted to find a more comfortable position. But it wasn't the hard floor keeping him awake. His mind was spinning with the messages and the visions of Sooni and Jesus. The Sooni images especially confused him. The first one he had seen, the ghost-Sooni that had appeared in the ritualistic gathering in the underground, led by the disturbing being, the entire experience unnerving. That Sooni had led him directly into danger. Had she been conjured up by the bizarre ritual, to kill him? It made no sense.

The voice of Jesus had warned him of being misled by evil. He had never thought of evil as a living force; to him, it had always been a concept. It was just a way to explain the absence of good, of righteousness, or to define its opposite. But could evil be something actively trying to mislead him, to keep him from achieving peace and enlightenment?

That might explain much of what he had experienced. The twisted force he had felt in the underground. The ghost-Sooni, leading him close to death. The false path through the fog. All could be the work of evil.

Jesus said anger was a weakness that allowed evil to enter one's life, and Win had certainly been full of anger. Had evil taken hold within him? Had his actions and desires allowed evil to enter his inner spirit?

Yet the next image of Sooni he had seen, the woman in green, had been much more corporal. That one too had led him seemingly into danger, to the burning building. Yet he had survived without a scratch, safe in the embrace of a powerful light and the voice of Jesus: *'Pain leads to guilt, because you confuse that which you can change from what you cannot.'*

It was not danger that this Sooni had led him toward. She had led him to a place he needed to be, to an experience he had to undergo. And he saved Varshan and his son in the process.

He was not able to help Varshan save his daughter; that was something he could not change. Just as he could not change the fact that Sooni was dead. Varshan felt guilty that he had failed his daughter, just as Win felt guilty about Sooni. It made no sense, feeling guilty about her accident, what could he have done? But the guilt was still there.

'Guilt is an excuse for dwelling on something you cannot change instead of freeing yourself to face the challenges ahead of you and within you. I ask of you: if you have not even raised your sword, then what is there to be guilty of?'

Jesus was so right. Win had been using guilt as an excuse to keep himself safe and secluded in his self made prison of despair. There were many things that Win could have done better in life, things that perhaps justified an occasional feeling of guilt. But Sooni's accident was not one of them.

As Jesus had said, it was a waste of energy and spirit. Not the remembering of her, but wallowing in the pain. Seeing what Varshan went through was the message right in front of him, a message he could have easily missed because he was too focused on his anger and guilt.

The messages from the recorder—he could not explain how it was all happening, how the messages seemed destined for him. But certainly the messages were not random. On K'Turia, Jesus had spoken of faith, that the very belief in something could have a great power. Perhaps he just needed to accept it on faith that the messages were meant to be taken personally.

And perhaps for Aralyn as well. Was Aralyn here to help him, to show him something?

Certainly she had saved him. And her losses, so similar and yet so different from his, had helped him understand the lesson about anger. He had thought that anger helped him, that it gave him strength to face his loss, just as Aralyn's anger gave her strength to survive.

Yet the message they had just heard told him something very different. Anger was selfish; there was more loss in the universe than he could possibly fathom. It didn't make his loss, or Aralyn's, any less significant. It meant that those losses were part of the universe, not separate from it.

The rebel woman Listra was full of anger. Yet it was odd how her anger was affecting her so differently from Aralyn and Win. Aralyn trying to keep it submerged, only to have it burst forth at times of need. Win, using it to punish himself. Listra wanted to use it to hurt others.

He thought back to the Sooni he had followed to the burning building. What had she said to Aralyn about Jesus? That he was at the Core. That he was *inside*. Aralyn had been confused, since the Core wasn't a building, it had no inside.

Aralyn had misunderstood. Sooni *was* telling them where to find Jesus. He wasn't at the Core, the meeting place on Carthlana. He was at Win's core, inside him. Inside of all of them. Inside everyone.

A great warmth came over him, as if he had just emerged from a dark cave, one in which he had not realized he had been cold, and into a beautiful sunshine, the heat of the sun tenderly reaching for him and gathering him in.

A calmness descended upon him, a clarity and stillness in his thoughts he had not felt in years. Not a void, but rather a settling of the constant flow of disparate thoughts that had bombarded him day and night.

From this inner tranquility he saw Sooni, not the ghost-image or the woman in the cape, but the true Sooni of his past.

She was walking away from him, toward the light, following someone. The figure turned. It was Jesus, his arms out, inviting both Win and Sooni into his embrace.

Jesus spoke to him.

'Because you have followed me with the desire to know the Truth, you have found me again. Now do you understand what has been shown you? No one can face the pain of the world alone. And no one can face evil alone.

Anger brings energy to the forces of evil, and gives it the power to do heinous things. The way to overcome evil is to take away its sustenance.

Your journey is not over. You will continue to meet trials and challenges that will demand everything of you. If you choose to turn to me, I will help you.

And just as you are being shown the way, so too must you show others. Do not wait; just because you do not know all the answers does not mean you cannot help others.

In a flash of insight, Win realized Jesus was telling him someone needed help. Win's help.

CHAPTER 21

WIN AWOKE INTO DARKNESS. For a moment he was disoriented, then the empty stillness was gently broken by a deep breath. Aralyn, sleeping across the room. It all came back, the storage room, the rebel hangout.

He groped his way to the door, trying not to wake Aralyn where she lay half propped up by the wall. In the corridor, sunlight fought to make its way through some grungy windows high overhead. All the rooms he passed appeared empty, their doors hanging open. When he reached the common room they had eaten in the night before, no one was there.

He spun around at a sound in the corridor.

"Sorry," said Aralyn. "I woke up and you were gone. I got worried."

"I came to see what was going on out here. It seems everyone is gone."

"I didn't hear anything. I didn't realize I would sleep so soundly here. I must have been more tired than I thought." Aralyn walked over to one of the tables. "At least they left us some food."

"I wonder where they went?"

"I don't care," said Aralyn. "Let's just get out of here."

Win was thinking about the conversation he had overheard the night before. "Maybe they went to Azotus to do whatever they were planning. Let's see if there is anyone left who can tell us."

Aralyn shrugged and took a bite of fruit. "Suit yourself. I'm just going to grab whatever is left of the food to take with us."

Win looked into the front rooms. They too were empty, as was the room where Varshan had been recuperating. Retracing his steps to the back corridor, he passed where they had slept and worked his way deeper into the building. Each room he passed was empty; most looked like they had been that way for a long time. The few that appeared to have been used for sleeping contained no personal belongings, no clothing. Nothing to indicate that anyone was coming back. A few of the cubicles had makeshift beds made with old mattresses.

At the very end of the corridor one of the doors was closed. Win hesitated, knocked, then feeling foolish, pushed open the door. This room was much neater. The floor had been swept, boxes stacked and organized. A bed had been crafted out of some sturdy crates, made up with a tucked in blanket. On the bed, a single sheet of paper, held in place by a thin band, a ring.

Aralyn's voice echoed down the corridor. "There's nobody here. Let's go."

Something tugged at Win. Something about the room.

"Aralyn, come here, please? Just for a moment. I want you to see this."

As she came down the corridor Aralyn said, "Okay. But let's be quick. Who knows what these rebels are up to. Even Varshan is gone. Maybe they found out the government knows about this place." She peered over Win's shoulder. "What is it?"

"This room is so much neater than the others. And that —." He pointed to the bed.

"Let's see what it says. Maybe a note for us?"

"I doubt it," said Win. "Probably something personal."

"Then why leave it on the bed? Looks like whoever left it meant it to be found."

Aralyn sat on the bed and picked up the ring. "Looks like a wedding band." Fingering it, she read the note to Win.

" 'My dearest Von. I have waited long enough. The time has

come to make them understand that we won't take this any more. Demonstrations and attacks on government property haven't worked. Your death proves that. While we try to bring down buildings and equipment, they are killing people. We must confront those who abuse us and attack them where it will hurt them equally. There must be a balance of death if we are to get attention, get people to rise up. And for justice.

" 'Perhaps with you by my side I could have gone on, accepting the repercussions, as long as it didn't really hurt us too badly. But look what they have done to me—to us. Maybe someone will read this and understand what pain the war is really causing, and why it must be stopped in any way possible.

" 'I'll be with you soon. I have taken off my ring, for I would not have needed to do what I must if you were alive, and I would not want to do it if you were still with me. It is my decision alone.' " Aralyn looked up. "It's signed Listra."

"She's the woman I was talking to last night, the one who lost her husband."

"She sounds angry," mused Aralyn. "You were right, the rebels are going to attack somewhere. Maybe today. She must have gone off with them."

Win looked around the tidy room. Kesh had told him that this building wasn't going to be used as a hideout any longer. Why clean up a place that wasn't going to be used?

Setting things in order. "No," said Win. "She's going somewhere to die."

* * *

Aralyn stuck her head under the pipe, running her fingers through her hair, then using the blanket to clean her face and dry off. "I need a good bath. It's hard to keep from smelling like smoke in this city."

"We have to go to Azotus," said Win.

Aralyn turned to him, the water still dripping from her hair.

"You're crazy. They are probably going to blow up some building. I told you there is a data center there, I bet that is what they are after. We can't get involved. You would put us in danger to save some building?"

"It's not the building I'm worried about. It's Listra. The note she left —. She's not going to just blow up a building. She is going to hurt people."

Aralyn turned away. "People get hurt all the time. We can't stop it."

"If no one does anything, it will never end." Win reached over to the pipe and covered it with his hand, stopping the dripping water. "No matter how bad things have been, Listra wants to escalate it into something worse. If we act now we *can* stop it." He turned the tap on full and the water forced his hand from the pipe. "A steady drip of actions like hers will become a torrent. And then it will be too late."

Aralyn reached past him and turned off the tap. "You are talking about a war. You can't turn it off just like this."

"But we *can* do something," said Win. "Listra is consumed by anger. She is blinded. She is going to do something she would never have done—she admits that herself. If we don't stop her she will destroy not only herself but others as well."

Win remembered what Jesus had said in his vision, something he didn't fully understand at the time, but now seemed clearer. *"Anger brings energy to the forces of evil, and gives it the power to do heinous things. The way to overcome evil is to take away its sustenance."* Evil, something Win had always thought of as a concept, was becoming more real to him. And Jesus was saying that anger would make it stronger. How much stronger would evil become if fed by Listra's anger, an anger so great it would force her to kill innocent people?

Aralyn shook her head. "The message from Jesus said we have to accept things. Maybe we just have to accept that this is going to happen."

"That's not what Jesus meant. I think he is talking about

accepting yourself, of not blaming yourself for things outside your control, of understanding what it is you can and cannot do." He spoke as gently as he knew how. "No one expects you to accept the war, or to forget your parents. But would you have everyone who lost someone they loved then go out and kill others?"

"*I'm* not going to go kill anyone," said Aralyn. "We can't change what others will do."

"And how will you feel if we didn't at least try? I know you try to help people, I've seen you do it. Listra wants to do something very public, something everyone will hear about. How will you feel if she kills a lot of people, and we had a chance to prevent it?"

Aralyn twisted her lip. "Now you are making me feel guilty for something I might *not* do. Pretty funny for someone who seems to believe that we shouldn't feel guilty about things."

"I have to try to stop her," said Win.

"You said you came to find Jesus. Ever since you got here you seem to be doing anything but that."

"I know. But Jesus has a way of—guiding. Of telling each of us what we need to do. I think he wants me to help Listra." Win smiled. "Besides, how do we know Jesus isn't in Azotus?"

* * *

Aralyn waited until Win was busy filling their water bottles, then she slipped back into Listra's room. Other than the bed, nothing in it hinted that someone had lived there, that someone had thought of it as a home. Except for the note and ring, it was empty of any personal things. No clothing, no photos. Nothing to suggest that Listra was coming back.

Was this how one planned to die? To leave behind an empty room?

Just the note. A note addressed to her dead husband, but obviously meant for others. Aralyn read it again, feeling the anger and the pain. She didn't need the note to help her to see the pain of the war, she already knew that. Yet she felt another pain, the same pain as Listra, for the unfairness of it all. They were the same, her and Listra. They had both suffered a terrible loss from the war.

Listra had decided to do something about it. Win might be right, Listra was probably going to do something bad. Was that worse than doing nothing at all, than just hiding, hoping it would all go away, that someone else would make it stop?

She carefully placed the letter and ring back on the bed. They were the only things left of Listra, and gave the room some feeling of life.

Aralyn wasn't sure what she should do, what she could do. But Win was right. She'd feel terrible if she didn't try. She had not developed enough toughness to overcome her parents' lessons. Maybe she never could.

She would go along with Win, at least for now.

* * *

At the river, they found a small boat easily enough. Aralyn explained that the fighting had been bad around the river, so most of the small fishing boats had been abandoned. They scavenged the other boats for oars and even managed to find some padding for the seats.

The pier was a shambles, the wood rotting and unmaintained. The street which paralleled the river was deserted, the buildings empty husks. An odor of rotten fish hung in the air.

"No reason for anyone to be here anymore," said Aralyn. "Although we might see some people on the river. Try not to look too dangerous if we do run into anyone."

"Everyone here seems pretty accepting of offworlders," said Win.

"It's the government and the rebels who have caused all the problems, not the offworlders." She handed Win an oar. "I hope you know something about boats. Azotus is downstream, but we still need to steer."

Aralyn rowed them out into the deeper part of the river, where they picked up the current and began to move steadily downstream. "I guess the rebels are going to Azotus the same way we are," she said. "They probably took a bunch of small boats and left at different times so they wouldn't attract attention. They might not be very far ahead."

"Unless they left in the middle of the night."

"That would be more suspicious if anyone saw them," said Aralyn. "And there are government patrols at night." She stopped rowing and let the current carry them. "You don't have much experience in sneaking around, do you?"

Win thought about his time on K'Turia and his secret mission there. He had been only partially successful in blending in. Jesus had seen through his disguise immediately. Or had seen through Win.

"Not much, I'm afraid. I'm actually a scientist."

"What do you study?"

"Nothing that seems important now. Science is—a way to keep me busy."

"So you won't think about your wife?" said Aralyn. When Win looked away she added quickly, "I'm sorry."

"No, don't be. Your directness is refreshing. It reminds me of a good friend. And you are right. That was why I turned to science."

"When did—when was her accident? If you don't want to talk about it, I understand."

"It was many years ago. I know it sounds trite, but it still feels like yesterday. I remember more about every minute of that day than I do about things that happened a few days past."

Aralyn sat still, watching the water. "I never expected that offworlders would feel the same way we did about things."

"I've been to a lot of different worlds," said Win. "Two things always amaze me. The first is how different everything can be.

How people look, what they eat, what they find beautiful or ugly, how they deal with conflict. But the other thing I am amazed at is how similar beings can be. How they all seem to understand and experience love. How they deal with loss. What brings them pain. Everything that is superficial is what can be different, but the inner things, the important things, are all the same."

"Why do you think that is?"

"It's not something I think science can explain. There is a woman I know, a very smart scientist. She set out to analytically prove that there are linkages between different worlds, linkages that are based on a belief in a higher power. She found it hard to find anyone to take her seriously. Most of the people in her scientific community don't accept the idea of some connection between science and religion."

"So she gave up?"

"At first she did. Her work jeopardized her career. But then something happened which gave her what she thought was the proof of her theory. That there is such a universal linkage, there is some power that connects us all, no matter where we are." Win dipped his hand in the water, thinking about his vision of Jesus in the lake, the water running through his fingers.

Aralyn leaned forward, interested. "Really? What was it that happened?"

Win looked up at her, feeling the water, feeling the Truth. "She found Jesus."

* * *

Aralyn was quiet for a long time. She began to pull on the oars, a steady and peaceful cadence that moved them gently along. The sound of the oars dipping into the water sounded like a heartbeat followed by a deep breath.

Past the city outskirts the river widened, the banks muddy, leading up to dense brush. They slid by abandoned boats and flotsam, pieces of buildings and other trash, all covered in silt.

They had yet to see anyone else on the river.

"What do you think about Jesus?" asked Aralyn. "Do you think he is some kind of higher power?"

Win listened to the sound of the oars, the whisper of the water flowing by. "What I believe is complicated. And my beliefs have changed—Jesus has changed them. So I'm not sure yet what I believe exactly. We Trebs have a concept that is very important to us, something we call *ana*. It is our life goal. You might think of it as reaching enlightenment, if that term means anything to you."

"Is that your name for a higher power?"

"I think it depends on what you mean by a higher power. We feel that our enlightenment comes from within. From knowing yourself. Not just understanding who you are, but fully knowing everything within your being, and then accepting it, while still trying to know more, to be more."

"That does sound complicated. What else is there to know if you know everything?"

Win smiled. "I know it does seem to be a contradiction, but think of it this way. Knowing yourself does not mean the journey is over. Achieving *ana* doesn't mean you've arrived at a place, it means you are well prepared for a never ending journey."

"To the higher power?"

"On a lot of the worlds I have been to, beings tend to think of a higher power—whatever they call their gods or God—as something only external. Something or someone outside of them, someone *out there*. We don't use the word God on Treb, but if we did we would think of our higher power as something shared across and *within* each of us. One power, but unique in how it affects each of us."

"How does Jesus fit into that?" asked Aralyn.

"Remember how the message we heard the other night seemed to be meant for you? That is what Jesus is able to do. Every time he speaks, I hear him speaking to me, as if he knows me. Yet other people hear the same words and think the words are for them. How is that possible?"

"Maybe you just listen for what you want to hear."

"Maybe. But it doesn't feel that way. Think about yourself. You seem—naturally skeptical. Yet something about the messages made you interested in finding Jesus, even at risk to yourself. This is the effect he has on people. You want to learn more about what he says, because he is helping you learn more about yourself."

"Like your *ana*."

"Yes, although I had not exactly thought of it that way before." Win had thought that there was a great difference between the Treb *ana* and what Jesus was teaching, that he had to find a way to choose one or the other. Aralyn had pointed out something he had not considered, that they might not be so different after all. Or that they might be one in the same.

Maybe this is what had hindered him from fully understanding and accepting Jesus while on K'Turia. He was starting from a mindset that accepting Jesus, as Prentiss had done, would mean the rejection of *ana*. But what if Jesus was showing him the path to—or even beyond—what Trebs thought of as enlightenment?

What if there was a universal God, and Jesus had just been using a different way of describing it? Or if the true goal of *ana* was the discovery—and acceptance—of the true God?

That would be a momentous truth, not only for him, but for all Trebs. For everyone.

"Tell me more about Jesus," said Aralyn.

Win hesitated, immersed in his new understanding. How could he explain it? "I don't think anything in my own words will really help you understand him. So let me try to repeat a story I heard him tell." He thought for a moment, remembering the words easily, as always seemed to be the case with what Jesus had said. " *'You are walking on a road through the hills, and you reach a crossroads. You do not know which way to go. You see me there at the crossroads, and you ask of me: Which of these roads will lead me to Paradise? And I say to you, as long as you stay on the road that I will show you, they all do! Thus each of you will walk the path a little differently, for the path is one of sacrifice, and helping others. Each of you will make different sacrifices, each to your own gifts. This is why I say that you can be shown the paths, even though you are not blindly led.'* "

Aralyn's brow furrowed. "I hope we aren't going to have to make a big sacrifice in trying to stop Listra."

"I don't know," admitted Win. What would they have to give up in order to help Listra?

Aralyn stopped rowing. "We're going to find out pretty soon. That's Azotus up ahead. Help steer us over to that side of the river."

Win held an oar in the water to pivot the boat. The river turned a small bend and the outskirts of the town came into view. It looked a lot better than Devatus. The banks were clean, the buildings near the river unmarked, their windows unbroken. A pier ran along the river, the moorings filled with small boats. Workers were busy up and down the pier, and the unmistakable smell of fish, this time fresh, drifted their way. A series of canals ran in from the river toward the city.

"Doesn't appear to be much damage," said Win.

"I haven't been here in a long time," said Aralyn. "But I know the government forces have much more control in Azotus. I bet they have a lot of troops to guard the data center. That's probably where the rebels mean to attack."

Win immediately thought about Listra's note. "The troops. That's who Listra will be after."

"Are you taking sides now? Do you want to help the government forces?"

It wasn't so long ago that Win wanted to avoid a war as well, the war he had been forced to take part in by his own government. Aralyn reminded Win so much of himself, being thrust into a tremendous conflict, when she was just trying to get along, trying to survive, trying to lead her own life. Hoping that the tumult and pain and destruction going on around her would go away if only she could stay out of it.

"It's not about taking sides," he said. "It is about helping people. Not only Listra, but everyone else it may affect. Who knows what may come about if she is successful? How much pain will be caused? How many other people will do terrible things? It's a spiral. Once it starts, it gathers strength. It gets worse and worse."

"Everyone makes their own choices," said Aralyn, a bit of cynicism creeping back into her voice. "We can't do anything if they choose to do something bad."

Win thought about evil again, about what Jesus had said about evil gaining strength from anger. Anger could certainly lead to hate. Could evil become so strong that it would feed on itself, and then achieve power over others to do more evil?

"Remember what Jesus said about the two neighbors fighting. They could not keep their fighting to themselves. Sooner or later others get involved. After a while it doesn't even matter what started the fight. People's choices are affected by what is going on around them, by what they see and hear. Just as Jesus is affecting my choices—our choices. Not making the choices for us, but helping us see the choices and figuring out what to do." Win reminded himself of how Aralyn had been forced to grow up so fast, of how young she really was. "This is your planet, your future. If people like you don't act, who will? It's not about the government versus the rebels, it's another choice you have to make."

Aralyn shook her head. "I can't do anything by myself."

"No one expects you to," said Win. "And no one can do it all. But you can start, you can take a first step. You can do your part, whatever it is. And I'll help you if I can."

"Why would you do that? What's this place to you?"

Win looked around. The planet, unfamiliar, yet like any other place. Filled with people just like him, with their own suffering, their own desire for a peaceful life.

"Let's just say that doing nothing is worse than doing something, even if you fail. Doing nothing is not really a decision, it is an escape."

"So where do we begin? What good can we do?" asked Aralyn.

"For a start, let's see if we can stop something bad from happening."

* * *

No one bothered them as they docked the boat and made their way along the pier. They followed a wide road which ran along one of the canals, the water gently flowing toward the city. The canals fed a row of cisterns and tanks, connected by a series of thick pipes which ran along the roadway. Win didn't see any other offworlders, but no one paid him much mind. Once past the river area the streets became busier, a steady bustle of activity and commerce.

"Do you remember where the data center is?" asked Win.

"I think so." Aralyn led the way, keeping the river at their backs. After a few blocks she turned right onto a wider street. "What are we going to do when we get there?"

"Look for the Listra and the rebels. If we can get to Listra maybe we can talk her out of whatever she is planning."

"I wouldn't count on that," said Aralyn. "She sounded pretty committed. And don't forget about Kesh. You don't know what he might do to protect his cause. If he thinks we are going to ruin his plan he's going to be really mad. These rebels have killed a lot of people."

"Let's worry about that when we find them," said Win.

"*If* we find them. We might not have seen everyone in their group. We might not even know what they look like."

"I'll remember enough of them. Let's focus on Listra. Somehow I think she is planning something different from the rest of them. Something worse."

Aralyn grimaced. "What could be worse than blowing up a building full of people? More than just government people will be in that building or around it."

"You are right," Win admitted. "'Worse' isn't the right concept. They are both bad." *Evil,* he thought. *They are both evil.*

"Even if we do manage to stop her," Aralyn said, "the rest of the rebels will cause way more damage than she will on her own."

"We have to start somewhere," said Win. "We'll worry about the rebels later."

Aralyn looked up at the darkening sky. "It's going to rain soon. People will head inside."

They increased their pace. Around them, everyone seemed to sense the coming change in the weather, and some started to drift indoors. All totally oblivious to anything that might happen.

"Maybe we should warn these people," said Win.

"And say what? That we think there are some rebels here, and they might be trying to blow something up? Even if they believed us, then what? They'd likely take us to the government forces for questioning."

"I guess you're right. Let's hurry."

Win saw some offworlders who seemed to know their way around. After a few blocks the streets were noticeably less crowded, more people taking shelter from the oncoming storm.

"There, that's the data complex," said Aralyn, pointing to a low slung, windowless building set back from the street. A wide set of stone steps led up to the entrance where four guards watched the street. From where Win and Aralyn stood they could not see the back of the building, but at the far corner two more guards were visible.

Win slowed down and tried to see as much of the building with his peripheral vision as they walked past. At the corner, they turned and checked out the other side. It was much like the front, except the back entrance was much smaller, although still commanded by four guards. There were no stairs here; the back of the building faced a wide plaza that led to another building. This one was windowed, uniformed soldiers coming and going in and out.

They turned away from the buildings and headed off half a block before stopping. A few drops of rain began to fall.

"Now what?" asked Aralyn. "That complex looks like it will be hard to attack. Maybe they are not planning a bomb. I don't see how they would get it in there."

There were few people left on the streets, none of whom looked like any of the rebels. The complex did seem pretty secure. Stymied, Win said, "I don't know."

"What about mortars?" asked Aralyn.

"It would have been hard to bring mortars down by boat and then walk up here without anyone noticing. Unless they are hidden somewhere nearby." Win thought for a while. "The building at the back, I think that is a barracks. It will be filled with troops. That will be Listra's target."

"Why?"

"She wants revenge. She'll want to get to soldiers, not the data center."

"But the troops there will have weapons. It would be a suicide mission."

"That's probably her plan," said Win, thinking about the note Listra had left. "Come on."

They retraced their steps back toward the troop building. The rain was heavier now, people pushing past them, intent on getting out of the rain. The wind began to pick up.

"If we stay outside we're going to look pretty suspicious," said Aralyn.

"I know. But Listra should be easier to find. Let's go past and then look for a place to watch from the other corner."

As they crossed the street Win glanced over at the entrance to the barracks. Soldiers were running in out of the rain, some coming from the data complex, others from the streets. The sky had darkened in just few moments, foreboding, making the city suddenly seem dangerous.

On the far corner a cloaked figure ran toward the barracks, hunched over, clutching a large parcel. The person looked no different from any of the others trying to stay dry. But near the barracks, the figure stood up straight and tall, ignoring the rain.

The head turned slowly, first to the right, and then toward Win and Aralyn. A woman. Her eyes met Win's, her body stiffening.

"It's Listra," said Win.

"What's she doing?"

"Nothing good. I'm going to stop her."

Aralyn grabbed Win's arm. "There are guards all over the place," she hissed. "What can you do?"

Listra began to walk toward the entrance, no longer hunched over, intent.

"Whatever it takes," said Win, pulling away, his eyes locked on Listra. In that moment he fully understood the true meaning of sacrifice, and what it might take to stop one. And the difference between a good sacrifice and a bad one.

He ran across the street, yelling over the sound of the rain. "Listra! Don't!" He called over his shoulder to Aralyn. "Wait there!"

The woman stopped, staring at him. But it no longer looked like Listra. It was Drason, the man who had led Win to the ritual. Drason's face was distorted in anger, an anger so great it bordered on madness.

Win stopped in his tracks, stupefied by the sudden change. Where had Drason come from? There was no one else there, no time for someone to appear.

Win wiped the rain from his eyes, and the face changed again. This time it was the man who had been leading the ritual, the one with the dagger, the one who had conjured up the ghostly image of Sooni. Where Listra's hair had been a black inkiness now seemed to hold the rain at bay, allowing Win to clearly see the face. The eyes, deep pools tinged with red, bore into Win, freezing him. The creature smiled, as if amused, and then made a gesture toward Win, beckoning him. Win felt himself pulled, and he staggered forward, the being morphing into Listra once again.

Win reached the end of the plaza, yelling, but Listra ignored him and walked slowly toward the entrance.

Win was almost there . . .

His eyes were torn away from Listra by a flash of light from above, so powerful that he fell to his knees. He looked up into a dazzling white, no rain reaching his face. For a split second everything stopped for Win. There was no rain, no street, no buildings. Nothing but the light.

As quickly as it came it was gone. When Win looked back at the barracks a man had appeared at the far side of the plaza. The man was limping terribly, trying to run toward Listra. He stumbled, one leg dragging stiffly behind him. The man stopped and looked directly at Win, emphatically holding out his hand, warning Win away.

Varshan. Even in the rain Win knew who it was.

The door to the barracks opened and two soldiers came out, stopping in surprise when they saw Listra. One held up his arm for her to stop. Listra froze, her eyes on the soldiers who were blocking the doorway, apparently unaware of Varshan. She reached into her parcel.

With an obvious effort Varshan threw himself at Listra, wrapping his arms around her body. Her head swung around toward him, her eyes wide, glazed.

At that moment Win was blown backward, the force of the blast knocking him on his back. A huge metal beam passed right over his face, so close he could feel the mass of it, and it crashed into the building behind him, impaling itself in the wall.

Dazed, his ears ringing from the explosion, Win rolled over toward the barracks. Listra, Varshan, and the soldiers were gone, and so was most of front of the building.

The rain fell hard, hissing as it hit the fire, creating a dark smoke that wound its way outward, its tendrils creeping into the heart of the city.

CHAPTER 22

WIN STOOD, SHAKING, his hearing still deadened by the blast. The air was dense with grit from the building, the rain forming into soot which stung his eyes.

Still groggy, Win watched armed troops pour from the barracks, more of it intact than he would have expected. The soldiers who had come out of the building had stopped Listra before she had a chance to get inside, and Varshan, wrapping his arms around her, had probably muffled the blast. It had saved most of the building, and probably Win as well.

Across the plaza two soldiers clanged a huge gate closed on the back door to the data complex. Behind Win, a siren blared, and an armored vehicle pulled up in the street he had just crossed. Four more soldiers piled out, and another vehicle, this one with a mounted gun, pulled up behind the first.

The soot was so thick Win could barely see across the street. Aralyn was gone.

Win had to muffle his scream for her as the soldiers from the vehicles came up fast, directly toward him and the barracks. Win realized he was the only one around not in a uniform and was sure they would stop him. After one last frantic look for Aralyn he unsteadily turned and walked as calmly as he could away from the complex, trying not to draw attention. At the end of the plaza he crossed the street. He wanted to get back to Aralyn, but to do that he'd have to walk right by the soldiers.

Win forced himself to instead go straight, down another block. Even here sticky soot floated in the air, carrying the unmistakable odor of an explosive. His feet crunched on broken glass, slippery from the rain. Slowly he picked his way down the empty street. At the corner he turned left, hoping the blocks were laid out in a grid so that he could find his way back to where he had left Aralyn.

A few people were peering out of doorways, eyes nervously darting about, disappearing quickly when they saw Win. In the distance, more sirens, undulating in and out over the pouring rain. Win's nose was filled with dirt.

The next street was wider and allowed him to turn left again. Relieved, he started to run, tentatively at first, not trusting his balance. No sooner had he taken a few steps he heard another explosion, muffled. Then a second, followed by the rat-tat-tat of gunshots somewhere ahead of him. He slowed, keeping close to the buildings. More sirens, then the roar of an engine, and another explosion, definitely ahead of him, this one closer. At the end of the block a group of fighters passed the corner, not toward him, but backing down the cross street, firing toward the data complex. One of the fighters dropped to a knee and fired a mortar, the flash hazy in the rain.

The fighters cleared the street, and for a moment Win could see no one, but then a truck rumbled past, following the fighters, and Win suspected the ones on foot were the rebels, maybe even Kesh's group. They had probably come to attack the data complex. Had they known about Listra's plan to kill the troops? Win didn't think so. And Varshan, what was he doing there in his condition?

Just as Aralyn had, Varshan had appeared just in time to save Win's life. Listra had said that Varshan had always been trying to find another way, a less violent way, to change things. And he had, but to do so he had made the ultimate sacrifice.

Another troop carrier came into view, and this one turned up the street Win was on. He involuntarily turned away, knowing he'd never be able to explain his reasons for being there, even if they bothered to ask before shooting him.

The first doors he tried were locked, but the third opened. Win slammed the door behind him and slumped to the floor out of sight as the troop carrier lumbered past.

* * *

Win found himself in some kind of small store. A counter ran off to the left, meeting up with shelves lining the walls. In the middle of the room, a few tidy racks and tables. He could not read the writing on the signs, but some of the packages were clearly recognizable: bandages, tape, ointments. A pharmacy. At the rear, a service counter formed a separation to another room.

He locked the door. "Hello? Anyone here?" The entire front room was empty, so he crossed to the back counter. Behind him, the sound of fighting continued, and another truck rolled by.

Win peered over the counter and was surprised to see an old woman crouched on the floor, her hands held out in front of her, as if to ward him off.

"I'm not going to hurt you," he said gently. When the woman made no attempt to get up, Win took half a step back, holding up his arms. "I'm sorry. I didn't mean to startle you. There was some kind of attack and there is fighting in the streets. It's a bit— dangerous out there. I just wanted to get somewhere safe and out of the way."

Shakily she stood up, her eyes never leaving Win. Her white hair was neatly coifed, her skin surprisingly smooth, her Carthlanian veins milky. A red scarf peeked out over her collar. She leaned on the counter for support and slowly set herself on a stool.

"When I heard you come in I thought you were one of the shooters," she said. "We don't see many offworlders in Azotus. No offense."

"None taken," said Win.

"What are you doing here?" The woman's curiosity appeared to overcome her fear.

Win didn't think it would help to mention that he had been trying to stop a rebel attack. "I came to your planet to find another offworlder. I just got caught up in the fighting."

The woman looked over Win's shoulder. "What is going on out there? Is it the rebels? We don't get many rebels either. This is a government controlled area. There are too many soldiers around."

"I think that is why the rebels are here. I was told there is a data complex."

The woman sighed. "I wish they would all just go away. The rebels, the soldiers. I don't know what is worse, having the data or not having it." She looked Win up and down, her eyes sharp and appraising. "You're a mess."

"There is soot everywhere. With the rain . . ."

"Come back here," said the woman, lifting a hinged door on the counter. "There is a washroom in the back. I don't have any clothes that will fit you, but there are towels and plenty of soap."

"That's very kind of you, but I can't stay. I was with someone, a young Carthlanian woman. We got separated. I need to go find her."

The woman shook her head. "You're looking for a lot of people, aren't you? Well, you can't go out there now. The soldiers keep the peace here by shooting first. They don't even ask questions later. If they see you wandering around after a rebel attack, you won't be safe. Whoever you are looking for is probably in hiding too."

Win turned his head back toward the door. "I should go look for her."

"You won't find her if you're dead."

Win thought about the soldiers he had seen shooting indiscriminately back in Devatus City. "I'll stay for a bit. Just until the fighting dies down."

In the washroom, Win cleaned himself up as well as he could.

When he came back the woman had set some dried fruit, salted meat, and a bottle of water on the counter.

"I don't know what you eat," she said. "But you are welcome to this."

"Thank you," said Win, and as he reached for the water a huge boom shook the walls. Something fell from a shelf in the front room. Then another explosion, bringing drifts of plaster down from the ceiling.

Outside, the sound of running feet, and gunshots, much closer now. The woman ducked down behind the counter again. A brief silence, the shots fading down the street, followed by shouting.

The building shook again. Win edged his way to the front of the store and peered out the window. The rain had let up. Some small arms fire crackled, and he caught a glimpse of a gun flash from a shop across the street. To his left, armed soldiers were making their way up the street toward the pharmacy, followed by a tank. The tank turret turned toward a building across the street and fired into one of the shops. When the smoke cleared the door and windows were black holes. The tank swiveled to the next shop and fired again.

Win ran to the back room. "It looks like the rebels are fighting from some of the shops. I think the troops are going to blow down the whole block to get at them."

"My shop," she groaned. "I didn't do anything to them."

"I don't think they care. Is there another way out of here?"

The woman got back to her feet. "How much time do we have?"

"They seem to be working their way down the street. Not much."

"Maybe they'll stop before they get here," she said hopefully.

"I don't think we can take that chance," said Win. Then he added, "I'm sorry about your shop."

The woman took a look around the store. "It's all I have." She pulled up straight. "Damn them." She reached under the counter and handed Win a large sack with handles. "Put as much food and water as you can in here. There's more on that shelf behind you. It's mostly dried snacks, but it will do. I'll get some medicine and bandages. People are going to need them. There is a back exit to a service alley that will get us out of the shopping district." She grabbed another bag and bustled out into the store, grabbing items as she went.

* * *

The shopkeeper, whose name was Miera, was surprisingly spry once she got moving. "I don't own a pharmacy for nothing," she had explained. "And I only sell medicines I know that work. Although I do get stiff from sitting in one place."

Miera had led the way out the back door into a dim alley. As she locked the door she said, "I don't know why I'm bothering, they'll probably destroy everything."

The boom of the tank continued methodically, muffled only slightly by the building between them and the main street. As they walked quickly down the alley a few other doors opened, more shopkeepers piling out into the alley, some with families. They all seemed to know one another.

Win overheard enough of the conversations to understand that the rebels had come into some of their shops to use as cover. No one seemed to have much love for either side. He received a few curious looks, but perhaps because he was with Miera no one appeared especially bothered by his presence. Some of the children stared at him and Win thought again about the boy Breal. Varshan had been so despondent over the loss of his daughter. Why would he leave Breal alone, without any family?

Varshan was dead. Obviously he had tried to stop Listra the only way he could. *Would I have been willing to do the same?* Win wondered. He had not consciously thought about what he was going to do as he had tried to reach Listra. If she had not listened to him, would he have wrapped his arms around her to save the soldiers?

Varshan, who had been one of the rebels, had been willing to save his enemies. Win remembered how Aralyn had berated the man, and how Varshan believed that he and the rebels were responsible for some of the effects of the war. Is that why he had stopped Listra? To make amends? Or because he thought her way wasn't right? Win thought it was probably both.

The alley opened up into a cross street. From the left came the sound of the tank gunfire. To the right the sky was dark with smoke from the barracks. Here too people spilled out onto the street, carrying packs and bags, gathering into small groups. Many streamed into another alley across the avenue, the continuation of the service lane.

Win hesitated. "We can't stop here," said Miera.

"I have to go find Aralyn—the woman I was with," said Win, looking over his shoulder. "She was back somewhere near the data center."

"Is she smart?" asked Miera.

"What? Yes, quite."

"Then she isn't there," said Miera. The old woman pointed down the street. "Everyone is coming this way. She will too."

"Unless she headed off in the other direction," said Win. "We came from the river." He didn't want to consider that Aralyn had been hurt in the blast. He couldn't bear the thought of losing her. Especially to an explosion.

He was jostled from behind, the street crowding up, everyone funneling into the narrow alley across the way. The boom of the tank grew closer.

Miera grabbed his arm. "Come, offworlder. These alleys run for many blocks. Once we are clear of the fighting you can go look for her. She may even be ahead of us."

Win allowed himself to be led along. His only consolation was that Aralyn could have seen him walk past the barracks, and he would be heading in that direction. If she fell in with the mass of refugees, they might even find each other.

And, she was a survivor.

* * *

Crammed into the alley, the fleeing civilians barely kept ahead of the fighting. Win strained to find Aralyn in the growing mass of people. Miera had tried to be helpful, asking anyone who slowed enough if they had seen someone matching Aralyn's description, especially back by the data center. "No one is hanging around there," one harried man told them. "The soldiers are all over the place. Everyone is leaving the city until things die down."

At the entrance to the next alley a small group had gathered around a man lying on the ground. Miera pushed through the crowd. The injured man's clothing had been cut away to reveal a deep puncture wound on his back, blood oozing from a makeshift bandage. Miera dug into one of her bags and pulled out a bottle. "Someone take off that dirty bandage," she ordered. She probed the wound gently with a pad soaked in the liquid and the man groaned. "What happened?"

"Some shrapnel I think," someone explained. "But I couldn't see anything in the wound."

"Probably sliced him as it flew by. Could have been worse. How much blood did he lose?"

"Not much. He was walking on his own and just collapsed here."

"Maybe in shock." Miera poured more of the medicine onto the wound and the bleeding slowed considerably. Deftly she wrapped the man in a new bandage. She pulled another bottle from her bag and shook out a few pills. "These will help him with the pain. Keep him still for as long as you can here, then he should be okay to move. You may have to carry him until he gets his strength. And give him water."

Win was still searching for Aralyn in the crowd streaming toward them. Miera was right, Aralyn would not be forcing her way through the crowd in the other direction, and would hopefully assume that Win would follow the flow out of the city as well. Unless she had headed back to the river right after the explosion. If he did not find her in the crowd he would search there next.

Win helped Miera up and they continued on into the next alley. In the narrow space the sound of the fighting faded. After three more blocks it had receded into the background, and all appeared quiet ahead. Within another block the alley ended, opening onto a smaller street. Most of the people turned right, then disappeared around the next corner.

"That street parallels the river," said Miera. "There is a large park not far along, and if you pass through it you'll be back at the river. Most people will head to the park and set up camps. They'll leave us alone there. I hope."

Win took a long look the other way, but no one was coming from that direction. Once again he reluctantly joined the procession of refugees. The streets grew noticeably shabbier. Some of the buildings had gaping holes and the shops were deserted.

"There was a rebel attack here a few years ago," explained Miera. "The soldiers tracked some rebels to this street. After the attack was put down, the government left the street like this to remind us what happens to anyone who joins in the uprisings."

The mood was somber, the rundown buildings dampening the mood of the entire procession. A few blocks ahead the buildings thinned, with a line of trees visible in the distance.

At the end of the burned out block Win noticed a man near one of the houses. He was whistling, carrying a stone paving block from a pile to the house, where he set it on a rebuilt part of a half missing foundation. The man picked up a trowel and ladled some mortar onto the new stone, carefully packing in the joints.

Something about the man's calmness amidst the chaos caught Win's attention. Like a sturdy tree that somehow managed not to sway in a tempest. He stopped and watched the man as he returned for another stone and repeated the process. On the next trip, the man nodded to Win and Miera, who had stopped when she noticed that Win was no longer following.

"Someone you know?" asked Miera.

"No," said Win. "But he reminds me of someone." He turned to Miera. "You go on ahead, I'll catch up with you." He held up the sacks he was carrying. "Can you get someone to help you with these?"

Miera gave him a strange look. "You shouldn't be wandering around alone."

"I'll be alright," said Win. "I appreciate everything you've done for me. You should go to the park. There might be other people who need your help."

Miera stared at him and then shrugged. "I'll ask around for your friend. You said her name was Aralyn? Where should I tell her to find you?"

"I'll be here for a little while and if I don't see her go past I'll come to the park."

"There is a reflecting pool at the far side, toward the river. It is a good meeting place and easy to find." She took the bags from Win and gestured to a few men passing by. "Help me with these please," she said. "I have medicine to share." She kept one of the bags and gave it to Win. "This one has some of the food and water. Just in case you need it." She hesitated. "The one you came to find on Carthlana. Must be someone special for you to go through all this."

Win nodded. "He is very special."

"Who is he? Maybe I've seen him."

"His name is Jesus."

"Never heard of him," said Miera. "But I hope you find him."

She touched Win's arm briefly and headed off toward the park. Win watched her blend into the crowd and then turned back to the man who was working on the building. The man had stopped and was looking at Win, a small smile on his face.

"Are you lost?" asked the man. He wore workman's clothes made of a sturdy fabric, spotted here and there by mortar stains. It was hard to tell his age. He wasn't old, yet he moved with a relaxed manner of maturity. Though he was not brawny he had picked up the building stones without apparent effort.

"I am looking for someone," replied Win. "We got separated in the fighting."

"Fighting does that," said the man.

"Forgive me," said Win. "But shouldn't you leave? The fighting could come this way. Everyone is trying to go somewhere safer."

"Safety is a matter of perception, don't you think?" asked the man.

"Some threats are real," said Win.

"This is true," said the man. "But often one strident threat conceals a greater silent one."

A loud boom in the distance made Win jump. The man appeared unperturbed. "Do you see? A lot of noise, and yet we are safe. It is not the obvious that one must fear, but the insidious." He picked up another stone. "That woman you were with, did she bring you here?"

"She was helping me get away from the fighting."

"So she helped you get to where you needed to be."

"I guess you could say that," said Win.

"Well, this is where *I* need to be." The man returned to the wall, gently laying the stone and tucking in the mortar. The wall facing the street was now complete, and the man finished the tuck work on the corner of the foundation.

Win looked back over his shoulder. The people leaving the city continued to head past him. He noticed a few more injuries, and many carried heavy bags, as if they did not plan on returning for some time. Most were headed toward the park; he hoped Aralyn was already there. He was torn between looking for Aralyn and talking to this man, who for some reason reminded Win of Jesus. Not in the way he looked, but in his calm energy, his palpable sense of tranquility.

If Aralyn had already reached the park, she would be safe. If she was heading there, Win would see her pass by from where he was. He decided he could spend a few more moments here.

He set down his small bag of food and picked up one of the

paving stones. It was much heavier than he had expected and he almost dropped it. Without looking up from his work, the man said, "Some things are not always what they seem, are they?"

Win lugged the stone over to the foundation and the man indicated where it was to go. Win set it down and the man gently tapped it into place, the first stone in the rebuilding of the next wall.

"Every house needs a good foundation," said the man.

"I have just seen entire buildings totally destroyed," said Win, somewhat exasperated. "From the threat you seem to take so lightly."

"Tell me something." The man paused from his work, resting his elbow on his knee. "Would you let every storm drive you from your home? Would you give up what you have just because it is threatened?"

"Is it only the house that keeps you here? Would it not be better to simply move on?" Win asked.

"I am moving on." The man turned back to his work.

"That seems like a contradiction. How can you stay here and move on at the same time?"

"Because I am adding to the foundation. It is changing, moving on in a way, just as it remains stationary." The man gently organized the stones, lining them up perfectly. "As I strengthen it, it is more able to withstand any kind of threat. I only need add one stone at a time, and the entire foundation becomes stronger. As it does so, it becomes a core, it becomes one with the core. For it is what is within that is important, not what is on the outside."

The core, thought Win. Once again everything seemed to be tied together, connected in some way here on Carthlana. The meeting place called the Core that Win had first gone to, thinking it would have the answers. The words the mystery Sooni had told Aralyn, about Jesus being at the core. And now this man, talking about the importance of the core, a core much more than what was inside a house.

"What is your name?" asked Win.

"What is in a name? I am called many things, depending on who is calling. Right here," he said, indicating the wall, "I am Tekton."

Another boom, this one much closer. Somewhere behind Win someone cried out, a wail of despair.

Tekton stood. "Perhaps it is time for you to move on, as well."

"What will you do?" asked Win.

"There is nowhere else I would be safer. I have my protection." The man grabbed onto the wall and pulled, the stones unyielding. "See? My foundation is stronger already." He looked at Win. "Living in hard times, living with difficulty—all that is part of living. It doesn't matter where you are. Safety comes from within. If everyone understood this, their inner peace would extend outward, and there would be no room for fear or destruction."

Tekton looked up at the sky. "Looks like it might rain. Another difficulty of life, sometimes."

Win picked up his bag. "I hope you stay safe."

"I will," said Tekton. "And I hope you find all that you seek."

CHAPTER 23

THE PARK, THOUGH JAMMED WITH PEOPLE, was surprisingly neat and orderly. Some of the refugees had come prepared, erecting makeshift shelters and tents, separated by open lanes. Tall trees provided a deep green canopy.

For all the mass of people, it was relatively quiet. Most eyes were turned back toward the city, and each blast brought nervous whispering.

As new people arrived they seemed to head to a specific location, and Win realized that the groups were organized in a grid. More people were at the center than the edges. He began to walk quickly up and down the lanes, looking for Aralyn. As before, he received a few curious looks.

After quite a while Win still had not found her and was beginning to despair. Maybe she had not come here after all. Yet he still had more of the park to search, and refugees were still arriving. He realized that he'd have to start all over again at some point, as he could not know if Aralyn would be among the new arrivals.

He thought again about how his life had become one of constant searching. Years ago, searching for an escape, then searching for any kind of peace. And later, Jesus had started him on a search for truth. Then, returning to K'Turia, the cycle started again, searching for Jesus. And now Aralyn; his search for Jesus not forgotten or set aside, but rather somehow all a part of what he seemed to be doing every day. Another connection, this time across an entire galaxy.

Miera had told him about the reflecting pool being a place where people would meet. Perhaps someone had told Aralyn the same thing. He headed off deeper into the park, following a wide gravel lane. A lot of others were going the same way, and some were returning, carrying jugs of water.

Wide, well sculpted decorative trees lined the lane. The walkway opened into a large rectangular mall of grass surrounding a shallow reflecting pool, with fountains at either end, a line of people waiting to get water.

The blasts from the city had continued, more or less constantly, since Win had been in the park. Some were far off, sensed more than felt. Others were much closer, and with each the water in the pool muddied, distorting the reflection of the sky and the people around the edges.

Win circled the pool twice. After the second circuit he wearily sat on the grass, tired and hungry. He chewed on some of the dried food Miera had given him without really tasting it. It was well into the late afternoon and soon he'd have to make a decision on what to do if he did not find Aralyn by nightfall. He wasn't sure he could accomplish much at night, and he would have to use the rest of the day to search the park again and then either check by the river or take a chance and go back into the city.

After just a few minutes of rest he was back on his feet. *Moving on,* he thought. Just like Tekton said. If only he could put Tekton's words into action right now, being able to stay in one place to rest while still moving on with his search. To find everything he was seeking by staying still.

He took one last look around the reflecting pool. A lot of people obviously waiting to meet someone, or trying to find someone. Just like he was. No matter where he went in the universe, that was another constant. People were always searching, trying to find some comfort in someone they knew, or trying to discover something.

Taking a deep breath, Win headed back toward the refugee camp. He fell in step with a short man who was limping, struggling to carry a large jug of water.

"Can I help you with that?" asked Win.

The man stopped and grimaced, but still managed a smile. "Thank you." He bowed his head and gratefully handed the jug to Win, who shifted the small bag of food to his shoulder.

"Did you get hurt in the fighting?" asked Win as they resumed walking.

"What? The limp? No, I've had that for years. I don't really notice it anymore, except when I have to carry something heavy, and then it unbalances me. When we left the city I took a few empty jugs since I knew there would be water at the fountains. I'm bringing the water to my family in the park."

"It sounds like you've had this experience before," said Win. "I mean, escaping from the fighting to come here."

The man shrugged. "Now and then. It had been quiet for a while. But these days, we all expect it to start up again sooner or later. The ones who are fighting don't seem to care about us common folks. It's kind of like my limp, you learn to live with it." He looked at Win, curious. "What are you doing here?"

Win explained what had happened. He ended by describing Aralyn, and asking whether the man had seen anyone looking like her.

"No, I can't say I have. Although we were all pretty intent on getting out of the city. I saw a lot of people I didn't know. Where does she live?"

"She's not from here—she's from Devatus."

"That's too bad. Everyone kind of organizes themselves in the park along the lines of where they live in the city, so we can find each other. I'm not sure where people from other cities would go. Does she know anyone here?"

"I don't think so. That's why I came to the reflecting pool."

"That was a good idea. When we get back I'll ask around about your friend. My family can help you look. I know it must be hard to not be able to find someone you are looking for."

Win gave a brief smile. "Yes it is."

* * *

Back in the park, Win followed the man to his family. They thanked him profusely for his help and offered him some food, which Win politely declined. When it was clear none of them had seen anyone like Aralyn, he set off again, determined to make one more pass through the park. The fighting had died off for a bit but now the gunfire started up again, sometimes sporadic, other times in a long fusillade.

Partway through his search he realized he was not going to be able to check the entire park and still have time to make it to the river and back before nightfall. He retraced his steps back to the reflecting pool, circled around it, and kept on, growing increasingly anxious. Past the far end of the park, he found himself in an industrial looking area, filled with long low buildings. A few workers were moving boxes inside and closing up the doors. The fighting did not seem to have spread to this area.

He angled off to his right, heading back toward where he thought he and Aralyn had landed. He felt the river before he saw it, the slight change in humidity. There were very few people here and he wondered why, but when he turned a corner and the river came into view there was a large contingent of soldiers on the dock. One glimpse told him that they were guarding the pier area. He retreated back around the nearest building before anyone had seen him.

It was unlikely that Aralyn would be there, unless she had been captured. Given how good she was at avoiding troops, he hoped she had stayed away. Resigned, he hurried back to the park.

This time he did not search the crowd but instead walked quickly along the wide lane back toward the park entrance. It had not taken him as long as he expected to go to the river, so he still might be able to make it back into the city to search there.

People were still arriving, though fewer than before. Still no Aralyn. Win was one of the few heading in the other direction and he felt exposed. The sound of the fighting still continued on sporadically.

Small groups clustered at the wide park entrance, a few soldiers amongst them. They were all armed but held their guns loosely pointed down and watched the people with little more than casual interest. A few carried on conversations with the soldiers, but most of the refugees gave them a wide berth.

Win had still not seen a single offworlder since that morning and wondered how the soldiers would react to his presence. He did not want to take the chance they would detain him so he kept as far away as he could.

After leaving the park he turned back onto the road that led into the city. There were fewer refugees but the late arrivals were more laden with goods and possessions. Almost all were on foot. The few in vehicles were bypassing the park and continuing on away from the city, where they were lined up at some kind of checkpoint.

Win resumed his walk back toward the city, thinking to stop and talk with Tekton again. Halfway down the street he stopped short in amazement. A small group had gathered around the building that Tekton had been repairing. Tekton was nowhere to be seen. But instead of a low wall under repair, the entire foundation now stood completely rebuilt, so perfect that it was impossible to tell where the original wall had ended and the new wall began.

The gaping holes had been replaced by new windows, clear and clean. They reflected the light of the late day sun, searing into Win's eyes with dazzling brilliance, casting a warmth onto him all the way across the street.

* * *

Win stared at the building, not believing his eyes. How could it have been rebuilt so quickly? He had not been gone that long.

Win stepped forward, and as he did so the angle of the sun on the window shifted slightly, and the bright reflection disappeared. He crossed the street and stood at the back of the group, watching a bearded man wearing a large hat who was running his hands over the wall. Suddenly the man pushed against it, testing its strength. The wall didn't budge. He stepped back and looked up, the top of the foundation higher than his head.

Someone in the crowd said, "I thought you said your foundation was destroyed, Tu Vos?"

The bearded man turned to the crowd. "It was, I tell you. I was here just yesterday. It was only this high," he indicated with his hands, "and the windows were gone."

"That's true," said a woman. "I was past here yesterday."

"Couldn't have been yesterday," said another man. "This could not have been repaired in one day."

"I saw a man working on it today," offered Win. The group turned to look at him, surprised.

"A man? What man?" asked Tu Vos.

"He said his name was Tekton."

"That's not a name," said Tu Vos. "It just means builder. A mason."

"I thought this was his house," said Win.

"It's my house," said Tu Vos. "I've owned it for a long time."

"He must have had a lot of help," said the other man who had spoken. "Who else was here?"

"No one," said Win. "He was alone."

"That's impossible. It would take days for a full crew to do this."

Win didn't want to argue. "I only saw the one man."

"Maybe they came after you left," said Tu Vos.

"That's right, a gang of government workers came and rebuilt your house for free!" someone said, and the crowd laughed.

Tu Vos was running his hand over the wall again. "I don't know what to believe," he said. "Except that this is good work. I can definitely rebuild my house on this foundation." He turned back to Win.

"What did this man look like? I need to thank him."

For some reason Win could not picture Tekton in his head. He usually had a good memory for faces, but although he could remember the man, his peaceful demeanor, and his words, he inexplicably could not clearly picture his face.

"He was wearing working clothes," said Win, perplexed. "I— I can't quite describe him. Not too young or old. He seemed very good at the work. And he was very strong. He picked up the foundation stones easily."

"I need to find this Tekton and get him to work on my house too!" someone said, and again the crowd laughed.

"If I see him again I'll pass along your thanks," said Win. "I'm heading back into the city now." He turned to leave.

"You can't," said Tu Vos.

Win stopped. "Why not?"

"There will be a curfew at nightfall," said Tu Vos. "No one on the streets. Around the park it will be okay, but if it is like the last time there was an attack they will not let people in or out of the park after dark."

"I really need to find someone," said Win. "We got separated in the attack and I'm worried about her."

"Another offworlder?"

"No, someone from here. But not from Azotus."

"She'll find her way here," said someone. "Everyone does."

"It will be dark soon," said Tu Vos. "You can stay with me tonight. Part of the back of the house is undamaged." He laughed. "You can tell me more about this mystery man Tekton."

Win looked back toward the street. The flow of refugees heading from the city had dwindled. He would look out of place going the other way, and the curfew would be a problem. As if to help him make his choice, a long rain of gunfire split the air.

"Very well," said Win. "I don't seem to have much of a choice."

* * *

Win wanted to make one more attempt to find Aralyn in the park before it was closed, and Tu Vos offered to help. Win wasn't entirely sure that his description of Aralyn would be enough for Tu Vos to recognize her, so they did not split up. Hopefully Aralyn would be on the lookout for him as well, and Win was sure he stood out as he walked up and down the lanes. It occurred to him that if Aralyn were asking around for him, someone surely would have remembered seeing an offworlder. The thought brought a new wave of despair. She must not be in the park after all.

He did find Miera, busy applying an ointment to the leg of a woman who had suffered a burn.

"Did you find your friend?" Miera asked.

"I'm afraid not," said Win.

"Hopefully they'll let us back in the city tomorrow," said Miera. "Although I'm not sure if I'll have anything to go back to." She stared off toward the city wistfully.

Win wasn't sure what to say. He wasn't one for platitudes. "That man," Win said, pointing at Tu Vos, who was talking to some other refugees. "Do you know him?"

"No, but I've seen him around," Miera said.

"He has offered me a place to stay tonight. He has a home just outside the park. I'm sure he would let you stay as well."

Miera shook her head. "Thank you, no. I have been finding injured people all day and there are only two doctors in the park. I have to stay here and help."

Win thought of Jesus' message of helping others to the best of their ability. "You are a good woman, Miera. I am glad to know you. Good luck."

Miera glanced up at Win before returning her attention to her patient. "Good luck to you, also. I hope you find your friend."

Back at the park entrance, Win and Tu Vos lingered until dark, watching the last of the refugees arrive. The flow finally stopped;

Win suspected that the curfew had begun. Only a few of the buildings on the street showed any lights. The rain had started up again.

Two small rooms in Tu Vos's house, those farthest from the street, were relatively undamaged. Both were so full of furniture and provisions there was barely enough room to move.

"Sorry about the mess," said Tu Vos, moving boxes off of a chair. He had taken off his hat, revealing a full head of dense white hair, the Carthlanian veins on his forehead disappearing into the locks. "I salvaged everything I could that wasn't damaged. We are right at the edge of the area that the government will let us rebuild. Farther from the park it's a mess, worse than this if you can believe it. There was a rebel attack a few years ago, and the government thought that the people who lived there had helped the rebels, so they've decreed that the families cannot go back. The good news is we have plenty of food, and I have an extra bed you can use. A cot really, but it is better than sleeping on the ground, especially with this rain. We usually don't even get any rain this time of year, it's not the rainy season. Very odd. Could cause some flooding in the canals."

"I have some food as well," said Win, offering up his sack.

Tu Vos looked in the bag and sniffed. "This isn't food, it's a bag of snacks. I'll get you something better to eat." He bustled around the room, opening boxes and setting plates on the small table. "Can you tell me more about this man who called himself Tekton? I still don't understand how my wall got rebuilt so fast. It's a miracle."

"I think I told you all I know," said Win. It was still bothering him that he could not hold a clear image in his mind of what Tekton looked like. Every time he tried to picture the mason, the visage changed just a little. Not in an unnatural or bothersome way, but one that made him focus more on what the man had said rather than on what he had looked like.

"I'll ask around tomorrow," said Tu Vos. "Who knows? Maybe we'll wake up and it will be destroyed again."

Win thought about the wall, solid and strong. Surprisingly certain, he said, "I think it will be fine."

* * *

Win lay awake long after Tu Vos had gone to bed. He was both physically spent and mentally fatigued, but he could not fall asleep. So much had happened in one day, so many images vivid in his mind. The last painful steps of Varshan, throwing himself on top of Listra. And the face of Listra, turning into an abomination, a grotesque mask of anger and hate. First looking like Drason, the one who had led Win to the creepy ritual, and then looking like the being leading the ritual itself, who now seemed more creature than man. Did that being have a hold over Listra? Had it forced her to do what she did?

Win was suddenly back in the underground station, hearing the chanting, seeing the dagger come up . . .

Win began to sweat, the image more terrifying than any nightmare, a whispered wondering forcing into his consciousness, the question of whether there was something, someone, who could make another do the unspeakable, to not only be driven to hatred, but to strike out, to hate something so completely that all reason was overwhelmed.

He was terrified that he might be made to do something against his will. Or even worse, affect him in such a way that he would choose to do something evil.

The darkness surrounding Listra's head just before she died, the black fog he had been surrounded by in the street, the inkiness of the room, clutching at him even now, reaching for him, smothering.

The rain, pelting on the roof, pounding in his ears, sucking out all other sound.

He jerked up, throwing off the coverlet, his arms out, groping, reaching for something, anything, feeling the very darkness, thick and terrifying.

He stumbled to the floor and crawled to where he thought the door to be, in his panic forgetting the jumble in the room. His head cracked on a crate, stunning in its intensity, a flash of light in his head.

Then suddenly a clear voice, calm and quiet, yet so assured that it cut through the rain, and with it a ray of light that forced aside his panic. *'You must be where you need to be.'*

Crashing into a box with my head is where I am, thought Win. And it did seem just where he needed to be, for it had forced away the dread. He started to laugh, his relief overcoming the spine tingling fear, freeing him from the clutches of darkness, from the sheer terror of being controlled by something evil.

Totally spent, he leaned against the crate and fell asleep.

* * *

And dreamed. The day flashed past: awakening in the rebel hideout, the river journey, the explosion, the fighting, the search for Aralyn. Everything moving fast. This time, the image of the evil creature who had seemed to take over Listra did not affect him as it had before—there was the same sense that he was seeing something totally unnatural, the same blackness, but it was as if he was protected, for the dread could not reach him.

And then he was at Tu Vos's house, coming upon the man working on the wall, the mason who had called himself Tekton. But this time, when he turned to look at Win, it was not Tekton, but Jesus. Now the face was crystal clear, his eyes holding Win's as they had so often on K'Turia, his words touching him in a way no one else's ever had. Not even Sooni.

Jesus turned to his work on the foundation, trowel in hand. Win picked up a stone, surprised that he could lift it so easily now, and set it on the wall.

"Now you see," said Jesus, "that a strong foundation provides protection not just from the elements, and from physical threats, but also protects you from the darkness of evil. This," he patted the wall, "is what protects you from the physical. But here," he said, pointing to Win's chest, "this is where you build the protection to keep the evil at bay. It is the foundation at the core, the foundation of faith."

"You told me something of this on K'Turia," said Win. "That I needed to think of more than the physical, that there are other threats. I did not know what you meant."

"You were not ready," said Jesus, leaning on his knee, just as Tekton had earlier that day. "Before you could begin to see, there was more you had to learn. And though you had seen terrible deeds, you had not witnessed true evil."

"The creature I saw, the one leading the ritual. Is he evil?"

"What do you think?" asked Jesus.

"Anyone who could cause another to do something so horrible, that must be what evil is."

"No one can make anyone do what they do not want to do," said Jesus.

"So I—I cannot be made to do evil?" asked Win, afraid of what the answer would be. He had never before thought he could be changed by evil, but after seeing what Listra had done, had seemingly been driven to do, now he was terrified.

"People will do evil things, but not by being forced. Yet they can be tempted, they can provide the fuel for the eruption of actions beyond comprehension. For the wrong fuel will create darkness instead of light."

"What is the wrong fuel?" asked Win.

"Anger, hatred, envy, guilt. These and others are like cancers which attack and weaken. Once weakened, it is hard to resist unless the foundation is strong."

"Is this what happened to Listra?"

"It can happen to anyone. You felt her anger. It opened her up to evil, which rushed into the void." Jesus' voice sounded sad. "By herself, she was not strong enough to resist. I could have helped her, but she did not call to me."

"If you can protect us from the evil," asked Win, "why don't you stop it?"

Jesus stood and picked up another stone. "Just as evil cannot force itself on someone, so too am I unable to force myself on anyone. The strength of faith is not given, it is built from within. But I can help." He set the stone on the wall, and it immediately melded into the other stones, becoming one with the wall. "You need not even see me, you need only to know that I am there, and have faith that with me, the wall will hold."

Jesus reached down and effortlessly hefted a huge bolder. Holding it high overhead, he cast it at the wall. There was a loud smack, the rock bouncing off, yet leaving not a mark.

"You see?" said Jesus. "Once the foundation of faith is built, even I cannot tear it asunder."

"So if I have faith, that will protect me?"

"Not from the temptation," said Jesus. "For the temptations will always be around you. Anger, vanity, selfishness, guilt. But faith will help you keep them at bay, and will help you make the right choices, and choose the right path."

"I am still confused," said Win. "What does this have to do with me? What should I do now?"

"I have already told you. You must move on."

"From where? From here?"

"From what is holding you back. From what is weakening you. From what is keeping you from building a foundation so strong you can reach the peace you have been seeking."

Anger, guilt. Win knew about those feelings, so powerful they had dragged him down into years of malaise. He knew they brought sadness. Could they also make him vulnerable to evil?

And how could he give up those feelings without losing Sooni? If he felt no emotion about her loss, what would that mean for him? For their connection?

Had you really loved someone if the emotions you felt after they were gone lost their intensity? If they did not affect you so much that they changed you, even if for the worse?

"I do not know if I have the strength for that," said Win.

"You do not need to do it alone," said Jesus. "As I have told you before. Remember, you cannot be strong while you carry the burdens of the past. You know what you must leave behind."

"You mean Sooni? I cannot leave her."

"But you can leave behind the anger, the guilt. This is what you must move beyond. The past cannot be changed. Yet it can be a source of learning, the source of the stones in your foundation of faith. You still live in the past, instead of experiencing the lessons of life, the lessons I bring you, in the clarity of the here and now."

Jesus stepped toward the wall, and just as the stone had before, he melded into the foundation, becoming one with the stone. It shimmered, alive and radiant, throwing off the darkness. The room vibrated, a wave of warmth filling the air.

Win was alone, and everything became sharper, his hearing more acute. Instead of a hum of white noise, he heard each rain drop fall, singing a symphony, enveloping him in a warm, whispering peace.

CHAPTER 24

WIN JERKED AWAKE at the scream. His eyes darted around the room, picking out the clutter of Tu Vos's house in the early morning light. Nothing moved and the only sound was the dull drumbeat of the rain.

He must have dreamt it.

The scream came again, a sound of sheer terror, like nothing he had ever heard, so chilling he shrunk down on the floor, cringing. The third time it came it held longer than any being could have yelled, somewhere outside, coming closer, closer. Then, impossibly, the sound of running feet, which should have been drowned out by the scream and the rain. Yet unmistakable.

The terror still gripped him even after the scream ended, and in the muffled stillness came a scornful laugh, followed by the tread of a heavy footstep. It stopped just outside Tu Vos's door, and Win cowered, his rational mind telling himself not to fear, but his body shaking uncontrollably.

A voice just outside the door, whispered, yet carrying over the rain and into the room. "This one is closer." A pause, and then the same voice, which sounded vaguely familiar, "As you command, Beros."

The footsteps receded, and the fear lifted just enough for Win to uncurl himself. Slowly he dragged himself to the door. He waited, still afraid, then cautiously reached out and touched the door, as if it was a living thing that could help him understand what was on the other side. His *gheris* told him nothing, it was as empty as he had ever remembered, an emotional void.

The door was but a door. Gingerly he cracked it open. A dark gray sky greeted him, the rain blowing into his face, puddles in the muddy street.

Someone, perhaps a man, was walking away from him, toward the ruined part of the city. His thin garments billowed behind him, seemingly impervious to the rain. His steps were steady and full of purpose, the footsteps Win should not have been able to hear, and they beat an odd cadence with the rain. The man crossed the street, heading for a blackened building, the doorway a dark shadow, drawing Win's eyes.

A woman broke from the doorway into the street, racing away, her scream cutting into Win like a knife, the same scream that had awakened him, a scream of terror. Yet Win's *gheris* sensed nothing; he should have been overwhelmed by her fear. He shied back nonetheless; his body feeling what his extra senses could not.

The man reached for her, grabbing her cloak and ripping it from her, but she managed to slip away. He laughed, the laughter as terrifying as the scream. He tossed aside the cloak, the rain shoving it to the ground, the mud overwhelming the green fabric.

A green cloak.

Sooni.

Win ran into the street, yelling, he didn't know what. For an instant everything froze, even the raindrops seemed to still, as if caught in a giant flash. Both the woman and the man turned to him.

The woman, unmistakably Sooni, her face pleading, begging. And the man, emotionless. Drason.

Drason turned back to Sooni, walking toward her but covering more distance than he should have been able to at that pace, as if he was carried by the rushing water. Sooni, her eyes locked on Win, unmoving, until Drason was almost upon her, and then she tore herself away, running down the street, buffeted by the sheets of rain.

Win was running, not thinking, the rain a curtain clawing at him, his feet slapping through the puddles. A wind blew down the street, whistling as it flew in and out of broken windows and cracked walls.

Win stumbled on, barely able to see Drason, Sooni a mirage, in and out of sight. He ran as fast as he could, yet he could not close the distance. Block after ruined block led him deeper into the city, the streets strewn with stone, timbers, glass. Heedlessly he kept on, dodging, jumping, falling, never daring to lower his eyes.

His breathing became ragged, his eyes stung. He had lost sight of Sooni. Drason flittered in and out of the rain, pulling him along.

Drason rounded a corner, and when Win turned he stepped into a vortex, the wind a fist. Debris flew at him, picked up in a whirlwind, slapping at his flesh. He covered his face, but the debris tore at his hands, slicing him raw, his blood sliding away, blown by the wind and the rain.

He peeked out between his arms and something flew at his face, grabbing at him, a grisly rodent, scratching at his hair as it blew by. Then another, and Win fell to the ground, shaking, uselessly pushing away at the air as gruesome black carrion birds flew at him, their claws digging. An acrid smell of blood filled his nostrils. He felt something on his leg and he kicked out, a snake-like, gelatinous abomination with bulbous eyes, slithering through the water. He screamed, scrambling up onto the sidewalk, frantic, his willpower to follow Sooni torn from him by the creatures.

The whirlwind spun, sucking the air from his lungs, pulling at him, the vacuum so strong it inhaled the rain, the vortex spinning, growing, and coalescing in the middle of the street, forming into a being, not of substance, but outlined by the void within the whirlwind, which swirled around it.

Overhead, the rain continued to fall, but it was absorbed into the vortex, and the street fell into an eerie quiet, still but full of tension, the whirlwind a giant spring fully wound and ready to snap.

The being was a man and yet not a man, a silhouette of a man, a black hole in the vortex, yet with eyes which Win could not bear to look upon, more painful than the rain. Drason was on one knee before the being, his eyes downcast.

"My lord Beros," said Drason.

Beros gestured to Drason, but his eyes were on Win. "It has taken you a long time, but you have come to me, Trebor Win."

Win recognized the voice. The being in the subway station, the one leading the ritual. The impossibly black bloodshot eyes, the same eyes that had sneered at Win from the visage of Listra before she killed herself.

Win was frozen in fear, a fear unlike any he had ever felt, a level of emotion he had not thought possible. His *gheris* reflected his own fear upon himself, suffocating, threatening to crush him. "Who are you?" he managed to say, his voice weak and trembling. "What do you want with me?"

"I am called many things," said the being. "Here, they call me Beros. But it is not what I am called but rather what I can do. For you, I am what you have sought. It is not I who wants you. You are meaningless to me. It is you who wants me."

"That isn't true," said Win, the very disagreement unbearable, inviting some kind of retribution.

But Beros only laughed. "You have fooled yourself into thinking you were looking for someone, some lord of light. But it is I who can change you. It is I who can fulfill your true wish, and free you from your pain."

"You know nothing of my pain," gasped Win.

"Don't be a fool," said Beros. "I know all about pain, and what great power it can bring. I feed it, and feed upon it. Else why do you cringe so in fear?"

"It is the unknown," said Win, not believing his own words, feeling the fear of what was right in front of him.

"You are wrong again," said Beros, disdainfully. "That fear

goes away. It is the known you fear, the knowing deep down inside of what you are, what you can be driven to, what you are capable of."

Beros held out his arm, and in his hand appeared a head, the face of Listra. Not distorted, as Win had seen her before she had blown herself up, but instead calm, smiling.

"This is how she looked before her anger took her," said Beros. "Before I had nourished the seed in her that you all have, the seed of chaos. It took but a single event, the death of her husband, to not only sprout the seed but grow it into evil." Listra's face changed, becoming that of Drason, and then shifting into the image Win had last seen, just before the explosion, distorted in anger. Beros dropped his arm and the face disappeared into the vortex.

"You did that?" said Win. "You made her blow herself up?"

"She did that on her own. I but helped her free herself."

"Death is not freedom!"

"To her it was," said Beros. "For her it meant forgetting. Her anger is what made her strong."

"Committing suicide and killing innocent people is not strength," said Win, not knowing where he got the will to argue.

"Who are you to know what innocence is? What strength is? Strength is not what you think. It is the power to overcome any nature, to lead one to do something they would not otherwise do, and to do it of their own accord. Just as I have led you."

"I do not know you," said Win, trying to sound more confident than he felt. "You have led me nowhere."

Beros voice was filled with scorn. "You say the words, yet deep inside you are troubled. You thought you were on a path to what you think of as enlightenment, some dream world. Yet with all your study and meditation and search for harmony, you are torn by anger. By guilt. By denial. You have built your own prison of despair. You curl up in the corner of your mind, hiding. You don't even want to escape. But you are not at peace. You will *never* be at peace. I have seen this confusion in you, this opportunity for me. I will hasten the seed which you have allowed to take hold within you and put you onto a new path. Onto *my* path."

"I will never do that," said Win, but he was uneasy, deep inside he felt something pulling at him, tearing at his soul.

"You already have," said Beros. "Before the loss of your Sooni, had you ever felt such guilt? Such anger? Had you ever felt such agony, such pain?"

The very mention of Sooni cut into Win. Hearing her name from the lips of this evil being angered him so much it briefly overcame his fear. "That was a normal reaction. I had lost someone I loved."

"And what of the suicide woman? Was that a normal reaction? You are but a breath away from her. The way just needs to be shown to you, the anger cultivated. Can't you feel it even now?"

Win felt it rising in him, the anger he thought came from hearing Beros mention Sooni. Could Beros be causing his anger? Could he really affect Win, guide him, drive him into the same kind of hatred that consumed Listra?

Beros said, "Like her, and everyone, you are weak, susceptible. You do not have the strength to fight me, to fight my temptations. They will serve as your excuses, excuses you will use as your justification to be led by me. Such is my strength."

"Just because some may not be able to resist does not mean that all are weak." Win was thinking of the enlightened ones, of Sooni. Surely she would have been able to resist such temptations.

And Jesus. Jesus would have the power. Jesus had spoken of a path that would take Win away from these temptations, these evils.

"All can be tempted," said Beros. "Look at you. Why are you here? In this place? You think you have followed someone who will lead you to peace, but can you ever have that peace? You don't know it for sure. You don't believe. What you really want is your Sooni back."

"That is impossible," said Win.

"Really? Certainly you think it might be possible. What have you been chasing across the city? If it was so impossible, if it was not what you really wanted, why did you run after her? Even when she led you into danger?"

"She didn't lead me into danger, not every time," said Win. "She led me to the fire, and I was able to help save a man."

"Ah, that one," said Beros. "A mere deceit, nothing more. If she was real, then where did that Sooni go? And why weren't you able to save the girl? You see visions, bringing you what your mind wants to have, what you want to see and believe. Yet I can bring you what you truly want."

Again Beros held out his arm, and another whirlwind spun there, dark, whipping, forming into a woman, into Sooni.

Real flesh and blood, before him once again. Win stared at her, his desire rising up, uncontrollable.

Was this his hidden wish, that through some power of *ana* she could return to him? Or an unimaginable nightmare, that *ana* was a delusion, or worse yet, a darkness, controlled by evil?

Win tried to step forward, but the water around his feet instantly froze, turning his legs numb, trapping him.

"Here is what you want, isn't it?" said Beros. "See what I have the power to give. Or to take away." The arm of Beros grew large, his hand encircling Sooni's neck, lifting her effortlessly, her legs dangling, her body jerking. Win could only watch helplessly, unable to move even his mouth.

Beros shook Sooni by the neck. "Be still," he ordered.

She fell limp, all but her eyes, the same look of pleading, reaching out to Win. Wanting him? Or warning him? He could not tell. Yet in those eyes he saw, or thought he saw, a glimpse of what was Sooni.

Or was this what he wanted to believe?

"Be still," Beros commanded again. "All of you."

Sooni's eyes glazed over, rolling back in her head, and when she again looked at Win they moved but had no life.

Beros let Sooni go, and she fell to the ground. The ice

cracked at Win's feet, and he ran to her, reaching for her hand.

It was cold as ice, alive yet lifeless. He helped her to her feet, and she stood, the soundless wind swirling her cloak.

Everything about her was Sooni, the body of the Sooni he remembered, the same hair, the same lips, the same eyes.

Yet when she spoke, it was her voice and not her voice. The same pitch, the same timbre, but without the feeling, without the joy.

"I am here, my love. Just as you wanted."

"Sooni . . ." Win wanted to hold her, to embrace her, but something held him back. "Is it really you? Did you find a way to come back?"

"Don't you know me?" She touched her face, ran her hands along her body. "Could you have forgotten so soon? We are to be together for eternity, aren't we?"

Win shook his head warily. With all his heart, he wanted it to be her and he wanted his life with her to go back to what it was. The woman who stood before him had all of Sooni's attributes and manners. But something was missing. "How is this possible?" he said through his tears. "This is not the eternity I thought we would share. The enlightenment. The *ana.*"

"Come with me." Sooni wiped at his tears, her fingers impossibly cold. "Our eternity can be whatever we want it to be."

And then it hit him, what was missing. This Sooni, she was without her *ana*, she was a shadow not only of what she had achieved, but of what she had always been. He stepped back, never imagining that he could ever pull away from her.

He tore his eyes from Sooni, forcing himself to look at Beros. "What have you done to her?" he screamed.

"Why, I have brought her back, just as you wanted."

"This is not Sooni, it is a mirage!"

"Is it? You can touch her. You can talk to her. She is as real as you are. This is my gift to you, for opening yourself to my temptations. To the guilt, the anger. Now you only have to keep making the right choices, and she will be yours forever."

"This isn't the Sooni I knew," said Win. "She had attained *ana*. She was happy, at peace."

"And who is to say she will not be so again? Do you doubt yourself so much? Think of what she can become with you at her side, and what you too can become. Watch!" Beros pointed at Sooni, and for a brief instant her eyes sparkled, her body relaxed. She reached for Win, and her hand was warm.

A breath later it was gone, she stiffened, her eyes darkened, her touch once again icy cold.

"You could bring her back," said Beros. "You keep hearing about faith. Aren't you willing to have faith in her?"

Win knew that it was all wrong, that Sooni couldn't be alive, that he could not save her, even now. Yet here she was, real, before him, in her eyes the beauty, the life she once had—and seemed to have again. Maybe he had been wrong about enlightenment. Maybe there *was* another way to eternity.

"What do I have to do?" he said, not wanting to say it, but having to know the price.

"Nothing special," said Beros, dismissively. "Just keep doing what you have been doing. Surrendering to your guilt. Running away. Despairing under your anger. All the things that keep you open to my power. Just live, and make a few more choices."

"What choices? What would I have to do to save her?"

"Just leave behind what is here, and follow her, and she is yours forever." Beros motioned with his hand, and Sooni turned and began to slowly walk away.

Win's eyes were on Sooni, his heart pounding. "Leave what behind?"

Beros was silent, and in the silence Win was frozen, unable to fathom what the true price would be.

Win couldn't bear the waiting, he had to know. "What must I give up? Tell me!"

Beros's voice was flat. "All that you seek. The way of light." Then, as if an afterthought, he indifferently added, "And, of course, those who you have found."

The silence was broken by the sound of running water behind him, and Win spun around, fearing a flood. Instead of the street, he found himself looking at a canal filled with water. He recognized what he was seeing, the canals back by the river. It was raining there, the water in the canal rushing into a huge open cistern, howling pumps struggling to force the water into the holding tanks.

Somehow he could see into one of the tanks, the water rising, and in the water a drenched girl desperately fought to stay afloat, reaching up, but unable to gain a hold on the slick walls.

Aralyn, in the water, reaching up to him. "Help me!"

Without thinking he stretched out his arm for her, but his hands met only the air of the mirage. He heard the water, he felt the spray of the rain, he felt the cistern beneath his feet, but it was not real.

Win spun back to Beros. Sooni was staring at him, waiting. "It's not real!" yelled Win. "None of this is real!"

"I assure you, what you see is happening," said Beros, his powerful voice rising over the watery crescendo. "Here, the love of your life stands before you, waiting for you to join her once again. But—I see your friend seems to be in trouble." Beros's mouth drew into his wicked smile. "She will die soon unless you go to her. This is your choice. Save the one you love, or save the one you barely know. The one who you believe who had found the way, and the one who doesn't even know what she is seeking."

"You can't do this! You cannot make me choose!"

"I don't have to make you do anything. You will do this on your own. Will you do nothing? Will you lose both of them? You have seen what I can do. I can bring back your Sooni, place her in your arms, and you will be free to do what you can to make her what she was. You can be free of the guilt you have for not saving her the first time, because she'll be back with you.

"Or you can save the girl, and Sooni will be lost to you forever, and the pain will be so great nothing you have felt so far can even hint at it. There will be no running away, no peace. You will feel guilt like you have never felt, and your anger will burn, first at yourself, for missing this one chance, and then at the world. And who knows what may happen then?

"You pretend the young girl needs you. An innocent, you think of her. A tragic child, caught in the grips of war. The death of her parents, brought on by all the hatred, the war nothing but the end result of the wills of those who are swayed by me. The weak. You can save her, and surely you cannot think she is an illusion. Yet she is nothing to you. Will you really care if someone you barely know lives or dies? If you had not come here you would never have known her, would never have known she even existed."

Beros reached out both hands, pointing, one to Sooni, the other toward Aralyn. "Here is your choice before you. Choose your path. Choose your reward, and your pain. And no matter what your choice, you will be one step closer to me."

"Why me?" pleaded Win. "Why are you doing this to me?"

"Don't flatter yourself," scoffed Beros. "It is not just about you. You are nothing special, nothing at all. I bring this upon everyone, everywhere. I have tempted everyone, even your prince of light. *Everyone* must face the choice."

Win fell to his knees, crushed, wishing it was just a dream, a terrible nightmare. The mere thought of having Sooni in his life once again was tearing him apart, at this moment more than ever. And now Aralyn had been sucked into the nightmare, through no action of her own, other than following Win. He was responsible. And he had to choose.

This was not a choice anyone should ever have to make. This was a choice of evil.

Beros was not done with him. "Your Jesus has said that all choices have consequences. Now you will learn how terrible they can be."

The whirlwind raged, and with it came the roar of the wind, the rain pelting him, driving Win down, yet above all that noise he heard Aralyn pleading for him, and the sound of Sooni's voice calling his name.

The wind tore at him, pulling him, dragging him toward the vortex, toward Beros. He tried to fight, but he had nothing to hold onto, he didn't have the strength. He could not do this alone.

He cried for help, to the only one he believed would have the power. "Jesus, help me!"

For the briefest instant Win saw surprise in Beros's eyes. A crash of thunder split the air, the reverberation overwhelming the vortex, pushing Win to the ground.

The echo of the thunderclap lingered long, and when it finally ended Win slowly raised his head. The rain and the wind had stopped.

The street was deserted.

CHAPTER 25

A RAY OF LIGHT cleaved the dark clouds, throwing a spotlight on Win, warming him instantly. Though the street still ran with water it parted around him, both it and the rain held at bay by the cone of light surrounding him.

Win lay on the ground, saved from the precipice of fear, yet still weak. His first thought was to run, to take advantage of the respite from the terror wrought by Beros. To escape, just run away.

That's what Beros had said he would do, just as Win always had since Sooni's death. Tried to run away, to hide.

Yet the choice he had been given by Beros could only have been offered up by one of evil, the evil that Win had never known as being truly real. Now he knew. He had felt it, it had shaken his entire being, he had seen what it could do. For an instant the terror clawed at him again, the cold, the fear, the doubt.

But the light warmed him, and a lucid thought filled him: *If Beros wants me to hide, then hiding is what I must not do.*

He did not have the strength to stand, so he tried to enter *nore*, the state of Treb awareness. It was not the *nore* he sought, for he was not sure if he could cope with a closer awareness of the terror. He wanted to find the calmness before the *nore*, the preparation, the readiness, a calmness he so desperately needed now, to give him the strength to decide what he must do.

He had to choose: Sooni or Aralyn. A test with no answer, a precipice he stood on with disaster in both directions.

He slowed his breathing, trying to empty his mind. But it was no good. The touch of Sooni, the scream of Aralyn, they were too real. How much time did he have before both were lost to him?

He raised his head, even that taking a huge effort. He could see no one along the street beyond his cone of light. Was Sooni still there, just out of reach, waiting for him to follow?

And if he did, then what? The Sooni he knew was dead. Yet in that one instant when Beros released her, she was back, alive again, joyous, wanting him.

Could Beros really have such power, to bring Sooni back, to create a corporeal container for her spirit? Or was that what Win wanted to believe? True or not, he was certain Aralyn would drown if he did not help her.

It was all his fault. He had led Aralyn here, he had led her to believe if she found Jesus she could find her answers as well.

He had come so far to find Jesus, and where had it landed him? He seemed to be worse off than ever. Was it too much to hope that Jesus could be the answer to all his problems?

He had always had doubts. Not like Prentiss, who had come to believe, who had cast her doubts away. She too had been a scientist, but it was Win who really demanded the proof, the confirmation that Jesus could bring him peace.

He and Prentiss were different. She had accepted, and he had doubted.

Maybe Beros was right. Maybe Win did not want to escape his prison of despair. Maybe he wanted to punish himself forever. Maybe he deserved to be punished forever.

That thought hardened him. Not with anger; he had just enough rationality left to know that anger was his enemy. But with determination. If Beros reveled in Win's despair, then Win would try as hard as he could to fight it, to free himself.

Yet deep in his heart he knew he did not have the strength. Maybe no one could fight off such evil alone.

He thought of Listra, and how she had succumbed. And of

the words of the builder Tekton, whom he now knew had been speaking the words of Jesus: *"I could have helped her, but she did not call to me."*

Win fell back to the ground, prostate, his hands reaching to the sky, to the beacon of light, the opening in the heavens. "Jesus," he called. "I do not know if my doubts are fully set aside, I tell you truly. Please, help me see."

* * *

The stone beneath his feet was warm and solid, making Win feel more rooted than he had ever been. It was as if he were one with the stone, the rock stretching out before him, all around him, as far as he could see. Every inch was illuminated with a comforting, even light, bright yet easy to look upon. Overhead, the sky was a deep blue, luminous, yet, oddly, Win could not see the sun.

A high wall circled him, close enough to feel protective yet not so near as to feel pressing. The wall was made of stones, each closely demarked, yet held together seamlessly, without mortar. The stones were of many different sizes, yet they formed a wall of beauty and strength. Though the wall was solid, Win was somehow able to see past it, to the great expanse beyond.

Jesus sat peacefully atop the wall, smiling at Win. His figure cast no shadow on the rock below.

Win stood, his strength returned. Awed, he said, "Where am I?"

"You are where you need to be, at least right now," said Jesus.

"But how—?"

"You called for me. You asked for my help."

"Is that all it takes? To escape—to escape the evil?" He saw Beros in his mind, but the terror did not grip him as it had before.

"I can help you, as I have said to you many times. But I cannot *be* you. I cannot live your life. That you must do." Jesus traced his finger along the top of the wall. "Evil is not something you escape. It is something you rise above."

"Then I have to go back? To make the choice?" Win panicked.

"Just as I cannot live your life, I cannot free you of your choices," said Jesus. "They are what define you."

"I'm not strong enough," said Win. "*You* are. Why can't you go instead?"

"Would you have me take from you what makes you who you are? Your free will?"

Win felt the anger rising up. "How can you expect me to face evil if you won't?"

Jesus' smiled faded. "I face evil every day. For this great battle takes place not on the outside, but within, within not only you, but in every being across the universe. Each must make a choice, to decide which path to follow. Were I to force you or anyone to make that decision, you would be nothing, your soul would be only a fantasy of the body. This is a truth you must understand.

"Beros was wrong. It *is* about you. About every one of you. The outcome of this battle will be determined by the choices people make. By the choices *you* make."

Win sought a way out of his dilemma. "But the choice I have been given, it is not between something good and something evil. There is pain in both choices."

"Are you so accepting of the way the choices have been presented to you? Is this how you see the world, your choices defined by that which you know is evil?" Jesus sounded sad. "I thought you were beyond that."

"I—I had not thought of it that way," said Win. "I see what you say, but all I feel is what I will lose."

"You can take many journeys but make no progress toward any destination. You have come on a journey to find me, but what you really seek is the Truth. Such is your destination. I have seen the progress you have made. You have made choices here on this planet which are even now changing you, continuing to define you. You will always have more choices to make."

"When will it end?" said Win, hoping to get the answer he longed for.

"It will never end," said Jesus. "Especially the choice between the light and the dark. For evil will not rest, it will always be there, seeking a way to offer temptations. It will not always be the stark choice you are faced with, like that between Sooni and Aralyn. Rather it will be the smaller decisions you make, the things you allow yourself to do. To be angry. To be envious. To be jealous. To feel or impart guilt. Evil seeks defect instead of purity, division instead of harmony, disturbance instead of stability, tumult instead of peace. These are the insidious weapons of wickedness, the hidden root of evil."

"How can these temptations be resisted?" asked Win. "They just come. I thought I was well on my way to enlightenment, and still I have succumbed. With one word you give me hope, and then you tell me it will never end."

"The temptations are roadblocks on the path to what you call enlightenment," said Jesus. "Others call it heaven. The word does not matter; they all share the light of Truth, they are defined by it and through it. For some, these roadblocks are so difficult that many do not even know that enlightenment is possible. For others, temptations are the challenges to overcome. The temptations are just a few of the weapons of evil, for evil becomes stronger whenever anyone turns from the path of light."

Jesus voice grew softer. "Evil can tempt anyone. Even me."

Win remembered what Beros had said. That everyone had to face temptation, to make choices.

After a moment Jesus continued: "Yet with an understanding of the Truth, evil can be held at bay. It is strong while it is hidden, but when exposed for what it really is, evil dissolves in the light. It becomes first a shadow, and then but a wisp, something you can blow aside, a hindrance less than a fog about your feet. But the light, even the blackest darkness cannot absorb the light, it cannot overcome the Truth. The light will always be able to push the darkness away. With the light, the darkness is nothing."

"I do not want to follow the path of evil," Win said softly. "I do not want to have anything to do with it. Yet I feel I am in its grip."

"Evil is like a climbing weed, it must have something to cling to. To what does it cling? To the cravings, the temptations. And the longer it is allowed to hold on, the stronger it becomes. Evil seeks to create chaos and terror, constructing an oblivion which will hide the Truth. But evil can be cast off, for it has no true root, it is nothing like the Truth, which is the root of all things."

"I hear what you say," said Win. "But how does this help me? I still do not know what decision to make. I still feel the fear, the pain, and am terrified of the evil."

"Evil may seem real, but it is not true," said Jesus. "It can cloak itself in beauty, it can masquerade as something bright, but that does not make it real. You cannot ignore evil in any form, you must face it and overcome it, but you can only do that from inner strength, from knowing the Truth. Once overcome, evil will show its true self, its hollowness, and you will pass beyond it.

"Just as you might awake at night from a frightful sound, imagining all forms of phantoms and terrors, only to turn on a light and find nothing but a branch scraping against the window, so too does the light of Truth illuminate and thus erase the evil. For evil has no substance in the light of truth; it's promises are but illusions, fictions, impossibilities in the light."

"So will understanding the Truth help me make the right choice between Sooni and Aralyn?" Win was hopeful. Perhaps there *was* a way out.

Jesus smiled and effortlessly dropped off the wall, making not a sound. "As I said, you have come very far in your search. You begin to understand what you truly seek, something to guide you in the choices which make up who you are and who you will become. I can show you the way to the Truth which will help you make these choices."

Win hoped Jesus would take him somewhere, or tell him more. But Jesus simply waited. Win felt overwhelmed, desperate. "But why do I still feel this way? I do not understand how I will find the Truth which will guide me in this choice."

Jesus said, "You still accept the choices that you have been presented. Who has told you those are your choices? You say you want nothing to do with evil, yet you let evil define your decisions? There are only two paths, what you will do, and what you will not do. If you understand the lessons you have been shown, you will know what to do."

"But this choice I have, I cannot see how I can reject it. There is death in both choices!"

"Death comes not with the final breath. True death comes when one cannot even accept that the Truth is what is real, that the Truth is what is everlasting. And before you can recognize the Truth, of what lies beyond, of what may be the outcome of your choices, first you must recognize the Truth of what is right before you."

"But I have seen what evil can do, what Beros can do, or lead others to do," argued Win. "I can't take the chance that what I have seen is not real. I have seen too many people die already."

"Tell me, then," said Jesus. "What do you see in the choice you think you have to make?"

"I see pain and loss. I see death."

"Are these truths?"

"If Beros is showing me what is really happening, I believe Aralyn might die. She might already be dead."

"That has not happened," said Jesus. "For if it had, you would not be faced with a choice."

"Can *you* save her?" asked Win.

"Is that what you would have me do? Save everyone? Keep everyone from dying? Bring loved ones back from the dead?"

"You mean Sooni."

"You did not answer my question. What is the truth in the choice you feel you face?" Jesus waited calmly, as if Win had all the time in the world to answer.

"If Aralyn dies, I will not be able to forgive myself, because I might have been able to help her. But if I lose Sooni again, after being this close, if I miss this one chance to be with her, I will fall further than I have already fallen. I don't know how I can go on living. But now I can rescue her, and travel with her beyond the physical to another place, where she can be what she was. I have a chance to make it happen—to fix my mistakes. To have it all made right."

"So this is your truth? You fear making a choice that will make you feel either guilty or sad?"

"No! I fear that Aralyn will die, and what was Sooni will be lost for all eternity, that she will be under the spell of evil!"

Jesus shook his head. "You use this truth as a way of justifying the actions you wish to take, which instead seem to be for you, to make *you* feel better. Tell me, do you make the choice for yourself or for them?"

"For them!"

"Now you have come to the heart of it," said Jesus. "What sacrifice will you make? Tell me truly."

"I would give up anything to save both of them!"

"Except your doubt," said Jesus.

The words slammed into Win, turning everything around, shifting the focus and the definition of his choices. A way of looking at his challenge that he had not even considered, the implications too profound for him to immediately grasp.

"You strive for certainty in an uncertain universe. Remember what I told you on K'Turia. Often there is no solid bridge for the crossing of the chasm. Sometimes you must simply have faith that you will take the right step into the unknown, because someone will be there to reach out to you, to help you."

"But that is why I have come all this way! To learn these things from you, so that I can be at peace," said Win.

"You have pursued me, but you have not accompanied me. You do not yet walk in my footsteps, or understand the Truth so that you can make the choices and sacrifices you need to, for the right reasons. You see what is right in front of you, yet you deny the Truth within you. You do not accept what you have been shown, what you already know."

"I have learned so much," said Win. "And yet I still feel trapped."

"You think you have to sacrifice either Sooni or Aralyn," said Jesus. "But instead, you have to sacrifice *your* wants, *your* desires. Only when you have sacrificed everything you want will you understand the Truth, for only the Truth will remain. Then the right choices will be as bright as day."

Win felt his doubts rise up. "I still don't know if I am strong enough."

Jesus pointed to a section of the wall. Slowly the stones darkened, the mortar became visible, and cracks began to appear, a ripping sound tearing at the harmony of the stone. "Chaos begins when the evil of the world exceeds the belief that it can be conquered. Tell me, Trebor Win, what Truth do you believe?"

Win watched the wall start to crumble, the shadow spreading over the stone, edging out, grabbing at the sheer beauty of the wall, threatening its strength. The wall of protection, of faith. The power to breach the abyss, to overcome the adversity.

He thought of Prentiss, staying behind on K'Turia at great risk, because she believed in Jesus. Of Varshan, who died believing he could save others. Of Aralyn, seeking the Truth that would lead to peace on her planet. They all believed something they could not see, something without proof.

"That there is a power in belief itself," said Win, suddenly understanding. Not all of the Truth perhaps, but what he needed to understand. "That I must have faith that I can do the right thing."

Jesus smiled, and swept his arm toward the assaulted wall. Slowly but surely the edges of the darkness began to retreat, the stones reforming into their seamless mass, the ripping sound muted until it was no more, and once again the wall stood as before, no, even higher and stronger than before. Not a hint of darkness remained.

Jesus turned to Win. "Now go, and let not faith slip to hope."

CHAPTER 26

BITTER RAINDROPS SPLATTERED WIN'S FACE, cold hard pavement beneath him. He was lying in the street, the dark gray sky once again overhead. He lurched to his feet, spinning around, the memory of Beros slamming into him.

But the street was deserted, the wind whipping through the empty buildings, pushing him toward where Sooni had gone. He fought to hold his place, knowing he needed to move, to make his decision, but not wanting to be forced.

He thought he understood what Jesus had told him, that he should not let Beros define his choices, the choices that made him who he was. Yet he still could not see how to escape the trap Beros has set for him. He was certain that Aralyn would die if he did not save her. And he was also certain that he would be ending his life as he knew it if he did not follow Sooni. She was dead in a physical sense, he knew that, but he had also dedicated much of his life, as did all his people, to the search for the everlasting, confident in a belief that the physical body was just a temporary aspect of life. That there was an everlasting soul, bound up in the infinite universe, a being that needed no body.

He never imagined that it would be Beros who would offer him the way to that everlasting life. How could one as evil as Beros be the means to such immortality?

The wind strengthened, pushing him forward, farther into the city, closer to Sooni. Pushing him to make a choice.

Win did not like being pushed, he never had. Yet his own choices had brought him here, had put him into Beros's trap. Win had chosen to come to this planet, and that is how he had met Aralyn. And he had chosen to run from his pain, to live a life of despair, and that is what made him susceptible to the temptation of getting Sooni back.

His own choices had not helped him. He thought he had been willing to face some difficult decisions, but now things seemed worse than ever. Maybe he should just once go with the easy path and see where it took him. Allow himself to just mindlessly float along.

The wind gave him another shove, and he let himself go, taking a step, and then another. It was so easy.

Getting Sooni back is what I have wanted since the day she died. This is what I have needed.

What *I have* wanted. What *I have* needed.

He froze, the stark reality staggering him. So obvious, yet so easy to ignore. It had all been about him. The sadness, the despair.

His wants and needs. Not Sooni's.

What did *she* want? He could not possibly know. Sooni had achieved her *ana*. What could he possibly give her that she needed? Who was he to say that she needed him at all?

It was Aralyn who needed him. He needed to help her, not because it would free him from guilt, but because she was in the grip of evil, she was in a danger she had not brought upon herself, a danger and a power she might not have the strength to overcome.

Facing this danger required not physical strength, but spiritual strength. It required faith.

Aralyn might not know to call for Jesus, to ask for that kind of help. Jesus' words came back to him: *'Do not wait; just because you do not know all the answers does not mean you cannot help others.'*

His wants and needs were not important, they should not be driving his decisions. And yet that is how he had lived his life since the loss of Sooni. That is how he had ended up in this dilemma, facing this impossible choice.

He had but to give up his own desires, his own selfish wants.

'Only when you have sacrificed everything you want will you accept the Truth, for only the Truth will remain. Then the right choices will seem as bright as day.'

Win turned into the wind, away from the false promise of the conjured Sooni, away from his wants. The wind pounded in his ears, the rain suffocating. Yet in the distance he thought he glimpsed an opening in the storm, a light in the darkness. He couldn't be sure.

But he could have faith.

He pushed into the rain, each step a battle. The wind kept trying to spin him about. If he turned, accepting the easy path, it would be so much easier.

Yet the easy paths had not helped him in the past. He had followed what he now knew was the counterfeit Sooni, a sham dangled in front of him that led him first to the underground ritual, which had threatened to engulf him, and then almost into the rocket falling on the rebels. Only Aralyn had saved him from that. And again, when the black fog had tried to push him down the street which would have led them right into the arms of the soldiers.

The other paths he had chosen had been hard. The decision to come to Carthlana. The decision to follow the other Sooni, surely not one created by Beros, to help Varshan.

These other paths, the hard ones, had brought him to where he needed to be. To learn the lessons that he had been too blind and unable to learn on his own. Lessons that he could only understand when they surrounded him with intense, stark reality. The loss of Varshan's daughter. Varshan's unnecessary and misplaced guilt, so like Win's. The useless anger of Listra.

He took another step, forcing himself into the wind. It took so much energy that he didn't have the strength to look up, to face the wind head on, to look for the light ahead.

But he had faith it would be there.

* * *

Win struggled on, one step at a time, the wind and rain unrelenting, his clothing smothering him.

Behind him came a call, his name carrying over the wind, in that one word a whole message of promise. Sooni's voice, recognizable even over the tumult. He ignored it as best he could, the sound tugging at him, promising him relief.

Another step, and then he felt an arm on him, spinning him around, bringing him face to face with Sooni.

"This way!" she said, her eyes bright. "We can escape together!"

The rain did nothing to mar her radiance, to take away from her beauty. Win felt a huge hole in his stomach, a pain of emptiness and longing. She was back.

"Escape to where?" he asked.

"Where we always wanted to be. Together. Forever."

"It would not be real!" Win cried. "You want me to join you in some forged imaginary world. I've already been living in a world like that, a world of hopes and dreams. That's not reality. I can't do that anymore."

She reached for his hands. "You can! Who cares how we get there? We're being given this great gift, why won't you take it?"

Win suddenly felt sadder than he ever had in his life, sadder even than when Sooni had died. The Sooni he knew would never say such a thing, would never take a gift from evil, no matter how beautiful.

"Who are you?" he said, each word a dagger thrust into his own image of the Sooni he was trying to recreate.

Her eyes reached out to him with promise. "I am everything you want."

It was what Win feared she would say, erasing his last vestige of doubt. He pulled his hands away. "And that is why I must let you go."

He turned away, pushing into the wind, and did not look back even as she cried out his name.

* * *

Debris flew by Win's head as he ran down the street back toward the park. He did not know if he still had a chance to save Aralyn. But he had to try.

A building toppled into the street just in front of him, and he barely had time to take cover from the cascading walls. He pushed on, scrambling over the shattered remains, dodging everything in his path.

One by one the buildings fell, crashing in his path, as if trying to stop him. Without thinking about it, just knowing he had to believe he could make it, he kept running, believing he would somehow find a safe path.

The last building on the left fell, the broken bits billowing up into the air to create a massive cloud, blocking his vision.

The wind swept aside the smoke, revealing Tu Vos's house, unblemished, standing strong, amazingly unfazed by the maelstrom, even its glass intact.

Win ran through the park, most of the people gone, a few tents tied down tight against the wind. The gravel lane was flooded, the water grabbing at his legs as he splashed through, past the overflowing reflecting pool.

He almost got lost in the industrial area, the buildings all looking alike in the rain. He started to panic, the vision of Aralyn struggling in the water, the water certainly rising with all this rain.

Then he was at the water storage area, a series of covered holding tanks, cisterns fed from the canals. They all looked the same, and he could not match it with the vision Beros had shown him. Which one was Aralyn in?

He ran up to the first tank, the top just out of reach. There was a small gap between the top of the tank wall and the cover, perhaps an emergency opening to let the water out in case of an overflow. But it was a mere sliver, not enough to escape from, not enough to allow someone to breath even if they managed to keep their heads above the water. Win remembered Aralyn's fear of closed spaces, and knew she must be suffering.

"Aralyn!" His voice was swallowed by the rain.

He climbed up on the pipe which fed water to the tank. The slit at the top of the wall was just out of reach. He leapt, fingers grabbing for the crack, missed, falling to the ground. He climbed the pipe again, the metal slippery. This time he managed to catch the lip, pulling himself up to the opening, the pain in his arms excruciating. A mossy smell of mold filled his lungs. He could see nothing in the darkness of the tank.

"Aralyn!"

He held on as long as he could, then fell back down, smashing into the pipe and falling painfully. He staggered to his feet. There had to be a way to get into the tank! He ran around it, but it was solid. The opening must be on the top.

Could he shut off the water? The pipe ran through a wheel valve. He pulled at the valve but it would not budge. Frustrated, he ran to the next tank.

"Help! Help!"

A woman's voice, blown by the wind. Or was he imagining it?

It came again, from another cistern, muffled yet full of fear.

"Aralyn!"

He ran to the tank. The plumbing was more complex, pipes coming in and out. He climbed, able to get much higher, enough to look into the slit at the top of the wall without jumping. He put his lips to the crack.

"Aralyn! Are you there?"

"Yes, yes, please help me," she was crying, the panic clear in her voice, floating in the darkness. "I don't have much room left . . ."

Win looked around frantically, trying to figure out a way to get her out. "Hold on!" He grabbed the edge of the lid and swung his leg onto the top of the tank, then struggled upright, fighting to stand in the wind. In the middle of the tank cover was a door with a metal ring. He grabbed the ring and pulled, but it didn't move, the cover was much too heavy. He heaved, with no effect.

He stuck his head over the edge, his face at the slit. "Aralyn, I have to go find something to get the cover off." Trying to keep his voice calm.

"Don't leave me!"

"I'll be right back, I promise."

He dropped to the ground, thinking there must be some tool to open the covers. He circled around the tanks, finding nothing; half the ground was covered with water. He ran back toward the storage buildings. Next to a shed he found a stack of long heavy cylindrical rods and grabbed one, hefting it across his shoulder, racing back to the tank with all the pipes.

Just before he reached it he heard her voice again, pleading for him. But the sound seemed to come from a different direction.

He stopped, perplexed. Did he forget which tank she was in? Then the voice again, unmistakably coming from his left, from a tank with only one pipe, like the first tank he had climbed.

He closed his eyes, trying to remember. Had he become confused?

"Win!" This time it was from the tank right in front of him, the one where Aralyn was. But then the voice again, from the other tank, calling him. Two voices.

Two Aralyns.

* * *

"No!" Win screamed, not at Aralyn, but at everything, at the choice he had to make, at the universe. For a heartbeat he froze, the voices pulling at him from two different directions. Another choice, forced upon him.

He stood there in the rain, somehow knowing that a wrong choice would be the death of Aralyn.

On one side, the tank from which he had first heard her voice, filled with fear, clutching at him. On the other side, a mere hint of what might be, only a voice calling to him.

A stream of water cascaded from the slit in the cistern in front of him, running down the side of the tank. Win spun around; water was escaping from the other tank as well. Both were almost full. The rising water would crush Aralyn against the top.

The tank with the one pipe would be hard to climb. He would have to blindly throw the bar onto the top, hoping it did not roll off, and then pull himself up by only the strength of his arms.

The other tank with the extra pipes would be easier since he had been able to reach the top; he could place the bar on the lid and easily climb up again.

The easy path.

"Win, help me! I'm going to die!" The voice frantic, pleading.

Suddenly he smiled, a ray of relief overcoming his panic. The answer, as Jesus had kept trying to tell him, over and over, was right in front of him.

The easy way was so tempting. It was not a difficult choice, it was a false choice. It was something to fall into, an excuse. It was a choice defined by someone else.

The hard way, the way that seemed impossible, that was his challenge, his roadblock. His rejection of the temptation.

A choice that he would define. His options.

His choice.

He turned toward the tank with the single pipe, knowing in his heart it was the right one. Leaning the bar against the wall, he climbed up, struggling with the wet surface. Balancing precariously, he grasped the heavy bar and pushed it over his head onto the lid. With a deep breath, he leapt up, his eyes blinded by the rain, reaching out with his fingers for the handhold he could not see, trusting. With a strength he didn't know he had, he pulled himself up onto the top of the tank.

He slid the bar into the iron ring and levered open the door. Reaching down into the water, he grabbed Aralyn's outstretched hand and lifted her up out of the darkness.

CHAPTER 27

THE REFLECTING POOL WAS COMPLETELY STILL, sharply mirroring the bright blue sky. The gray stormy clouds had only been gone a short time, but they were a distant memory, completely overtaken by the warm bright sun.

Win set Aralyn down on a bench by the reflecting pool. He had half carried her from the water tanks, and after her ordeal and the challenge of getting her down she could barely walk. Other than to find out if she was harmed, Win did not try to talk to her on the way, she seemed so weak.

A few people milled about the reflecting pool, and many more were arriving. Win hurried off to the fountain, found a ladle, and brought some water to Aralyn, but she shook her head.

"I swallowed too much already," she said, coughing.

"We should get you to a doctor," said Win.

"I'm fine. I mean, I'm really tired, but I think I'm okay." She held out her arms, splattered with muck. "I could use a bath, but I don't want to be in water for a while." She tried to smile. "How did you find me?"

Win dabbed at her arms with his sleeve. "It's a long story. I'll tell you about it when you are feeling better." He looked around. "We need to get you some dry clothes. Maybe I can ask someone in the park; I met a few people."

"Don't leave me," she said, her lip quivering. "Please, not right now. The sun feels good, I'm warmer already."

"Okay." He sat down on the ground next to the bench. "What happened to you? If you feel up to talking about it."

"I don't know. The last thing I remember was watching you from across the street near the data center. You were running toward Listra. I saw someone else coming from across the plaza. Then a flash of light, and the explosion. I don't remember anything after that until I woke up in that tank. The water started to come up so fast. I couldn't get out. I started to panic, I hate small spaces . . ." Her voice grew distant, and she started to cry.

Win touched her hand. "Shh. Don't think about it. I'm sorry I asked."

She shook her head, still crying. "It's okay. I—I was so afraid. I've always been afraid of dying that way, trapped in a small space."

"You're safe now," said Win. And though there would be challenges, he believed she would be. And he would be safe too. The sun was shining, the cold wind and rain were gone. Tired and hungry as he was, he felt better than he had in years. His mind had awakened from a long dullness. His heart still ached for Sooni, but he knew he had made the right choice.

It would not be easy, making the choices that would keep him on the right path. There would always be the temptations. But now it was clear to him that sometimes the choices that seemed to have no answer came about simply because of how one looked at them. Jesus was right. He could not, he would not, let Beros or anyone determine his choices, his path. His life.

"I want to sit up," said Aralyn. "Can you help me?"

Win helped her up. She raised her face to the sun, her eyes closed. "That feels better already," she said.

Win waited, basking in the warmth, feeling the light renew him. It seemed forever since he had had a chance to just rest.

After a while Aralyn opened her eyes and looked around. "Where are we?"

"Just at the edge of the city. There's a big park over on the other side of the pool, where those trees are. A lot of people camped there during the fighting that broke out after the attack."

"You mean the bombing? That was the explosion?"

"Yes. But something strange happened. The man you saw on the plaza, that was Varshan. He stopped Listra from getting inside the barracks. He muffled the bomb with his body." Win took a deep breath. "He saved my life. And many others, I'm sure."

"Why would he do that? He was a rebel too."

Win was thinking about what Jesus had taught about sacrifice. On K'Turia, he thought he had understood, he thought it had to do with giving up material things. But that was just part of it. Listra, overcome with anger, so susceptible to evil. Making the wrong kind of sacrifice. "I think Varshan didn't want to see any more needless killing, especially killing driven by hatred."

"What good did it do? You said there was more fighting after the explosion."

"There was a rebel uprising. Maybe Kesh and his group, and probably others who were already here. The soldiers cracked down on them hard."

"Then Varshan wasted his life," said Aralyn. "And what about his son Breal? What happened to him?"

"I don't know," said Win. "When you are feeling better I'd like to go look for him. He may still be back in Devatus. Although I don't think Varshan would have left him."

Aralyn was silent for a moment. "You think he saw his father die?"

"I hope not. I didn't see Breal anywhere around. Maybe Varshan left him with someone. Varshan probably didn't know what he was going to do when he came here. Maybe he just came with the rebels as part of the attack, and changed his mind when he saw what Listra was planning." Win was thinking about the bright light just before the explosion. Maybe something had opened Varshan's eyes to the true horror that was before him. A light, illuminating the Truth, giving him guidance and strength.

For a while they sat quietly, soaking in the sun. The area

around the pool was quiet, the others there silently taking advantage of the respite from the fighting and the rain.

"I'm hungry," said Aralyn. She reached into her pockets. Instead of food she pulled out the recorder. "I thought I had a few food bars. They must have fallen out in the tank." She looked at the recorder, playing with it aimlessly in her hands. "I can't believe I still have this."

The recorder came on. Not the voice of Jesus, but a radio transmission, a news broadcast. *". . . head of the old civilian government authorities, has replaced the Chief of the Army Forces. The government has also announced that it is declaring an immediate cease fire and has reached out to the various rebel factions to discuss a possible peace agreement, with an invitation for the rebels to be part of a new democratic process. Already there are reports of both soldiers and rebels in some cities laying down their arms. We will bring you more details as soon as they become available."*

A great shout went up from the direction of the park. Aralyn looked up at Win. "I don't understand. Does this mean the war is over? It can't be that easy."

Win was smiling. "It won't be. But I think some people are starting to make the right choices."

* * *

The people around the reflecting pool began heading back into the park, where the sound of jubilant cries filled the air. Soon the area was empty except for Win, Aralyn, and a small figure on the other side of the pool, facing toward the park, looking forlorn even from the back. A child.

"I don't know how to thank you," said Aralyn. "You saved my life."

Win shrugged. "Well, you saved mine, too."

Aralyn was looking at the child across the water. "I was just like that a few days ago. Lost. You found me."

"In fact, you were the one who found me," said Win.

"I guess we found each other. Before I met you I had nothing. I was just surviving. I didn't think much about the future, just each day. There was nothing to hope for. I had this," she held up the recorder, "but I didn't understand the message, what Jesus was saying. I'm not sure I understand all of it yet, but you helped me see. You helped me get past the words to the meaning."

"You were angry," said Win. "I have been angry too. It's hard to get past it. It's hard to even think straight when you are angry."

She looked up at him, her eyes a mixture of hope and fear. "You're going to leave, aren't you?"

"When it's time."

"Will you go home?"

Win looked up, thinking about his birth planet Treb, where he had lived with Sooni. About other places he had been, about where he had been living before coming here. Where was home now? Whatever he had on Treb was gone. Or still with him. It just depended on how he thought about it.

"I'm not sure. Probably."

"Should I keep looking for Jesus?"

"What do you think?" asked Win.

"I wanted to find him to see if he would be the one to help bring peace. It looks like we might get that."

"There might be other reasons to keep looking for him," said Win. "Maybe Jesus can guide you."

"I'm not sure I'd be able to understand him without you."

Win smiled. "Think about the recordings, how they helped us to decide what to do next. How they seemed like they were made just for us, when we needed them. Remember what I told you. The great power of Jesus is that whenever he speaks, it is as if he is talking just to you. All you have to do is listen."

Aralyn nodded. "Sometimes it's hard to really understand what is right in front of you, isn't it?"

The child across the pool turned. A little boy, his facing breaking into a smile when he saw Win and Aralyn. He ran around the pool and threw his arms around Win's waist.

"Hello, Breal," said Win. "We were just about to come looking for you."

Breal looked up at Win. "My father told me that if we got separated I should come to the reflecting pool. I had to ask someone where it was." His eyes filled up with tears. "I can't find my father."

Win knelt down and hugged the boy. He didn't know what to say.

"He's dead too, isn't he?" whispered Breal. "That's why he isn't here."

"Your father was very brave," said Win, as gently as he could. "He saved many people."

"Why did he leave me?" The boy's body wracked with sobs.

"He was thinking about your future," said Win. "He was trying to make things better for you, for a lot of people."

"Why did he have to do it? Why couldn't someone else?"

Win held the boy tight. "He was doing what he could. Everyone has to do what they can."

"I miss him! I want him back!"

Win fought to keep from breaking down, understanding this sadness, this longing. "You will always miss him. I won't lie to you. That will never go away. You can't have him back, not in the way you want. But that doesn't mean he won't always be with you." Sooni's love washed over his sadness, cradling him with warmth.

"I lost my parents too," said Aralyn, kneeling next to the boy.

Breal looked up at her. "You did?"

"Yes. They died in the war. I miss them, a lot. But I try to remember the times when we were happy." She looked away, wistful. The sound of singing came from the park. "Maybe things will be better now. Your father said you had stayed with relatives?"

"My aunt and uncle," said Breal. "In Devatus."

Aralyn looked at Win. "We'll bring you there." It wasn't a question. She stood up, a little unsteady. "First, let's see if we can get you something to eat. Maybe all those happy people in the park will share some food."

Before they had a chance to move Win heard his name being called. He looked across the pool and there was Miera, walking toward them with her spry step.

"I've been looking for you," she said as she approached. Miera stood in front of Aralyn, hands on her hips. "So. Is this the friend you were looking for? Aralyn?"

"Yes it is," said Win. "And the boy is Breal."

"You seem to have a knack for meeting people, offworlder Win," said Miera. "Is everyone so friendly where you come from?"

Win considered. "I think connected is a better word," he said. "Everyone feels connected." Even, he thought, when they were not together.

"We heard something about a cease fire?" asked Aralyn.

"Yes," said Miera. "It seems that the civilian leaders have been fighting amongst themselves, trying to decide between opening up to the rebels or cracking down more. A group of them were arriving in the city just as the attack started. They saw one of the rebels give himself up to stop another rebel from killing soldiers with a suicide bomb. It made some in the government think there was hope for a peace, that the rebels didn't want to just kill. It was enough to turn the tide toward reaching out to the rebels." She reached into her pocket and handed Breal a piece of candy. "Amazing, isn't it? If they hadn't been there at that time, maybe we would not have this chance for peace."

Win considered how that chance had come about. Someone seeing Varshan giving himself up, an unmistakable example of a sacrifice for peace, a rejection of hatred. He could not bring himself to think that Listra's actions had contributed to the chance for peace, for hers was a choice of evil. But Varshan's reaction—Varshan's decision—had lit the spark of hope.

A choice of a single person, coming about after a long connected series of other decisions, by many people. Leading off into a nexus of even more choices. Choices that could have gone many ways.

Win smiled, knowing he had just learned yet another lesson.

"What are you thinking?" asked Aralyn.

"I was just thinking about how everything is connected here as well," Win replied. People making the right choices, one at a time, each separately, but they all added up, they all came together. Choices of sacrifice, choices rejecting anger, rejecting hatred, forging a path toward . . . he could not define it. Perhaps a different kind of enlightenment, not just for one, but for all.

"Could we get Breal a decent meal?" asked Aralyn. "And me too."

"There's plenty in the park," said Miera. "A lot of people came back after the rain stopped, and while I'm sure everyone wants to get home, I think the celebrating will go on for a while. And you look a bit disheveled. I can help get you cleaned up. Come on."

"I'll be along in a bit," said Win.

Miera squinted at him. "You aren't going to disappear again, are you?"

"No," said Win, laughing. He couldn't remember the last time he had really laughed with joy. "I just need a few moments. I'll find you, I promise."

* * *

Win closed his eyes, breathing deeply, feeling oddly refreshed. The melodic swish of the water in the fountain melded with the air to form a whispered peacefulness. When he was younger, he had always been astonished at the beauty of the universe inherent in the small things, the sound of a single bird singing, the rustle of the wind through fallen leaves, the exquisite calm of meditation. The connection between all things, so central to the Treb way of life.

He had been blind to much of that during the years since

Sooni's death. Certainly the wonder was still there, but he did not notice it, he did not want to notice it. Yet here, even in the simple reflection of the pure blue sky in the reflecting pool, he could once again see the beauty all around him.

And the connections. He watched his three new friends walk along the path toward the park. Another connection forged, a connection that had brought two orphans together. He had no doubt that Aralyn would be a great help to Breal. And though she had not yet found Jesus, through some amazing series of coincidences, the peace she longed for might be at hand.

Or perhaps they were not coincidences after all. Everyone had made choices, the choices that had led to what had happened, what was happening, and ultimately, what would happen. Who could say what might have transpired if a single choice had been different? What terrible things might happen if just one person makes a wrong choice, a choice influenced by evil?

Listra had made a choice to kill. And Varshan had made a choice to save. Both choices led to pain, and loss, and taken together, the outcome was different than either had expected. But Varshan's choice of sacrifice had led to something larger, something better.

Win had made his own choices, choices that led him to where he was now, not just physically but emotionally and spiritually. He had never before considered that these choices could be so connected, that where he decided to go could affect what he would become. That how he decided to think about things could end up leading him physically to a certain place.

For certainly his reactions, and his decisions after Sooni's death, had brought him here, to this very place. His sadness and guilt had caused him to join the Science Corps. His search for inner peace had opened him to the words of Jesus, and had led him to search for Jesus. His choices, the totality of who he was, and much of what he had learned—especially from Jesus—had allowed him to confront evil and then make the decisions that saved Aralyn.

And perhaps himself.

Win opened his eyes. He was alone. Everyone had gone off to the park to join in the celebration. A soft breeze blew, the surface of the reflecting pool glimmering, yet somehow the reflections still distinct.

He looked down into the pool, thinking of the crush of water that had threatened to kill Aralyn. Here the movement of the water was gentle, yet this water had the potential for great power. He couldn't control how that power would be unleashed or whether it would be used for good or bad, yet he, and others, in the choices they made, could impact whether the spiritual powers of good and evil would thrive.

The water stilled, peaceful now, but with the promise of great power. Everything grew silent, as if waiting for something to happen. For Win to decide who he would turn to, who his mind would seek out.

Win smiled. This decision, at least, was easy. Win pictured Jesus in his mind, watching over Win, silent, yet filled with an immeasurable hidden power. The water began to vibrate, as if it could no longer contain the energy within, the energy of Jesus. Win felt himself resonate with it, receptive.

The water turned to shimmering ripples which eddied and spun, forming into the image of Varshan, standing next to Win in the reflection.

Win heard Varshan's voice. "Why does pain lead to guilt? It is because we confuse that which we can change and that which we cannot. If something brings us pain, or pain to one we love, our inability to do something about it, or prevent it, makes us feel inadequate. This is why to be at peace we must fully understand ourselves—we must understand what we can and should change about ourselves, and accept that there are things we simply cannot change. Guilt is an excuse for focusing on something we cannot change instead of facing the challenges ahead of us and within us."

Win turned. There was no one beside him. Only the image in

the water, a reflection of nothing other than Win, Varshan's words a reflection of Win's guilt.

"I see that now," said Win. He needed to voice his thoughts, his understanding. "I hid behind guilt. It kept me from healing. Is that why you did what you did? Because you felt guilty about not saving your daughter?"

Win wasn't sure if Varshan would be able to hear him, not sure at all if this wasn't just some trick of his own mind. After his time here, who could say what was real and what was not? Or what was a message from another power, a higher power, a message that, though heard only in his head, was just as real as someone he could touch?

"Some blame others in order to hide their own faults," said Varshan. "Others blame themselves when someone else has done wrong, or even when no one is at fault. All because of the fear of reality, the fear of what they might learn of themselves. Yet you cannot be at peace with yourself or your neighbor without first knowing yourself. Guilt is a heavy curtain around your true self. You cannot know why you do what you do, or what you should do, if you are shrouded in guilt. Guilt is a false protection against facing your own anger, and as long as guilt remains, you will never be able to move past your anger to achieve understanding and be able to move forward."

Varshan was talking about the need to know oneself. Win thought he had, even before K'Turia; his whole life had been a search for *ana,* and the first step on that journey was to know oneself. Yet knowing himself when times were good was one thing. He had never really been tested. Even the challenge of the Great Meet, the final test of *ana*, had not prepared him for the pain of loss and for confronting the force and form of evil.

Varshan continued, "Guilt leads to a spiritual barrier. It makes us retreat within ourselves, pulling a shroud around our emotions and our minds. We think we do this out of self defense, that the shroud is a shield, protecting us from harm and pain and evil in the world. Yet such a curtain cannot be selective; it will not let in the joy and beauty either. It will not keep us from being unhappy. And just as we are filtering what comes in, so to are we hindering the power we have to bring our gifts to others."

Win knew he had blamed himself, even though no one was at fault for Sooni's death. He had been adrift, not able to make even the simplest of decisions on K'Turia, because of the shroud that guilt had placed over him—the shroud that he had *let* guilt place over him. His choice. That was the lesson in what Varshan was telling him. Win had let the guilt blind him, had let himself focus on the past, on something he could not change. All his emotional energy sucked up by guilt and sadness and despair, leaving him no energy, sapping even his spiritual being.

The image of Varshan began to fade, the water churning briefly, muddied, then forming into the body of Listra.

"Anger is something everyone feels," said Listra. "Yet what we do with that anger is a choice. The easy path is to fall into anger, to be led by it, to be controlled by it. Once this path is taken, it becomes easier every time. Yet if anger is seen as a temptation and a threat, then it is possible to understand what is at work, the evil that causes not the anger, but how one deals with it. Each time this temptation is resisted it weakens the next threat. It may not keep you from being angry, but it will help you build the kind of energy you need to make the right decisions, to forgive, to be at peace."

"Some things are hard to forgive," said Win.

"Lashing out with your anger is easy. Letting anger swallow your energy is easy. Forgiving is difficult. I could not do it. I had energy, but I used it to cause pain instead of using it to give me the strength to forgive. Just as you have seen the connection between the spiritual word and the physical world, so too is there a connection between the spiritual and the emotional. Your spiritual strength can help you overcome the evils of being led by anger."

"Is that what happened to you?"

"The anger of my loss overwhelmed me. I was weak, but did not see that. I thought I was strong because I made the decision to act. Being strong is not merely doing *something,* it is doing the right thing."

Win had never really thought of himself as angry, even after Sooni's death. And yet he *had* been angry, at what he thought of as the unfairness of the universe. At the people who could not save Sooni. At the people who told him he could not go and find Prentiss. And at himself, for letting himself be so overcome with his sadness that he had lost years of his life wandering both physically and spiritually. What might he have been able to accomplish if he had not wasted those years? Who might he have helped?

The pool resonated again, the image of Listra absorbed. The vibrations were steady, harmonious, giving off no sense of judgment. The water cleared, still resonating with the vibration that touched Win to the core, strengthening, and now Win saw Tekton, the man who had been rebuilding the house. As before, Win had a hard time seeing his face; the water shifted to and fro, yet the movement was soft and peaceful.

"Just as bombs can destroy the physical, so too can the spirit be challenged by malevolent forces," said Tekton. "And just as the physical can be rebuilt, so too can the spiritual. It can be made ever strong, a foundation of protective understanding that allows you to stay in one place yet move ahead. Your decisions brought you to where you needed to be, both physically and spiritually. You have seen how you can make decisions that allow you to move past your troubles, not to forget your pain, but to move ahead with your life."

Win remembered Tekton rebuilding the wall, explaining to him how to move on, and for a moment Win saw himself, not Tekton, as the mason, a reflection within a reflection.

"And so I must let go of Sooni," said Win, not sure how he felt about that, not sure even now that he could do that.

"Letting go is not the same as forgetting," said Tekton. "What do you think you are letting go of? What you must really let go of is what you have allowed her loss to do to you. What would you rather have held in your heart, the joy she brought you or the sadness of her loss?"

"The joy, of course," said Win. He thought of Aralyn and Breal. Would he want them to live their lives overwhelmed with the sadness over their losses? Somehow it was easier to know the right answer for others than it was to take the lesson to his own heart.

The image of Tekton swirled and began to fade.

"Wait!" said Win. "I understand that the Sooni who kept leading me into danger was my temptation. But the other Sooni seemed to be trying to help me."

"If you could not see the truth in what is visible to you, how could you know the truth of the unknown?" said Tekton, as his image disappeared.

The water stilled, the reflection so pure that Win felt he could have walked into it. And within the perfection was the image of Jesus.

"Temptations of the world come in many forms," said Jesus. "Some are horrors, as you have seen. Yet others are hidden behind what you want, excuses you allow yourself to create. The Sooni you followed into danger was a conjuring of evil born of your overwhelming craving for her. The other Sooni, the one who led you to where you needed to be—you can think of her as a guide. She was not real, but her love, and the impact she has had on you, are real. And what is also real is what you have now, your friends, your search for the Truth. Your faith. The events here served as the catalyst which forced you to choose. Once you made the right choices, the illusions fell away."

"You spoke often of faith on K'Turia," said Win. "I did not really understand."

"Words are not always enough, even my words. You had to see these lessons, not just be told. The lesson of your temptations, of the decisions you had made."

"Is this true for everyone?" asked Win. "They need to see something?"

Jesus shook his head. "Many look but do not see, others listen but do not understand. Only when they are open to the Truth can it be understood."

"Like Prentiss," said Win. "She always felt, even before she knew you, that there would be a savior, someone who would allow people to grow, to advance. As a scientist she was thinking of the physical, but later she saw that it was more, that the growth was of the spirit, not just the body."

Jesus said, "A savior is not one who lifts his hand and all the hardships in the world disappear. That is an illusionist, and anyone who promises that a falsehood. You have seen what such an illusionist can do. A savior teaches you to grow by knowing yourself, by being at peace, by doing what you can to help others. Even great conflicts can be overcome this way, one person at a time."

"Conflicts like war?" asked Win.

"And smaller ones. Conflicts are the challenges of life, the other side of beauty and joy. But there are also the conflicts brought about by the instigation of evil."

"I felt them, but did not understand where they came from," said Win.

"I am the Light for all to be able to see what was hidden in darkness. I have shown you what is real and what is not in your worldly journey, so that you may see it for what it is. And now you know how the Light of Truth can also empower you to face evil. For the Light must illuminate the Truth before it can empower, and only then can evil be overcome.

"Many want to know the one way to act, the one path. A simple, effortless way. The easy way. Such a path would not prepare you for the challenges of the world. It would not reveal the power of sacrifice, of giving. Just as every being is different, so too will each have their own temptations, their own choices. Everyone must navigate their own worldly and spiritual journeys. Some will understand this better than others. Yet no matter what I say, some will choose not to understand, or may struggle to understand."

Jesus smiled at Win, the smile of a loving parent to a child. "You are a vessel filled with my teachings and my love. Now you too can help others see. Just as you have helped Aralyn."

Win finally understood all of it, the Truth as clear as the pristine water. No one pulled all the strings of the universe, not Beros, not Jesus. It was up to him—and everyone—to decide how to act, what to do next. And if he needed help, Jesus would be there. Perhaps not physically, but in spirit.

Like everyone else, Win would face difficulties. The experiences of life in his worldly journey. People would get sick, they would have accidents, they would die. These were not the actions of evil, they were the realities of life. He would need to get through them. Sooni's death was one such reality.

The important thing was not what happened, but how one dealt with it. Sooni's death had overwhelmed him. He did not move ahead in his worldly journey or his spiritual one. If he could not handle something so basic to life as death in his worldly journey, how could he possibly progress on his much more difficult spiritual quest?

For certainly the spiritual journey would be much more difficult, for it required both avoiding the temptations of the corporal world, and also achieving inner peace. So the two journeys were continually connected, making the other harder—or easier.

"Are you real?" asked Win, not sure if he wanted to know the answer.

"That is for you to decide," said Jesus, smiling. "You see me now because you realize you did not need to find me to know me. The ultimate test of faith, and its ultimate power, is to believe in something greater, and to believe in it so much you do not have to actually see it.

"You saw me on K'Turia, you touched me. Yet you did not believe in me. Here, you have not touched me, yet you have heard my message. One does not need to see me in the flesh to believe in me, to follow me."

Jesus turned and began to walk away. Behind him came

Varshan and Tekton. Win felt as if he was watching himself, that it was he in the place of Tekton who was following Jesus.

And there was Sooni. She smiled, and somehow Win knew she was at peace, and had been at peace all along.

He watched her go, reaching out to her with his own feeling and spirit. He felt her return the touch, not from the image in the water, but from deep within, the mysterious somewhere of his soul. He embraced her, holding her in his heart even as he let her physical image walk away.

"Jesus!" called Win. "Where will you go?"

Jesus pointed, and another image appeared, crouched in sadness and uncertainty.

"Where I am needed, everywhere and forever," answered Jesus. And he held out his arms to Listra and embraced her, and Win could see the anger drain from her face as she let herself be taken up.

The images began to fade, but Win did not feel he was being abandoned. Instead, he somehow knew that as long as his heart and mind remained open to Jesus, Jesus would always be with him. No matter what happened, whatever challenges he would face, Jesus would be there, catching him when he stumbled, guiding him along the way.

And helping him do what needed to be done.

CHAPTER 28

THE MELODIC SPLASH OF THE FOUNTAIN merged with the gentle breeze through the water fronds. Win's senses so acute, so in touch with everything around him, that the sound amplified everything instead of masking it. He heard the rustle of an unseen bird, high overhead, the skate of a dragonfly on the water. The veil that had been upon him for years had been lifted, the cloud over his mind and body brushed away. He was alive again.

The fountain here in the garden of Na-Shay reminded him of the reflecting pool on Carthlana, and all he had seen within it. Those images too were as distinct now as they had been there, impossibly clear reflections of his lessons, of what he had been through, of what he still needed to achieve.

Certainly he had come a long way. Physically to K'Turia, and then to Carthlana, and now back home. Not to his home planet of Treb, he was not quite ready for that, but to where he had lived for the years of his military service when not aboard ship. Not his real home, yet the comfort he felt here in the gardens was proof of what he had long been told but had yet to really experience, that home was a state of mind, not a place.

And beyond the physical journey, he had traveled spiritually. He had started as a learner, a believer in the Treb search for enlightenment, a search for understanding, for knowledge of oneself, all with the goal of *ana*. Something else he had long been told, that *ana* was not a destination, but no matter how one tried to understand that, it was difficult to not think of *ana* as a goal when he didn't have it. It was hard to comprehend the concept of achieving a process.

Now he understood that even with all his years of study, his understanding of *ana* had been too limited. Or perhaps *ana* itself was. In either case the result was the same; there was more to enlightenment than just self awareness. And there were risks and challenges greater than he had ever imagined, there were temptations and adversities. There was evil.

He also understood how this might scare some away from the search, or lead to dismay, or abandonment, as it had for him. Now, reinvigorated, seeing how he had let himself be pushed in the wrong direction, he was determined to try again. He recognized he needed to make this decision not out of anger, anger at whoever or whatever force had led him astray, but out of his own desires, his own volition of what was right for him. Getting back on the path out of anger would have been an insidious succumbing to the same temptations. He would climb back on his spiritual horse and ride on, but he would do it for the right reason, one that was strong enough that it could not be twisted or taken from him.

His journey to enlightenment, or whatever one called it, was not to be a destination. It was not a point or a place, but a Way. Just as Jesus had been teaching on K'Turia. It was not a path to a place, it was a means to a path. An understanding of the importance not only of the path, but how one walked it. A belief that while there was always something ahead, the focus had to be on what was right here, right now, and the choices one made.

Taken together, those choices always led to something more, something else to do, more choices to make. People to help.

Some had the gifts to help physically, to cure, to protect. Others helped emotionally, to comfort, to mend.

But only now did he understand there was another purpose, another need. To help spiritually. To help others define their choices, face their decisions, to gain the strength to choose the right path, especially when evil tried to color the outcomes, to confuse, to disrupt.

Win's physical journey had mirrored his spiritual journey. He had been lost spiritually, just as he did not know where to go in the desert, searching for Jesus. He had been challenged physically with fire and assaults, emotionally with pain, and spiritually with temptation.

He had not been able to overcome these challenges by himself. Others had helped him. His friends, new and old, had been with him on his journey. I'Char, the followers of Jesus on K'Turia, Aralyn. All of them had guided him in their own way.

Yet it was Jesus who had shown him how to live again. Not only through his words, but through the lessons he awakened Win to. He would probably never know if Jesus had caused everything to happen on Carthlana in such a way that Win would learn the lessons he needed. Yet it was clear that what Win had experienced was exactly what he needed to see; no amount of words would ever have done it for him. He needed to be a part of it. He needed to see the futility of Varshan's guilt, the chaos and destruction caused by Listra's hate. He had to make the choice to turn away from the temptations of evil. Only then could he understand Tekton's message, of how to remain fast, yet move on.

Others, he thought, could perhaps learn the lessons they needed without having to be thrust into such harsh reality. They just had to open a door in their mind and in their heart, open themselves to the possibility of a greater power. His experience on K'Turia was proof. People could grow spiritually, and find the path, from hearing the guidance, from having faith that it was there. Certainly Prentiss had.

A familiar figure emerged from the trail across the gardens. Familiar in feel, if not in looks, for today I'Char had shifted his features into a pattern Win had never seen. Yet Win still knew who it was.

"Welcome back," said I'Char. He gave Win an appraising look. "You seem different."

"I am, although I at least look the same," said Win. "You, on the other hand, look different, yet seem the same."

"For me, the outside is easier to change than the inside," said I'Char.

"I think that is true for everyone," said Win. "Although I've just learned a lot about that." He knew I'Char did not like physical contact, but he reached out and briefly touched the Illian's arm. "I'm glad you got back safely."

I'Char nodded and looked out over the gardens. In some way Win felt more emotion in that subtle movement than he had ever sensed from I'Char. As usual, Win's Treb sense of *gheris* told him nothing about I'Char's mood.

"Then you'll be especially happy to hear that Prentiss is back as well," said I'Char. "At least for a while. She agreed to return with me only so she could get some good recording equipment to bring back to K'Turia to document Jesus."

"I'm surprised the League will let her go back," said Win.

"They won't," said I'Char. "But she'll go anyway, because they can't order her. They've cancelled her funding and thrown her out of the Science Corps." I'Char looked over at Win. "Along with us."

Win felt a weight pushing on him, a weight that not long ago might have crushed him back into despair. "I'm sorry I got you into this," he said.

"It was my decision. You didn't force me to do anything. No one can force me to do anything."

Win smiled. "I wish I had learned that lesson before going to Carthlana. It would have saved me a lot of trouble. How do you know these things?"

"How does one know anything? From experiences, from watching others. From thinking, seeing. There are things going on all the time to learn from."

"Like what is right in front of us," said Win. "That is something I learned. Remember how Jesus spoke about the Way, the path? I kept thinking it was this one thing, this one way. One set of rules. It is and it isn't. There are an endless number of ways different people can come upon what they need to learn in ways that are best suited for them. I've learned it's not about learning rules in order to achieve some state of perfection or some ultimate dream."

"It's not about living in the past either," said I'Char.

"You mean me? Yes, I was doing that. Now I understand that I can move on, and that doesn't mean giving up what I had. What I knew. Who I loved."

I'Char's eyes followed the flight of a solitary tane overhead, a rainbow of color against the clear sky. "I was talking about me, too."

Win watched the bird, flying higher and higher, an arrow toward the heavens. "You once told me that you had a purpose, a reason in life. Or a series of them. I always thought that my purpose was to achieve enlightenment, to be one with myself, and with the universe. Never thinking that something that seemed so—grand—could actually be quite self centered. I think I have another purpose now. A calling, if you will."

I'Char was still following the bird, or at least it looked that way, because the tane was well out of Win's sight. "Really? What is it?"

"It has a lot to do with what happened on Carthlana." Win gave up trying to see the tane. "You haven't asked me what happened there. If I found Jesus."

"I figured you would tell me when you wanted to. But I am curious. Did you?"

"Yes and no. It wasn't what I expected. I'll tell you all about it sometime, but the most important thing I discovered was that I could find Jesus without having to actually physically see him. Jesus, and everything he teaches, is both within me, and everywhere else at the same time. On K'Turia. On Carthlana. Here. And yet he is not necessarily physically in any one of those places. It seems like a paradox, but it makes sense. It means anyone can find him. They can look inward or outward, but it means nothing if there is no understanding. On K'Turia I stood in the same room as Jesus and thought I understood. But everything I've been through shows that I understood nothing then.

"We are all the same, no matter our race, what we look like, where we call home. Yet we are all different in what we must learn, how we can learn, and in what we must do to become enlightened. Everyone will have challenges that will lie along the way, things that will make it harder to see the truth. The pain that I felt from Sooni's death was my challenge, my suffering, but it is no different, or worse, than the challenges anyone else may face, the pain that anyone else may feel."

"And your purpose?"

"To help others who are willing to listen, who want to understand this. To help as many people as I can learn the lessons that matter, as I have. To present the teachings of Jesus as I understand them, to help give people the strength to avoid the temptations that I have had, to make the right choices. I believe this is my calling."

"Here?"

"Here, anywhere." Win gestured upward. "Wherever."

The soft breeze caressed the water in the pool, the ripple of water a breath of song. Then it stilled, becoming perfectly tranquil, an infinite reflection of the sky above.

"Do you want some company?" I'Char's voice a promise, a commitment.

Win was momentarily dumbfounded. "I didn't think you believed in—well, I just didn't think something like this was for you. I'm not even sure I know what I'm going to do next."

"Well, if you're planning a trip you'll need a ship. I can help with that, as a start."

Win didn't know what to say. "Thank you," he finally managed. "That would be wonderful." He looked up at the sky, straining to see the tane, with no luck. "I don't know where this will take us, or how long we will be gone. Or what may happen."

"All choices have consequences," said I'Char.

Win smiled. "You do listen. And remember."

I'Char did not answer, his eyes still facing the sky.

"Can you still see that bird?" asked Win.

"Does it matter?" said I'Char. "I know it is there. What good is faith if you don't use it?"

Also by W. R. Pursche and Michael Gabriele

The Eternal Messiah: Jesus of K'Turia
(Book 1 of the Eternal Messiah Future)

Also by W.R. Pursche

Lessons To Live By: The Canine Commandments

The Book of Warriors: Dior
(Chronicles of the Third Reckoning Book 1)

www.EternalMessiah.com